Y0-CPB-604

Grim

Grim

ANNA WAGGENER

SCHOLASTIC PRESS • NEW YORK

Library of Congress Cataloging-in-Publication Data available

ISBN 978-0-545-38480-3

10 9 8 7 6 5 4 3 2 1 12 13 14 15 16

Printed in the U.S.A. 23
First edition, June 2012

The text was set in Adobe Caslon Pro.
Book design by Whitney Lyle

To Mom, for keeping my feet on the ground,

and to Dad, for showing me the stars.

Together you made me tall.

Prologue

I love my youngest child more than the other two, and God bless them but they all know it.

It's not that I don't love Rebecca or Shawn. I would die for them — let my ashes hit the ground a hundred times over. But Megan's special.

Shawn is so cold, so afraid to remember how things used to be. And Rebecca — she got her father's temper, his habit of burning and burying those around him. I hope that she's forgiven me. That she still loves me. I've never really been sure.

Maybe I'm only skewed because of everything that's happened. I might've been a better mom if their father had been a better dad. I might've been a better person if my husband had needed a better wife. I've never aspired to be much, myself, but I rise up to meet other people's expectations. I can't help it.

So no, I've never loved my children any less than a mother should.

It's just that I love Megan more.

Meg. So different from her brother and sister. There's so much guilt when I watch her sleeping, but there's a kind of pride, or maybe just relief, every time she laughs. Every time she promises to never, never change. Until you've been where I've been, you can't have any idea what a comfort that is.

Chapter One

Shawn pulled up to the impound lot before the rain, while the air still felt tight in his throat.

Behind the chain-link fence, cars waited in perfect rows, windshields facing the parking lot like soldiers at attention. He glanced to his left, where the small brick office sat, dark, locked, and shuttered, before leaning over to fish a set of spare keys from the glove box. Panic slipped into his stomach when he straightened again and measured up the fence. All around him, floodlights were throwing distorted shadows over the ground, and a thought lurked in the back of his mind: a yell, and a night patrolman's heavy footsteps quickening to a run. Breaking and entering, they would say. He closed the door as quietly as he could.

Seriously, Becca. Every single time.

Shawn hadn't expected better from her, but that didn't make things any easier. Still, when the buzz of his phone startled him, he gritted his teeth and answered. "What?"

"Hurry up, jerk." Rebecca's voice came through a haze of bad reception.

Shawn snapped the phone shut and headed to the padlocked gate.

Predictable. After all was said and done, he always ended up being the jerk.

The cuff of Shawn's jeans snagged on his way over the fence, but that was the least of his worries. He shook himself free and dropped onto the dirt lot. Crouching down to be less conspicuous, he hurried off to the left, where they kept newly towed cars. He planned to tell Rebecca how pathetic it was for him to know that.

When his phone started humming again, he almost ignored it — he'd already caught the gleam of Rebecca's Mustang anyway — but even on vibrate, it made too much noise and he knew that she'd just call again, over and over until he picked up.

"What?"

"Oh my God, Shawn, hurry."

He straightened up and punched the unlock button, and the car's lights flashed yellow through the dark. The Mustang's trunk popped open and his sister climbed out, all legs and too much skin, smoothing down her navy skirt. Shawn just shook his head.

Rebecca doubled over to fluff out her long hair, the blond almost silver in the dark. "Took you long enough," she said.

"Yeah, I guess."

"Jesus, it's cold."

Shawn knew, even without looking, that Rebecca's eyes were on his jacket.

"Yeah," he repeated. "I guess."

"Shawn."

"Fine." He shrugged off the coat and handed it over. "Happy?"

"Yessir. Now how are we getting out of here?"

"I'm parked out front."

"No, I mean *we*." Rebecca settled her palm on the Mustang's scarlet tail fin, fingertips caressing cold metal. She maintained an unhealthy relationship with that '97, but at least she could admit it.

Shawn crossed his arms. "I'm not breaking that out of here."

"Shawn!"

"What?"

"If I don't come back with it, Mom will *kill* me."

"Well, if Mom gets in from work and finds Meg asleep and *no one else home*, then we'll both be dead, Becca. So your car really isn't my first priority."

Rebecca pouted. "I'd do it for *you*, Shawn."

He shook his head and chafed his arms against the cold.

"Lemme call Matt," she said.

"There's nothing he can do."

"He's a captain, Shawn. He can do anything."

"He's got a badge, Rebecca. That doesn't make him Batman."

Rebecca stared at him, her eyes slit and her mouth hanging open. "Christ, you're lame."

"Hey, there." They both flinched at the voice. A high-powered flashlight burst on, leeching all color from Rebecca's face. Shawn felt a stab of déjà vu.

"Dammit, Becca."

Her palms were already flat in the air. "I need to make a call," she said. It came out so easily that Shawn knew it was habitual. Making coffee in the morning. Chewing hangnails until they hurt. Coughing up your Get-Out-of-Jail-Free card. All in a day's work.

Erika emptied another packet of creamer into her coffee and watched the sandy powder fan out and settle. She dropped the plastic spoon into the trash bin. The gas station's fluorescent bulbs glared against white wall paint and spotted linoleum floors, and oldies crackled out of a radio next to the cash register. Erika recognized the two women behind the counter but didn't know their names. She'd spent more time in this gas station than she'd like to admit, filling paper cups with strong coffee and excessive sugar and praying that the jolt would be enough to get her home in one piece. It was the only store for miles, pedaling its gasoline seven cents too high and lighting itself up like the Empire State Building of U.S. Route 30.

An automated bell sounded as a fellow late-night traveler came in, and Erika looked over. A man in jeans and a black sports coat strolled up to the counter.

"How do I get to Atlantic City?" he asked.

One of the cashiers eyed him over the edge of her magazine. "You want directions," she said, "you buy directions."

"You know, I'm going to be in big trouble if I don't get to Atlantic City soon, so if you'd just point me in the right direction I'd be much obliged."

The other cashier arched one slow eyebrow. "You want directions —"

"I buy directions," he finished. "Someone's having a bad day. And how much do you charge for telling me where the maps are?"

She pointed a mulberry-colored fingernail at the rack beside the coffee counter.

The man pivoted, eyes skimming over Erika. She offered a small, sympathetic smile.

He gave her a second look. "Have we met?"

He asked the question without malice, as if he really cared, but he'd come in with the late-for-a-business-meeting vibe of someone from the city, and Erika had gotten enough I-don't-know-you-so-why-are-you-smiling-at-me? looks in her life for the question to put her on edge. She'd grown up in Pennsylvania, in the country, and had never been able to wrap her head around the kind of logic that made pleasantries rude.

"I don't think so," she said, looking back down at her triple-heated coffee. She was too tired to be talking to anyone right now.

The man brushed past and pulled out one of the maps. He gave her a third look. When she caught him, he faked a smile.

"Do you know how to get to Atlantic City?"

"South to Walnut Street," she said. "Then get on the expressway. Forty minutes, tops."

He sighed hard. "No time," he said. "Where's the closest hospital?"

"Pomona." An awkward pause grew as Erika took her turn looking him over and he pretended not to notice. She took the bait. "Are you hurt?"

"No," he said. "Just looking for sanctuary."

"Then I think you'd be better off in a church. Plenty of those."

He smirked and ruffled his hair. "Thanks," he said. "I'll keep that in mind."

Erika paid for her coffee and left. As her car rumbled to life, she glanced up and saw the man leaning back against the counter with a thoughtful look on his face. He held a New Jersey road map open in his hands, but his eyes were set on her.

Police Captain Matthew Kingston felt his frown deepen. His broad hands, nails too short, summer brown just fading, tightened around the steering wheel. "And you still call them your friends?"

Rebecca focused on the phone in her lap. Dark buildings rolled past them as Matt guided his police cruiser down Hudson Avenue. Shawn had gone on ahead in his own car, anxious to get back to Megan and away from Rebecca.

"We were just messing around," she said quietly.

Matt groaned. "Beck," he said. "Getting into the trunk of your car without your keys is *not* messing around. It's practically suicide. You could've died."

"I had my phone."

He shook his head. "You have to grow up someday."

Rebecca nibbled her lips, looking sorry. Matt knew her well enough to call the bluff.

"What's on your mind?"

She shrugged. "What's on yours?"

"How to revive your mother after the heart attack."

Rebecca's neck snapped up so fast that Matt thought she might get whiplash. "You're *not* telling my mother."

"Oh, really?"

"She'll kill me!"

"She'll take your car."

Rebecca huffed.

"I'll tell her to, Beck."

The sky opened up. Fat drops of rain smacked against the windshield.

Rebecca glared at the rivers forming on the glass and let her voice go cold. "You wouldn't."

"I would," said Matt. "Look, Beck. It's been hard enough getting you out every time some party gets busted, and to clear your record after that stunt with the water tower. Now you're trying to sneak into the drive-in with people who find it funnier to leave your car in a tow-away zone? What the hell's next?"

For the rest of the drive, Rebecca kept her legs crossed stiffly at the knee, her mouth scrunched into a tight line. She watched as the rubber wiper blades skimmed clear a double arch. Back and forth. Back and forth. Matt pulled to a stop in front of the house on Mission Street and looked sideways at Rebecca.

"I'll be calling your mother," he said.

Her grimace vanished when she turned to him, desperate. "Please don't."

"Go inside, Rebecca."

"She'll be pissy and we'll all have to deal with it. You too."

Matt saw Shawn standing in the doorway of the house, waiting like an angry father, his arms crossed and the hall light throwing him into silhouette. If Rebecca's own brother could look that embittered, the city police captain certainly had a right to.

"Go inside, Rebecca," he repeated.

She got out. "Fine."

"Good night," he said.

"Whatever."

Matt gave a small laugh when Rebecca marched up the steps and gave her brother a death look so exaggerated he could call it from behind. Hair sopping, but shoulders back and her chin up like she owned him. Shawn shoved open the glass storm door, and Rebecca breezed past without a word. The downstairs lights were all on in ten seconds, warm against the rain. She really was her mother's daughter.

❧

Erika coasted down the highway, cursing under her breath. Her headlights turned the drizzle silver, so that the road looked like a mirror and a million flashes of light.

She hated driving in the rain. And driving at night. And this empty stretch of highway, where the only sign of life came from an occasional farmhouse, porch light winking through the trees.

It was too late for her to be out, and she knew it. The overtime was killing her. She could feel the tension knots all along her spine — one for each sleepless hour, and another for each caffeine-fueled drive home.

She wanted to be home, in bed, asleep, without a stack of unfinished reports in the backseat. She wanted to get the man from the gas station out of her head. Something about him made her jumpy, but a promise flickered in his eyes that said he wouldn't hurt her. That said he could become whatever she wanted.

In the passenger seat, her phone started glowing. She ignored it.

If she finished the reports tonight, she'd be done for the week. Or she could call in sick tomorrow and finish everything at home. She could have dinner with her kids for once, instead of leaving a twenty tacked to the fridge next to a list of take-out numbers. There was a chicken in the freezer. If she took it out before bed, it would be thawed in time to make soup tomorrow.

Her phone glowed blue again, playing a tinny version of Beethoven.

"Dammit, Matt," she muttered. She kept telling him not to call when she was driving, and he kept ignoring her. She reached over to grab the phone.

Light filled her windshield, white-hot and blinding.

"What the hell?"

A car shot over the hill ahead of her, high beams on. It took a few seconds for Erika to realize that it was in the wrong lane and picking up speed.

"Shit."

Her car fishtailed as she twisted the steering wheel, trying to get off the road. The rain-slicked highway slid like oil under her tires.

The scream of her horn died when the two cars collided. Their metal bodies crumpled together like construction paper.

Rebecca zipped up her jacket and checked herself in the hall mirror.

"And where are you going?"

She turned to look at her brother. "Ashley's picking me up," she said.

"At midnight?"

Rebecca rolled her eyes. "Yes, Shawn, at midnight."

"Why?"

"You're not my mother."

"Becca."

"Jesus, you're annoying. David still has my keys, okay? I want them back."

Shawn couldn't help but stare. "You don't have a *car* anymore, Becca. Don't you *get* that?"

"Oh my God, Shawn, shut up about the stupid car."

"You got it impounded, Becca. I know that you're not very intelligent, but please tell me that you know what 'impounded' means."

"Matt'll get it out tomorrow."

"And how will you get the money?"

"Mom'll do it."

"You're going to ask *her* to pay?"

"Well, yeah."

Shawn saw the headlights of Ashley's car flash across the front windows. He shrugged.

"Fine," he said. "Do whatever you want."

Rebecca gave him a dangerously sweet smile. "Thanks," she said. "I plan to."

She didn't lock the door on her way out.

Shawn slouched against the wall, feeling sick to his stomach. Even after seventeen years, he'd never gotten over Rebecca acting like a million-dollar bitch.

Rain drummed on the scrunched metal of the wreck, sounding hollow. Jeremiah peered into the spiderwebbed window of the other car. He tapped the glass out of his way until a pile of diamond dust covered the pavement, then stepped back and folded his arms, thinking.

The woman from the gas station slumped against the wheel, a trickle of blood running from her hairline down her cheek. The air bags almost looked like pillows, soft and plush as they began to deflate; she might have been asleep, except for the blood. Jeremiah sighed and wiped his palms against his jeans. Air bag powder dusted everything, like the finest breath of snow he'd ever seen. He shivered. The woods waited, calling, as his brothers sped closer, by now in West Virginia and gaining speed. He knew that they could feel him.

Jeremiah reached through the window.

Rebecca came back with her keys after three. The rain had let up and the whole night smelled of wet earth and grass. Some of the house lights were still on, waiting for her to come home.

"Bit of a drive to David's?"

She jumped. "What are you doing up?"

Shawn twirled the cordless phone facedown on the coffee table. "Mom's not home yet," he said.

"What?"

He repeated each word with added weight. "Mom is not home yet."

Rebecca pursed her lips. After a second, Shawn realized that she was stifling a laugh.

"Are you drunk?" he asked.

She thought about it and then giggled, putting a finger to her lips. "Shh," she whispered. "Maybe a little." She dropped her bag by the door and threw her keys on the table. They skidded over the glass to settle next to Shawn's forearm.

"Becca?" he asked.

"Yeah?"

"Why are you such a fuck-up?"

She blinked at her little brother. "Why would you say something like that?"

"Go to bed."

Rebecca walked over to the couch and sank down next to him. She leaned against his knee. Shawn tensed up at her touch, but, as always, she didn't seem to notice. Her drinking never failed to carry the sting of their father's whiskey breath.

"So where's Mom?" she asked.

Shawn picked up the phone. "I don't know. She won't answer."

"Have you called Matt?"

"She wouldn't be with him now."

"Why not? He was going to rat me out. She probably went over there to cry."

"Why are you okay with that?"

"Hell if I know," Rebecca said. "Guess I'm just a fuck-up."

She took the phone and started punching keys.

"Are you calling Matt?"

"Well, yeah," she said. "He's my guardian angel, isn't he?"

Shawn cracked his neck and knuckles. "You're a weird drunk."

Rebecca giggled. "You should see me stoned." She wedged the receiver between her chin and left shoulder so that she could check her nails.

Shawn tipped his head to the side and listened to the muffled ring of a cell phone. "D'you hear that?"

Rebecca put her finger to her lips again. Her face brightened as the line connected. "Hey, Matt?"

"Open the door, Rebecca."

She got up and went to the front door, phone still at her ear. The Christmas wreath tinkled.

Rebecca giggled again and turned off the phone. "Good timing," she said. "Mom get rained on? I'll grab a towel."

Matt took in the beads of water along the creases of Rebecca's jacket. He didn't miss the tang of cigarettes and discount beer.

"Beck."

"What? Does she want her bathrobe?"

"Rebecca," said Matt. "Where's Shawn?"

Shawn's head popped around the edge of the door. "What's up? Where's Mom?"

Matt's mouth opened too slow. Even tipsy, Rebecca stiffened.

"Matt?"

"Your mother," he said, so formal on the doorstep, facing these two kids and their blank faces. Kids he cooked breakfast for and gave birthday presents to. Kids he called by nicknames and got out of trouble, not only because of their mother but because of them. Because they were Shawn and Beck. And Meg. Oh, Meg. "Your mom was in an accident," Matt said. "I'm sorry."

Shawn put a hand on Rebecca's shoulder as she stepped backward.

"Is she okay?" he asked. "Is she in the hospital?"

"Shawn . . ." Matt's words collapsed in his throat, folding in on top of themselves in that too-small space. He looked at the tiles in the hallway and then back up at two pairs of wide eyes, bottle green like Erika's. "She didn't make it."

There was a long silence, and then Rebecca's jaw stiffened. "That's not funny, Matt."

"Beck, please," he said, in a whisper close to begging. "Please don't make this harder."

Her breathing came fast, with too many exhales, lungs desperate. She covered her mouth, and then her eyes, and then turned around and grabbed Shawn's shirt with one hand. "It's not — it can't. Shawn."

He hugged her. He couldn't remember the last time he'd hugged her, but he did now, clothes getting soaked by the rain on her jacket and hair. He stared at Matt like he needed something.

"What happened?" he asked, finally.

Matt started to answer when Rebecca jerked away and spun around again. "I want to see her."

The statement hung in the air before Matt cleared his throat. "I don't think that's a good idea, Beck. I've already been down. It's her."

"I want to see her," she repeated. "I want to see my mother."

"She's not —"

"Matt." Her voice, spine, shoulders slipped, crumbled. "Just take me."

Shawn tightened his grip on her arms. "Becca —"

"Don't." She shoved away from her brother, brushed past Matt, and stumbled down to the parked cruiser.

Shawn looked at Matt again. His thoughts were rolling in slow motion, but his heart punched hard against his ribs. "I have to stay with Meg," he said. "I can't leave her alone."

"I know." Matt hesitated. His left hand jerked, like he wanted to reach out but stopped himself. "We won't be long," he said.

Rebecca came back, with her mascara run to gray from rain and tears and her cheeks chapped red. Shawn let her push past him on her way up the stairs. He heard her door thud shut at the end of the hall.

"I'll stay," said Matt. "You kids shouldn't be alone tonight."

Shawn shut his eyes to quiet their burning. His building pressure headache made the whole world foggy; he could feel his body turning against itself, begging to split open. All he could think of was his mom's bedroom and how wrong it felt to intrude on this night, as if her things were mourning too. "Don't take this the wrong way," he said, "but I think we need the space."

Matt gave Shawn a long look before reaching out to put a hand on his shoulder. "Get some sleep," he said. "I'll be back in the morning."

Shawn waited for the cruiser's taillights to disappear around the corner before he locked the front door and headed to his own room. He decided to let Megan sleep through to morning. She deserved that much.

Chapter Two

Morning hit the eastern windows with a bite of frost. Shawn woke to the smell of coffee and a clatter of pans on the stovetop.

Through half-lidded eyes, he saw his mother pause in the hallway by his bedroom door.

"Matt's here," she said. The world snapped into focus and Shawn saw Rebecca in their mother's cream-colored bathrobe. Her hair was pinned up in a loose knot, her hand clutching the fluffy collar under her chin. Since the age of sixteen she'd been taller than their mother, and now the yellow cuffs of her pajama pants stuck out under the robe's hem. "He's making breakfast."

Shawn nodded. He wanted to pretend that this was normal. He wanted to believe that this was Sunday morning. That Rebecca's nose was pink from a cold. That Mom was downstairs, scrambling eggs.

"Meg will be up soon."

The weight sank back into his stomach. "How are we going to tell her?"

"Matt offered."

"No," said Shawn. "I want to."

Rebecca watched him, looking sorry. She nodded.

"I called Grandma." She didn't wait for him to ask. "She hung up on me."

"I'm sorry."

She shrugged. "I thought that . . . but whatever. She's just like that." She pinched the bridge of her nose. "I want the service to be on Friday."

"Today's Tuesday."

"Wednesday," she said.

"Are two days enough time?"

"Time for what? The coroner's done with the death certificate and report. We can go to the funeral home today to pick out flowers and a casket." Her voice died. She looked away.

"And the obituary? And food for a reception? Can we even get a priest by Friday?"

"People will bring food, Shawn."

The conversation felt wrong. The ceiling looked back at Shawn, same as ever, but too bright, lines of paint too clear. His throat felt dry. "It's not enough notice; people won't come."

"They will," Rebecca said gently. "Think about it and you'll see that they will."

Shawn covered his eyes with the crook of his elbow. "I've never done this before," he said.

"Neither have I, Shawn. We'll figure it out."

"I just think that it's too soon."

"I don't want to stretch it out for Meg. We can't afford anything big anyway."

"I know."

Rebecca flapped out the robe and cinched it again, tying the belt like their mother always did.

"Becca." Shawn rolled over to look at her. "Are you . . . I mean, are you sure that it was Mom?"

She stared at him, and then her face got rigid. "I think that after eighteen years I'd remember what my mother looks like. Yes, I'm sure."

"That's not what I meant."

"Yeah. Okay," she said, sharp with sarcasm. "Maybe you should go double-check. Make sure this isn't a practical joke."

"Becca —"

"Fuck you, Shawn," she said. "Fuck. You." She spun away. Shawn heard her footsteps fly down the stairs a few seconds later.

He shut his eyes and sank back into the cold plush of his pillows.

The man from the gas station faced the crackle of the fire, and his closed eyelids flickered gray and gold. The man from the car crash tapped the ground with a broken tree branch because the motion kept him awake. *Scratch, scratch, scratch* against hard-packed earth. The man who killed Erika Stripling wet his lips and tasted smoke. It reminded him of cremations.

Megan, Shawn, and Rebecca. He saw their names in her eyes. Smelled their memory on her skin. It lingered. It lingered longer than she did.

What did he owe her now? Everything, probably. Or maybe nothing at all. What was the punishment for a guide stealing a charge instead of waiting? There was none, because it didn't happen.

He heard the rustle of sleep-stiff limbs and opened his eyes.

"Feeling better?" he asked.

Erika blinked against the firelight. "Where am I?"

He was proud of her for not screaming. "You're safe," he said. "I promise."

She looked worried. "Why do I believe you?"

Because humans always believe us, he thought, *or we could never help them.* He offered her a placating smile. "I'm not sure," he said.

"You're lying."

The man cocked his head. "Truth bending," he admitted. "I'm sorry. I have an idea, but I shouldn't tell you anything. Is that better?"

She wore black business clothes, and when she rested her chin on the peaks of her knees, everything but her face slipped away. The gesture made her look younger, more vulnerable. Face small and lovely in the dark. "Where are my kids? Can you tell me that?"

"At home," he said. "You can't see them right now. I'm sorry about that too. But they aren't hurt." He paused. "How's your head?"

"My head?" Erika ran a hand over her hair. "Fine." She kept watching him. "It's a long way home, isn't it?"

"For you, maybe," he said. "For now."

Her eyes were green like clover in the firelight. "I feel dizzy."

"You aren't ready yet," he said. "Go back to sleep until you are."

"What?"

"Go back to sleep."

Erika lay down again. She tried to tell herself not to. She tried to tell herself that she should be terrified. That she should be screaming, or kicking embers in his face and running back to the road. It would be better to hitchhike than to sleep here, with this man watching her.

"Do you believe in soul mates, Erika?"

He seemed sweet for sounding so awkward. Like he had to know but was afraid to offend her. To scare her.

"No," she said. "I don't."

"My father never did, either."

"I think that you have to believe in souls first."

A smile slunk into his next whisper. "How ironic." He shifted his weight and prodded the fire. "Sleep well, Erika."

Erika shut her eyes and rolled onto her side. Then she heard herself ask for his name. She felt silly. It seemed like such a grade-school question.

"Jeremiah," he said.

The echo of empty air that followed was comforting. For once in her life, Erika Stripling embraced the quiet.

The king ran his palm along the edge of the wooden table and reached for another pen. His advisors stood in a line on the other side of the room, waiting for a word or motion from him. He ignored them and turned back to his work.

A request from the Upper Kingdom for Pellegrino Aretusi, with a commission for frescoes in a new public square. Next, they would be wanting Raphael himself. The king scribbled his assent and moved the paper from one pile to the next. If only he'd known, when he was younger, what the crown and Sickle really meant: years and decades and centuries of signing his name and transferring papers from one side of his desk to the other. The king glanced at the next appeal and then straightened. Lifted it up to look more closely at the red wax seal stamped at the bottom.

"What is this?"

"Highness?"

"The queen wants a new handmaid?" He shook his head. "She has twelve already."

The youngest of his advisors shrugged. "She wants another."

"An unlucky number."

"She wants another."

The king set aside his pen. "And are there any courtiers waiting?"

There was an uncomfortable hush.

"Well?"

The advisors shuffled against the wall.

"Highness . . ."

"What is it?"

"She says that her seraph court gossips and bickers and does not heed her to its best. She asks for a rogue."

The king picked up the appeal again and squinted at it.

"A rogue?" he muttered. "Ridiculous. The rogues are busy enough, ferrying souls into the Kingdom. And what will we do when the fashion fades? Cast him back into the woods?"

"Her, Highness."

"What?"

"Cast *her* back into the woods. Her ladyship . . ."

"Ridiculous!" The king waved his hand, brushing away the thought. "Are we to make one? There have been no female rogues in five hundred years."

"Highness . . ."

The king lifted his chin. He hated being corrected.

"An accident," the advisor murmured. "Last week."

"And I wasn't told? What is the point of advisors if they do not advise?" He snatched up the pen and signed his name to the order. "I married a spendthrift."

"Highness."

"Take it! Take it and your evasive answers!"

The retaining room cleared quickly, carrying the queen's order out in a wave of fur, silk, and heavy gold rings.

Shawn knocked on Megan's bedroom door before going in.

"Morning, Meg."

Megan was already sitting up, legs tucked under her comforter. Sleep tousled her hair, the ends of her bob tickling her round jaw. A collection of Hans Christian Andersen stories lay open in her lap.

"Good morning," she bubbled, shutting the book and dropping it on the carpet beside her bed. "Tell Mommy I don't like that shirt she made me wear yesterday. Katie called it ugly." When her brother said nothing, she gave his face a once-over. "What did Becky do?"

Shawn swallowed and wet his lips. He took the chair from Megan's desk and dragged it to her nightstand.

"You're eight, Meg," he said. "So you're a big girl, right? I can tell you the truth?"

"Shawn, what's wrong?"

"Meg . . ."

"Shawn, what happened? I have to get to school —"

"We're not going today, Meg."

The frantic climb of her voice settled. She closed her mouth and looked at him. She had brown eyes, like their dad did, and his dark hair too. But she already tipped her head to the side like their mom did when expecting answers.

"Shawn," she said. "What's wrong?"

Shawn drummed his fingers against the plastic back of the chair. He felt huge and clumsy on the miniature seat.

"Mom was hurt last night," he said.

Megan's forehead creased. "No," she said. "No, she wasn't."

"She was hurt really bad, Meg."

"No, she *wasn't.*"

"Becca and I are going to take care of you, okay? I promise that we'll always take care of you. She loved you a lot, Meg. Mom, I mean. Mom did."

Shawn was getting confused. The slow, plainspoken explanation that he'd planned on now muddled itself in a rush to get out. He shut up and stared at his hands.

"I'm sorry, Meg."

He could hear someone come into the room behind him, and knew that it was Rebecca. He wondered how long she'd hovered in the hallway, letting him do things the way he wanted them done. Or ruin things the way only he could ruin them.

Rebecca lowered herself onto the edge of the bed and pulled Megan into her lap. "It's okay to be sad, Meg," she said. "I'm sad too."

Megan tucked her head under her sister's chin. "But when is she coming home?"

Rebecca's voice caught. "Oh, honey." She laid her cheek on Megan's stick-straight hair.

Shawn sat down beside his sisters. "She's not coming home, Meg," he said. "She can't come home anymore."

"She's dead, Meg," Rebecca whispered. "She's dead."

Megan stared at the patchwork of her quilt. She knew dead. Dead was the cat her piano teacher owned, whose name was Remmy and whose tongue felt like sandpaper. Dead was the squirrel that Becky hit the first time they rode together, that they left wiggling in the middle of the street, each shouting and crying at the other all the way home. Dead was the bluebird that broke its neck when it flew into the garage door. Shawn dug it a grave in the backyard, under the hickory tree. Dead was a lot of things, but it wasn't Mommy. It couldn't be Mommy.

"Is she going under the hickory tree too?" It was the only thing that Megan could think to ask. Shawn understood, and he started to cry.

Shawn carried Megan down to breakfast, but the pancakes were already cold. Matt put them into the oven to reheat. When he heard Rebecca whisper that she felt guilty for eating, he made her the biggest plate. He said that he wouldn't leave until everything was gone, because he'd always promised Erika that the children would be safe. They sat around the glass-topped table, morning light pouring in through the big window that overlooked the backyard. Megan glanced from one face to another and back to her plate, but no one spoke. She chewed her lip and kept on eating.

"I called in to check you all out from school," Matt said when Megan left for the bathroom. He kept watching the doorway that Meg had disappeared through. "You know how kids are," he said, almost to himself. "I didn't want them asking about anything. Talking her down."

Rebecca sipped her coffee. "Are you going to work later?" she asked.

He turned to her, offended. "The town can mind itself for a day."

"I didn't mean that."

"I loved her too, Rebecca. Love her."

She had never heard it put that way: present tense last. She softened. "I know," she said. "I'm sorry."

Matt cleared his throat. "Let me know what you want for the service. I'll take care of it."

"We can do it, Matt."

"Beck —"

"I want to," she said. "I need to."

He put the dishes in the sink. "All right. If you're sure."

"I am. Take Meg to the park? Shawn and I have to talk."

"All right." He turned on the tap. "Let me do the dishes first."

"I can do those."

"I need to do something for you three."

"You have," Rebecca said. "Leave them. Please?"

"Okay." Matt turned off the faucet.

A few minutes later, Megan came in with her shoes. When Matt visited on Sunday mornings, this was their ritual — breakfast, park, grocery shopping. Nothing in her would break that pattern. Not even Wednesday.

Rebecca put the last dish in the drainer and pulled the stopper from the sink. She hadn't spoken since starting the chore, but Shawn wasn't about to interrupt her. This was her own ritual.

The last gulp of soapy water swirled away, leaving a mushroom of white froth in the drainer. Rebecca watched it for a while, listening to the soft *tick* of popping bubbles. She rinsed her hands.

"We should ask Matt to let her friends know," she said. "And call her office."

"Yeah," said Shawn. "And I'll tell Peter."

"Who'll tell Beth, who'll tell everyone else." A drop of acid sizzled in the comment. Rebecca didn't like Shawn's friends.

"So that takes care of the high school." She paused. "But I'll tell Ashley and them myself."

Shawn said nothing. He didn't like her friends, either.

Rebecca looked at him. "Who else?"

He sighed. "Well, you already called Grandma, so that about wraps up family."

She nodded, torn between the sting of the statement and the reality of it. They settled into thoughtful silence for a few more seconds. Finally, Rebecca cleared her throat. "I think that we should call Dad."

Shawn blinked at her from across the kitchen counter.

"Excuse me?"

"Dad," she said. "I think that we should call him."

He folded the newspaper on the counter in front of him, taking care to match the creases. "You know Dad's number?"

"Mom gave it to me."

"You've talked to him?"

Rebecca stared at the white grout between the counter tiles. "Not recently, no. Not really at all. She just wanted me to have it."

"Oh." Shawn stacked the newspaper sections, separating them: advertisements in one pile, everything else in the other. Their mother had always done this before breakfast, throwing out the coupons before the deflated paper even touched the coffee table. She'd hated coupons. "Why?"

Rebecca must have drifted too. She glanced up at him. "Hmm?"

"Why are you even asking me about this?"

"Because I'm not sure it's such a good idea," Rebecca said. "I don't want to upset Megan. Or Matt."

"Then don't call him."

"He deserves to come."

"No, he doesn't."

"Yes, he does, Shawn," she said. "He deserves to know, at least."

"He'll see the paper."

"He left town last month. He's in Hammonton now."

Shawn leaned away from his sister and took a deep breath. "Good for him," he said. "I'm glad that someone told me."

"Don't be stupid about this."

"You've made up your mind. I'm going for a drive."

Rebecca reached for his hand. "We need to talk about the service."

Shawn pulled away. "Why don't you ask *Dad* about it? I bet he'd love that. I can't believe you, Becca. He walked out on us. He walked out on Mom. You really want him there when we *bury her*?"

Rebecca glared at him. "I don't *know*, Shawn," she said. "That's why I'm asking you!"

"Then, no," Shawn spat. "No, I don't want him there. No, I don't think that it's a good idea. No, I don't think that he deserves it. Now I'm going for a drive."

He left her in the kitchen with the sparkling dishes and the neatly divided newspaper.

Megan knew that Matt watched her as she swung, kicking her legs out as far as they could go, wondering what would happen if she spun all the way around the metal bar above her and dropped her hands. Would she fly up to heaven, where Matt said her mommy might be?

No. Because things fell down when they died, and that's what Matt meant when he said that they would say good-bye soon. Her mommy, with her hair like a princess's, would go into a shoe box, but nicer, and never come back.

"My mommy's dead," she said to herself, tasting the words and how strange they felt in her mouth. "My mommy's dead."

She realized she was saying them too loud when Matt walked up and slowed her swinging. Made her stop. Came around to squat down in front of her.

She liked Matt and how easy he smiled and the way his hair perched too high on his head. It made his face look big, but he had a nice face, so that was okay.

"Are you all right, Meg?"

"Yeah."

"You can tell me if you're not."

Megan looked down at the dust on her white shoes. She wanted to say that she liked the pink shirt even if Katie didn't. That she liked the way her mommy smelled in the morning, when she came in and turned on the light and kissed her full of giggles. That sometimes she went into her mommy's bedroom just to hear her sleep, and then got into bed because they kept the house too cold, and that sometimes she got angry when her mommy hadn't come home, and what would happen now? But she didn't know if these were good things to say; if Matt would get sad about her talking about Mommy, because this morning she'd asked if they could have Mommy's special chicken-and-tomato soup for lunch and Rebecca had almost cried.

So instead, Megan said, "Who's going to take me to piano?"

Matt opened his mouth a little, and then closed it, and then said, "I'll take you, Meg, if you want to go."

Megan looked at him and how careful his eyes were, like he thought they might hurt her if he let them, and she said, "I'm too sad to go," because it sounded like something she should say.

Matt nodded and got back up again, and then he pushed her on the swing. Megan wondered what would happen if she jumped. If she could go deep down and curl up there until her mommy came to find her.

The forest floor was packed hard as brick and just as cold, the sun sleeping somewhere behind the horizon. No leaves rotted on the ground, but no life grew in the branches, either — just smooth earth and columns of naked trees, each a splotchy black against air that hovered gray and glassy and a little damp, like early morning in the Rockies.

Erika clutched her knees to her chest while Jeremiah stubbed out the fire. When she'd woken again, he'd told her that she was ready now, and she believed him. She felt rested, as if she'd just gotten up from the best sleep of her life.

Tall. Medium build. These were the things easiest to notice about Jeremiah in that dying half-light. Erika watched him, trying to catch the details that faded with the coals. He had a thin, straight nose and eyes like hers. Shamrock eyes, her mother called them. Outside of her family, Erika didn't know many people with eyes that green.

He might've been thirty, but he'd let his dark hair grow long, to curl around his ears like the art students' at the nearby college. His jacket looked expensive, and tailored well, but threadbare. His T-shirt underneath was washed thin, the lettering faded to a shadow she couldn't read. Keys jingled on his belt loop as he moved. It reminded her of her ex-husband.

Erika knew, from the way Jeremiah looked at her, that something had changed. He seemed calmer, happier even, but when he caught her staring, something like guilt flashed across his face. That conflicted feeling flooded into her stomach again, making her nauseated.

Then he helped her to her feet and, though he didn't say anything, Erika found herself reassured by his touch. She knew that he watched her in the dark, his hand still on the crook of her elbow, and something told her that he could see her far better than she could see him. He seemed to be measuring her up.

At last, he opened his mouth. "Do you trust me?" he asked.

Erika hesitated. She wanted to trust him, but the thought of giving up control terrified her. Unusual, since she had always lived her life as the one willing to be molded.

"Yes," she said, surprised to hear herself.

"Do you know why?"

The silence hung heavy. Erika could feel Jeremiah's breath on her forehead, but he wasn't looking at her anymore. Something crackled in the distance.

"No," she said. Her voice had dropped to a whisper.

"I'm not going to hurt you," he told her.

"I know," she said, sure that she *did* know. Afraid not of him but of what she allowed herself to do when he was there. She felt like she was drunk or dreaming, going through motions without sense telling her to stop.

Jeremiah pulled something out of one of his pockets and

took a few steps back. Erika followed him without a question. His hand never left her arm.

A *click* punctured the dark.

Jeremiah dropped his mouth to Erika's ear. "There's someone behind you," he said, "who wants to kill me."

Erika saw his hand flash up and almost screamed, but he yanked her close so that her mouth filled up with his jacket. His hand, fisted around a pocketknife, slammed into the tree beside them. The blade sank in up to its hilt and stuck. Jeremiah gripped Erika tighter, then drove her up against the tree as well, until her shoulders dug hard into the rough bark. Now she couldn't scream if she wanted to, because his free hand pressed against the back of her head and she could only think of how it felt like he cradled her, just a baby scared by too much sound and too much dark, and how he smelled of chocolate and oranges, and how the shape behind him — a shadow blacker than the trees, the size of a man — twisted and churned like cloying smoke.

"I'm sorry to drag you into this, Erika," Jeremiah said, his voice a whisper but loud in her ear.

Her knees buckled and Jeremiah had to hold her up, refusing to let go as she started to slip, pushing her harder against the tree like he wanted to shove her all the way through, but the more he tried, the more Erika realized that it didn't matter, because there was no earth for her to fall to, since the forest had dropped away, the whole forest, except for the skinny tree that made up her entire world, and the black, empty air rushing past them both. She thought about the smell of the sap biting into her throat, and tried to place it because it was so, so important. Sharp and smoky. Hickory. She could feel hickory bark sliding through their skin. When she started to fall, Jeremiah fell with her.

Chapter Three

Shawn stayed out late, and came home to find Rebecca's Mustang sitting in the driveway as if it had never left. House lights glowed through the curtained windows of the first floor. Shawn locked his own car on his way up the front steps. As he let himself into the house, his cell phone rang.

"You had better be on your way home," Matt said when he answered.

"I'm just going in."

"Good. Rebecca's a wreck. She wouldn't let me stay over there, but I put Megan to bed before I left."

"Thanks."

"What'd you say to her?"

"I didn't say anything."

"Don't lie to a cop, Shawn."

"She wants our dad to be at the service."

Matt fell silent. "That's between you two."

"You think that it's a bad idea too, don't you?"

"I'm not getting into this. I'll call back in the morning."

Shawn frowned. "Good night," he said.

"Night."

Shawn found Rebecca at the kitchen table with her head nestled in her arms. A cluster of beer bottles crowded near her elbow, their folded caps scattered across the floor. The room reeked of hops and vomit.

Shawn dropped the bottles into the trash and nudged his sister awake.

"Who came over, Becca?"

She blinked at him, mascara sticking her lashes together. There were trails of makeup down her cheeks and chin, mapping out her tears. "Ashley," she said. Her voice came out hoarse from crying.

Shawn didn't ask anything else. He didn't want to criticize.

They walked upstairs together, with Rebecca leaning against her brother. He dropped a blanket over her once she made it to bed.

"Shawn?"

"Yeah?"

Rebecca didn't open her eyes, but her voice came out soft, pleading. "Don't let Mom know, okay? She'd kill me."

His chest tightened as he sighed. "Okay."

"Promise?"

"I promise," he said. "Now go to sleep."

Shawn closed the door and checked on Megan before turning to his own room. At the end of the hall, his mother's bedroom stood open. He wanted to go in and soak up the smell of her air freshener. Rebecca had never let her spray it anywhere else in the house, saying that it gave her a migraine. Now the scent of bottled rain, light and cool, seeped into the hallway. For the first time, Shawn realized just how much he loved it.

Jeremiah broke away from Erika before they touched the ground. She found her voice in a scream as she slammed into the rigid clay floor. Jeremiah rolled to a stop and sprang to his feet. They were in a clearing, but the earth was still packed solid, the trees still bare and straight and lonely. A quiet wind chuckled through the stripped twigs and branches overhead.

Erika ignored Jeremiah's proffered hand and pushed herself up. "What happened?"

He shook his head. "It doesn't matter."

"What did you do to me?"

"I . . . I can't . . ." Jeremiah pressed the heels of his hands against his eyes. "Don't ask me, Erika. Please don't ask me."

"Tell me! Tell me what you did."

"I can't."

"Why not?"

"I *can't.*" He ran a hand through his hair. "We had to move quickly. Too quick for you. It's just a bit of magic."

"Magic?" she shrieked. *"A bit of magic?* Who *are* you?"

"No one." Jeremiah's voice was thick, afraid. "Just whoever you make me out to be."

"What do you want from me?" Panic tightened Erika's throat. She took a step back and choked out her last question. "What are you going to do to me?"

"Nothing," Jeremiah told her. "I've already done the worst. I'm sorry, Erika — I'm sorry. But I need to get home and I can't do it by myself."

"Get *away.*"

"Erika, please." He whipped out his pocketknife and flipped it open. "The Passing Woods only open up for human souls."

"Oh God!"

Jeremiah shrugged off one of his jacket sleeves. *"Look."* He sank the knife into the soft underside of his arm and ran it up toward the elbow. His skin pulled away from the blade, but no blood came to the surface. Instead, a thin ribbon of smoke seeped out and hovered in the air around him. He ran his fingers through it, dispersing the curls of charcoal gray until they'd faded. "There's nowhere to hide out there. I had to get back in. So I needed you," he said. "I'm sorry. I'm so sorry."

His cut sealed itself back into smooth skin. Erika pressed her palms hard against the nearest tree. Her mouth hinged open, her hands trying to grip the knobby bark.

When she found her voice, it came out muddled, half scream, half sob. *"What are you?"*

"I'm . . ." Jeremiah faltered, knife still in hand, arm still hovering in midair. "I'm just a guide," he said. "Just a guide."

"Don't touch me," Erika said, but she already sounded defeated.

"Do you think that I wanted this, Erika? I didn't. I've been running from myself for so long." He held out his hand. "I know that you've been doing the same."

"No."

"You can't lie to me, Erika. Give me your hand."

"No," she said.

"I can help you."

"No."

But her arm drifted up, fingers limp in the air, and she wasn't afraid.

"I can show them to you," Jeremiah said. He took her wrist, lightly, between thumb and middle finger.

Her baby's face shot through her veins. She could feel Megan, like a ghost, prickling the hair along the backs of her arms.

She opened her eyes and stared at Jeremiah's hand, and at the thin blade of his knife.

"I'll protect you," Jeremiah said. "I promise I'll take care of you, Erika." His eyes looked dead into hers, irises dark and drowning in white. "I'm the only one who will anymore." He snapped the pocketknife shut and laid it against her palm, pressing her fingers down around it.

She looked at the fat pearl handle and, after a minute, pried open the blade, studying its worn edges.

"Put it against your mouth," Jeremiah said. "Flat." He tried to demonstrate with his fingers. "Now breathe."

She did. He saw her eyes glaze as she lost herself in the wandering. Her breath glowed frosty on the steel, and then white-hot. Through it, Jeremiah could see the shadows of dreams. He took her shoulders in his hands and guided her to the ground, so that she knelt on the earth that so many souls had knelt on, walked on, wept on. He sat down a few feet away, letting his breath come slow, because he was alone now, and safe, and that was all he needed.

Shawn sat in a rowboat with his father, the lake all sapphire and silver under a sheet of duckweed. Water striders crisscrossed the surface on spindly legs, spinning trails behind them. He was saying something about school, but his father wasn't listening and it dug at him. He looked up from his fishing line.

"Don't you care at all?"

"Not really. We didn't want you, Shawn."

Shawn's mouth dropped open.

The boat rose and fell as if on the chest of a sleeping giant. He could see his mother on the other side of the lake. She wore her favorite picnic dress and a straw hat, wind playing with the hem and ribbons as she watched them. The same waves that lapped at her sandaled feet were making hollow sounds against the hull of their fishing boat.

"Mom would never say that."

"Mom doesn't give a damn about you." His father scratched at the stubble of his chin. "She's screwing that cop," he said. "But he's going to get it, because she's not in love." He smiled. "She's not in love."

"Don't talk about her like that."

"Why? Because she's dead?"

Shawn looked back at his father, his heart speeding up. This didn't happen. This never happened.

"Didn't you go see her? Rebecca saw her. Rebecca cared more."

Shawn saw the caps of the waves turn from white to pink. Rubies. Wine. The water started to jump and bubble like hot water in a kettle. Something bumped against the side of the boat, making it tip harder one way. He gripped the fiberglass seat.

"Don't you want to look, Shawn? Don't you want to see your mother?" Shawn shook his head, eyes shut tight. His father leaned down to breathe against his ear. "Don't you want to say good-bye?"

It felt like the years before his parents' divorce, when his father raved about the affairs and the empty bank account and the things that he'd given up to make this work. Shawn had never been sure what his father thought "this" was. The family, probably, or his marriage. Or maybe even his life.

"Look, Shawn! Stop being such a fag and look at her for once!" Shawn felt the heavy hands on his arms before he opened his eyes. His father slammed him against the bottom of the boat and dragged him to the edge.

"Little whore, little whore, little whore."

Her dress clung to her like a second skin, pale blue and patterned. Blood stuck her lips together like the cheap gloss that Rebecca had always complained about. Red hair sparked fire as it snaked around her face and neck.

Deep in his throat, Shawn's father chuckled. He shoved his son and let go.

Shawn saw his mother reach out of the water, but he was struggling to catch his breath and said nothing. He saw her put her pale, slick fingers over the edge of the boat. He saw her pull, hard, and felt the boat tipping up.

His father was gone, leaving him alone to his mother and her pruning fingertips. Shawn slid down toward the water. Crimson and steaming, it licked at his skin, but he didn't think to open his mouth. He just toppled forward, splashing into the lake and breathing blood and water and air. He let himself drown.

Shawn woke up in a cold sweat, choking on spit that tasted of lake water.

Jeremiah waited for Erika to come back. Her body sat behind him, lips barely touching the cold surface of the pocketknife. Her mind walked somewhere else.

Jeremiah didn't pry; she'd find her own way. He knew that

time seemed to pass more quickly while wandering, and that Erika would come back to herself without realizing just how long she'd been gone.

Though surrounded by steadfast twilight, the knife blade flashed like sunshine on water. A little bit of magic. Weak magic, old magic, but magic nonetheless. Still, it wasn't the enchantments that made Jeremiah hold on to the old heirloom. The knife had been a gift from the High Kingdom to his own homeland and to his own father, and it was the most precious thing that Jeremiah had taken with him when he'd been sent away from the royal circle. It was as much a part of Jeremiah as anything, and it brought him as close to his father's house as he could ever hope to be again.

The dusk hovered cool and silent, and the air smelled sweetly of pine sap and thawing soil. Jeremiah drank it in as he struggled to plan his next move. He was in his element, and nearly back home, but that was never enough. He always had to run. Running and running and running on and on and on since the day they deemed him mature enough to understand. Or at least to almost understand. He hadn't been all that old when the tricks turned dirty and the game stopped being a game. Running and running and running. The running would be a part of him, ingrained and tested, until he gave up and gave in and gave over.

Someone had told him, once, that he was lucky not to be too much like his mother, because spirits like hers bent too easily to fit the shapes expected of them. He was lucky also, they said, for having a father capable of pushing the ghosts back into the shadows, just beyond seeing. But they didn't understand: His father wasn't always there.

The knife fell out of Erika's grasp as she came to, and the polished handle struck the forest floor. She wiped her eyes with stiff fingertips.

"I want to go home," she said. "I just want to go home."

Jeremiah put the blade back into his pocket, his fingers lingering on the worn family crest. "I know," he told her. "But it's such a long way. You have to give me time."

"They think that I'm dead."

He took her hands between his own. She felt the warmth of his skin, and wondered at how normal he felt. As if blood moved underneath, instead of air. She didn't understand how everything could have gone so wrong.

"They think I'm dead," she repeated.

"You make it sound like the worst possible thing."

"Isn't it?"

Jeremiah smiled. "No," he said. "There are many things worse than dying." He squeezed her hands gently. "And half of those things are bent on getting rid of me."

"Take me home?"

"You'll see your children again, Erika," he said. "I promise you that much." He jumped to his feet, smooth as smoke. "We have somewhere else to be now."

Erika tried to catch another breath of the sweet smell clinging to his skin. "You remind me of someone," she said.

"Oh?" said Jeremiah. "I hear that sometimes." He pulled her up, but she wasn't paying attention anymore.

Again, chocolate stuck to the back of her throat. Coffee and citrus and the clean scent of soap. She thought of Matt.

In the morning, Rebecca came downstairs and found Shawn in the kitchen, leaning over a sheaf of notebook paper, his ankles hooked around the wooden legs of one of the bar stools.

He slid a line of old photographs across the counter. "Which one's best?"

Rebecca held the pictures out for judgment. "When did you get up?"

"Seven."

"Couldn't you sleep?"

Shawn glanced at her. "Could you?"

"Sure," she said.

She let three of the four pictures fall back onto the tiled countertop. "This one," she said, handing over the last photo. It was from last Christmas, Erika beaming in a thick, white sweater as she leaned over the kitchen counter, fingers protective around a yellow mug. Matt had snapped it while the kids whipped together a fancy breakfast. "She looks pretty," said Rebecca. "Happy."

Shawn nodded and clipped the photo to an envelope. "Remember how Meg forgot where she hid Mom's gift, and we ended up quietly tearing the house apart at two A.M.?"

Rebecca took a chipped ceramic cup from the drainer and filled it with water. While the microwave buzzed in the background, she rummaged for creamer and instant coffee.

Finally, she said, "Yeah. Of course."

There were lines being drawn, and both Shawn and Rebecca could feel the boundaries ink themselves in. They were agreeing on distance. They were agreeing not to say "Mom," not to connect her to the body on the coroner's table, not to hurry back to those images, now that they'd survived the first round. If things were calm until the funeral, then they could grieve.

Rebecca took her cup of hot water out of the microwave and spooned in coffee powder.

"Shouldn't we plan the service before the obituary?" she asked.

"It's done."

"What?" She set the mug on the counter, making a crisp *click* against the tiles.

"What did you think I was doing all day yesterday?"

"Getting high? How should I know? Shawn, you knew that I wanted to do this."

"You can do flowers. Talk to the priest. I just chose the casket and time. The funeral home is preparing everything today. I thought you'd be relieved."

Rebecca stared down at her swirling coffee, lips pressed into a thin line. "When is it?"

"Friday."

"Tomorrow? It's so soon."

Shawn didn't look at her. "Like you wanted," he said, tapping his pen against the paper. "Don't tell me that we don't have enough time."

Rebecca turned away from her own point. She stirred her coffee and picked up the bottle of creamer.

"Matt took me downtown yesterday," she said, sounding distant. "There's a will, did you know that? Dad wanted them each to have one."

"Oh?"

"The accounts are ours now." Shawn nodded along. Rebecca cleared her throat. "The house is his."

Shawn felt his stomach clench. "Matt's?" he asked, his voice spread thin.

"Dad's."

"You're lying."

Rebecca didn't even have the heart to be rude. "You know that I'm not," she said. "She never changed it after the divorce."

"He'll come and take it from us. You know he will."

"He wouldn't do that, Shawn. He's not as bad as you think he is." Rebecca dropped her spoon into the sink. "He's really upset about all of this."

Shawn laid his hands flat against the counter. "You talked to him?"

"They loved each other once," she said. "He deserved to know. I invited him to the service."

"He won't come."

"He said he'd think about it." Rebecca sipped her coffee. "Look, Shawn," she said. "Believe what you will, but you don't know everything."

"I'm not letting you introduce him to Megan."

Rebecca frowned but said nothing. Instead, she took a handful of gingersnaps from the cookie jar and left the kitchen. Her brother had drawn just one more line and she knew that whatever she said, this one would never change.

The queen's chambers had high ceilings and marble floors. When the king entered, his footsteps echoed, crisp and clean, against the polished tiles. His wife sat straight-backed on a gilded stool. Skirts in deep and violent red spread out around her; her legs, which he saw, touched, kissed only occasionally, hidden deep within a cage of silk and organza. Her neck, long and slender, tightened as she lifted her chin and ran her fingers down the side of her face: thin nose and painted cheeks, lips so red they matched her dress, jewelry glowing gold on sun-licked skin. She did not smile, but the king knew that she admired how she looked, even though she had not seen her own reflection since leaving the High Kingdom. Waving off her handmaid, the queen turned to face her husband, a hand perched to hide her half-curled hair.

"Yes?" she asked.

"I have business below."

"Give my regards to the duchess."

"Of course."

She turned away again, running a hand over her dark ringlets. "Was that all?"

"It was."

He'd fallen in love with her long after they were engaged, when he'd watched her feeding swans by her father's lake, and had realized how much she resembled the beautiful imported birds. After their marriage, he'd learned how deep the similarities went: so pretty to look at, so quick to bite. The perfect queen, and yet sometimes he forgot. To love her. To cherish her. To see her as a husband should.

"This is the rogue," she said, an afterthought, and flicked her wrist at the handmaid.

"Highness."

The king appraised the girl. Her eyes were green, he could see, and the red of her hair stood out against her skin. She wore pale pink, the queen's color, for her train. It didn't suit her.

"You come from the High Kingdom?" he asked.

"I do."

"It shows."

She blushed and turned away before the queen caught her.

"When will you come home?" the queen asked her husband.

The king's attention slid back to his wife. "Tomorrow morning," he said.

She lifted her chin. "Spend time with the boys when you do," she said. "They miss you."

"They are princes."

The queen frowned. "They are children."

The king gave a quick nod and turned to leave. "I'll give the duchess your regards," he said, and hurried to the door.

"Charmed," his wife muttered.

Her rogue took up the brush. "Madam?"

"I may lose him," the queen told her, "to that bottomland leech."

"I should hope not, madam."

"Shouldn't we all?" She sighed. "The world loves him too much, child. And to think that I asked for it."

Erika and Jeremiah walked in silence for a long time, but dusk stayed draped around them. Erika had adapted to the twilight here, and the odd way it lit itself without any stars. She kept hoping to see the sky brighten with sunrise. Her imagination had always been quick to add extra eyes and teeth to the black-and-white sweep of midnight. Ever since childhood, she had found daylight an escape.

They reached another clearing, where a line of downed trees edged out the woods like a flood levee. Jeremiah touched Erika's arm to slow her. She glanced up and saw, for the first time, a ripe moon beaming down from that blank, slate-colored sky.

Ahead of them, the smooth forest floor began to break up, fading into a path and then a patio of weather-beaten stone. A low wall, netted with the dry, twisting stems of wintering vines, served as a border between earth and stone.

A lake lapped at the eastern edge of the terrace while a shuttered cottage marked the other side. Between them stood a trio of statues, all spaced along a weatherworn pedestal sixteen inches high. The stone extended out into a smaller platform in front of each statue, with shallow steps to lead the viewer up.

Jeremiah climbed over the downed wood and into the clearing. Erika followed, cautious as they approached the statues.

"Aren't they beautiful?" he murmured.

Erika kept her eyes on Jeremiah. "They're stone," she said.

Jeremiah smiled.

They were women in the refined style of ancient Greece. All three were draped in robes that curled along their arms and fell in waves at their feet. Bursts of lichen bloomed in the hems of their dresses, and in the folds of their fingers and hair. Their heads were tipped forward in mourning. The first had her palms pressed against the hollows of her eyes. The second was the most serene, her hands buried in twists of perfect ringlets, her face stoic. The third clutched her mouth, as if to stifle her own weeping.

"They're creepy," Erika said.

"Lonely," said Jeremiah. "Sad."

He turned to her. "You need to be very quiet for now," he said. "You'll be my ears for a little while. Can you do that for me?"

She nodded.

"Good." He walked up the steps of the second pedestal and ran a thumb along the curve of the sculpture's closed eyes. "Don't be afraid, Erika," he whispered. "They're here to help us over." He pressed his mouth against the statue's parted lips.

There was a heartbeat of silence and then, with a sigh of stone scraping stone, the carved fingers slid away from their bed of curls. The statue moved slowly, her hands splayed like starbursts. Ropes of hair snaked between the thin fingers that she slipped over Jeremiah's skin.

Erika held her breath as she watched, transfixed and terrified. Her own hands pressed hard against the stone wall, her knees locked straight to keep herself from falling. She thought about running away, but realized that she'd become too dependent. This man, or ghost, or demon, was the only one who could tie her back to something she actually understood.

Jeremiah held still until the statue drew back, hair tucked cleanly behind her ears and a half smile on her mouth. Her hands hung in midair, poised as if in conversation.

Jeremiah turned to Erika, sharing the statue's vague smile.

"Are you okay?" he asked.

"What just happened?" Her voice came out a little desperate. With every passing hour, the world that she had always known was breaking to pieces in her hands.

Jeremiah looked at her a little while, silent, and then put a finger to his lips. He led her to the shore of the lake and untied a small wooden boat that waited there. She held tight to his hand as he helped her step offshore. The boat reminded her of the fishing trips that her ex-husband had been so fond of. They had never ended well.

Jeremiah took the oars and pushed away from the beach. Gentle swells fanned out behind them as he guided the boat farther and farther away from the shore. Above them, the moon sat bright and full in the sky. Its twin laughed softly in a bed of rippling glass.

It was a small lake, almost a pond, the surface littered with dark flecks of dead plant life and beetles. The spines of reeds and cattails ringed the shore, straight and sharp like quivers full of arrows. The only things alive were moonflowers that pushed down close to the water, blossoms clustered thick and brilliant white through the dark, mouths open and trumpeting to the twilight sky. Behind them marched the trees, bodies straight and slender in their sheer moonlit robes.

Erika turned away from the shore and stared at the water, her expression blank. She felt so drained, as if all of the sleep from before no longer mattered. Her shoulders sagged and she felt something like guilt and grief surge up from the bottom of her chest. It caught in her throat and settled there, heavy enough to make her sick. She wrapped her arms around her stomach and hunched down, breathing deep and trying to control herself. Jeremiah didn't seem to notice.

But of course he didn't notice, Erika thought. He knew exactly what was happening, even if he wouldn't tell her, so no panic pressed in to suffocate him. She turned over this idea, wondering why she wasn't more upset by his secrets, and tried to make herself angry. Anything to take away the nausea that came from thinking about her children. How long had she been gone? How could they possibly find her?

Across the shore, where the bones of more water plants split the surface of the lake, came a quiet splash. Erika rested her forehead against the back of her hand and tried not to dwell on the image of her own fingers, pale and slick, grabbing Shawn's collar and dragging him to the bottom of a bloody lake.

Jeremiah closed his eyes and kept rowing. His movements were steady, and the gentle pull of the water gave Erika a rhythm to focus on. Each stroke came like the rock of a cradle, smooth and easy, and brought back snatches of lullabies and sleepless nights. A mother's memories. Erika tuned every sense to the physical presence of the boat. She forced her breath to come slowly, regularly, and forced her mind away from her children.

They bucked forward. Erika's head snapped up. Jeremiah nearly dropped the oars.

"I told you to listen!" he yelled, tightening his grip, and tried to row faster.

A pair of thin, water-pruned hands slammed against the edge of the boat. Erika screamed, drawing back. She kicked at them and the fingers flew up, joints locked at odd angles.

"Don't touch the water," Jeremiah said sharply. He threw himself into his work.

The surface of the lake burst as if boiling, but the water that slapped Erika's face and arms was cold enough to hurt. She clenched her teeth and held tight to the wooden seat as the boat continued its erratic skipping. She felt it leave the water. Beneath them, the lake came alive. They splashed when they came back down on the frothing waves. Erika winced, her muscles so tense they burned. Jeremiah kept his head down and rowed hard.

The sun came out.

Erika squeezed her eyes shut when the light exploded around them, its arrival making her dizzy and confused. The world, so green and blue and brilliant after the dark of the woods, almost blinded her. The water continued to throw them into the air, splashing yellow-brown now instead of black. When Erika opened her eyes again, she could see something crisscrossing the lake bed: thin, black shadows streaking past like bullets.

They were nearly to the eastern shore.

Jeremiah got to his feet, knocking the boat into a sideways lurch. "Don't touch the water!"

He grabbed the coil of rope from under his seat and swung the looped end in wide circles above his head. A docking post stood onshore, short and squat and so far away. The rope rippled out from Jeremiah's hands. He watched it fly, desperately fighting for balance on the shifting floor.

He missed.

The rope flopped on the patchy grass, kicking up a fine breath of dust. Jeremiah's stomach jerked as he realized that he'd missed his only chance, and that he'd lost them both to the Weeper's lake. He could feel the boat tipping up at the bow, rising on the back of an unnatural wave. He hauled on the rope to pull it back, and hissed as the cord cut into his sweaty palms.

A sapling shot out of the earth and speared the improvised lasso. As the tree grew, it dragged the boat into harbor. Jeremiah clung to the rope until the hull struck shore. Then he collapsed over the edge, desperate for just one mouthful of air that wasn't tangy with fear.

A splash came from the middle of the lake and the surface turned to glass all over again. Erika lay curled in the bottom of the boat, still sheltering herself with her arms.

"Boy!"

She looked up and saw an old, summer-baked man standing beside the newly risen tree. He leaned heavily against a knotted staff and glared down at Jeremiah with sharp black eyes. It didn't seem that he'd noticed Erika yet.

"Every time, boy," he said. "You never bring no good here." His sandals scuffed the ground as he turned, and his staff kicked up dry dirt each time he jammed it down. "Help her along, poor thing," he said. "No idea, eh? You not telling her."

When Jeremiah reached out to help Erika to dry land, she latched on to his hands as if they were lifelines. Jeremiah draped an arm around her shoulders as she stepped onto shore.

He leaned down to her ear. "That's Baba Laza," he said. The pitch of his voice soothed her. "Or Laza, if you like. He's going to offer you tea."

Erika looked at the ground, thick and soft with grass, and at the trees that nearly buckled beneath the weight of their own fruit. Berries grew fat on shrubs, and bushes and flowers bloomed, yellow, orange, violet in any space not occupied by leaves. A cottage squatted on the rise ahead of them, small and made of cut stone like the house by the statues across the lake, but ropes of creeper turned this one green, and grapes like rubies bunched along its eaves. The air here vibrated with life. Erika looked over her shoulder at the lake and saw that the surface had stilled and, from here, the water had gone as French blue as the sky above it. The woods on the other side looked like the woods around her now — summer-drunk and thriving — but there were no statues, no moonflowers, no paved pathway to be seen. Jeremiah squeezed her arm and pulled her on ahead.

They found seats on an old vine-invaded bench until Baba Laza came out of his fairy-tale cottage with a clay bowl in each hand. He gave one to Jeremiah and one to Erika before stepping back to look at his two visitors. He took in Jeremiah, who still had an arm around Erika, and Erika, damp from the lake and covered in dust and sand from the bottom of the boat. She pressed herself into Jeremiah's side as if terrified of losing him. She'd traveled so far out of her element that Jeremiah was all that she had to anchor her. She could just about hate him for it.

"See her loving you," Laza said. "After you bring her through that." The old man shifted his weight, setting one hand on his hip and leaning heavily against his staff. "What would your brothers say?"

Jeremiah shook his head. "I can't hear you."

Laza's papery laugh came out through cracked lips and broken teeth. "You *are* your mother's boy," he said.

Erika took time to examine Baba Laza between sips of his spiced tea. His posture was all angles and his skin was all knots. There were fans of laugh lines at the corners of his eyes, and his mouth had stiffened out from frowning. His cropped hair was salted, the bristles on his chin were peppered, and each stood out against his red-brown skin, tough and burnished from gardening. Laza's mismatched appearance comforted Erika in a way that she couldn't quite place.

"I'm not a bad man," Jeremiah said.

Laza dropped his chin. "Our talk is one-sided. You cannot hear and you will not listen, so your company is worth nothing. No better than usual."

"We need a place to sleep, Laza," Jeremiah said.

"And you will have my floor." The old man tossed back a hand, rapping one dusty windowpane with his knuckles. "No better than usual."

Shawn and Rebecca avoided each other all day. It was easy to do after Megan got up, because Shawn took her to the park, and then shopping for a funeral dress, and then for dinner and ice cream, where he tried, and failed, to finally talk to her about their mother. She just watched him with her big, steady fawn eyes and broke the silence by asking for more chocolate syrup.

Shawn was angry, and wanted to be able to blame Rebecca. Drunk, sad, unhelpful Rebecca.

He and Megan came home to find the lights on, as usual. When he pushed open the front door, the smell of flowers struck him.

Rebecca stood at the kitchen counter with her ear to the phone and a pen in hand. Clouds of white and pink peonies filled the room, the air heady with their scent.

Shawn walked over to her once he recovered from the shock. "We can't afford this," he said, his voice low.

"Dad paid for it," Rebecca answered coolly. "He's coming, by the way."

Megan buried her face in a bouquet and came up smiling.

"He shouldn't be involved," said Shawn.

Rebecca covered the phone's mouthpiece with one hand and smiled at her little sister. "I bought you a new dress, honey," she said.

"So did I," said Shawn.

"It's on your bed and you'll love it. Go up and try it on."

As Megan's footsteps pounded up the stairs, Rebecca turned back to her brother.

"Sleep it off," she said. "You'll be less bitter in the morning."

Shawn rolled his eyes and left the kitchen. He still wanted to hate her.

Erika tried to sleep, but she was overtired. Her skin felt stretched over her bones and her muscles were worked sore.

She crept to Jeremiah's side and felt in his pockets for the little knife. His breathing went on slow and undisturbed even after she'd moved away. Curled tight in a corner on the other side of the room, Erika put the flat of the blade against her lips and let out a long, slow breath. She could feel the air funnel out along her cheeks and she could taste the metal of the knife. The light from the window thinned and then became a luscious, sacred white. Something sifted through the pores of Erika's skin and she wilted with relief. Everything in her flowed away.

❦

Shawn sat on a cliff, his legs dangling over the edge and his hands gritty with black earth. He could feel the wind grate the back of his neck, where his skin stretched tight with sunburn and where his sweat gathered in a tangle of hair. He could feel a layer of loose sand shifting under his weight, sticking to the backs of his shins, a little more each time he touched the crumbling ledge. He could feel his mother beside him — could smell her perfume — but was too afraid to look.

When he opened his mouth to ask a question, no sound came out.

"I miss you, Shawn," Erika said. "And I miss your sisters."

You're dead, Mom, Shawn wanted to say, but "Me too" came out instead.

"I want to talk to Meg," she said, "but I'm afraid to scare her. Is she okay?"

Shawn didn't answer. He stared at his knees and the world that fell away beneath them. He thought, briefly, about jumping.

His mother waited out the silence until she had to break it. "Tell her that I love her. That I didn't mean to leave."

"She knows, Mom."

More silence. Erika reached over to touch Shawn's shoulder, but then stopped. Put her hand back down. "It's not the same, is it?" she asked.

"No."

"I'm trying to come home."

When Shawn opened his mouth, he heard his own voice say, "Don't." As his teeth closed around the reproach, he felt a jolt of panic. What had he done?

Erika sat still for so long that Shawn began to wonder whether she'd disappeared.

"You're dreaming, Shawn," she said at last. "But I'm not."

He shivered. "Mom," he said. "Why are you here?"

"I miss you. I still love you. I still want to come home."

"We lost you, Mom. We bury you tomorrow. You can't come back."

"I'm not dead, Shawn. I would know. He would tell me."

"Who would tell you?"

Finally, she reached out a halting arm and put it around her son's shoulders. Her touch was cold. "You'll understand."

Shawn turned his face to hers, more out of shock than curiosity. Her skin looked caked on and her eyes were yellowed and bloodshot. There were sores around her lips, and the gums that held her brittle teeth were blistered black.

He could sense his mother's distress, as if she could only see herself through him.

"Why do you picture me like this, Shawn?" Erika asked, close to tears. "Why would you think this?"

Shawn tried to move away from her. Instead, he slid too far, to the edge of the cliff, and lost his hold. He seemed to fall forever, but his life never flashed before his eyes. All he could see was his mother, looking down from the mountain, not saying a word.

He was less than a meter off the ground when the man caught him. The man slipped his arms under Shawn's shoulders and knees to stop the long fall and the crack of a skull and the jolt of a broken back. For some reason, Shawn didn't feel at all thankful.

The man smiled, but the warmth never touched his eyes. He looked miserable.

"I'm Jeremiah," he said.

He sank down into a crouch and laid Shawn on the ground.

"What are you?" asked Shawn, looking up into his rescuer's troubled face.

Jeremiah took a pocketknife from his blazer.

He shook his head. "I'm sorry," he said.

The blade flashed down, glittering, and Shawn gasped as his throat split open.

He woke up on the floor in a tangle of blankets, his wrists crossed above his neck to block Jeremiah's knife.

Erika opened her eyes and found Jeremiah standing over her, blade in hand. He flipped it shut with an irritated *snap* and put the knife back into his pocket. Even in her embarrassment and anger, Erika watched closely as it slid out of sight. It drew her in, made her desperate. Jeremiah noticed.

"Don't do that again, Erika," he said. "It's not worth it."

"They're my kids!"

"You saw the way Shawn thinks of you. And telling him that you're coming back — don't you realize that you're scaring him?"

Erika pushed herself off the floor. "I am their mother and I have a right to see them."

He turned away and straightened his jacket. "I can't hear you, Erika, so stop. Stop all of this before you do something stupid. And don't steal my things."

The door slammed behind Jeremiah as he left the room.

Chapter Four

A rainstorm rolled in at noon, seething with a tension that made the city smell like cooling pavement.

Erika's children arrived at the interment site with armfuls of calla lilies. The flowers stood out against their black clothes and left smudges of pollen against their sleeves. When the children got there, their mother's coffin sat waiting beside the gaping hole, a polished cherry box with brass clasps and a lid draped with peonies and ivy. Shawn carried Megan from the car as she sobbed against his neck. Rebecca stood beside them, dark sunglasses hiding swollen eyelids. Only she knew why Shawn kept throwing worried looks at the gathering crowd.

Matt had come with them. He spoke quietly to the priest while the children waited by the coffin, watching the rows of collapsible chairs fill with family friends and a handful of Erika's coworkers.

The storm had not yet broken, but some mourners carried umbrellas with them, just in case. The pool of black suits and dresses broke in flashes of bright polyester, tucked quickly under chairs because the shock of color seemed inappropriate.

Thunder rumbled in the distance.

The priest cleared his throat and brought all extra talk to a close. He began by quoting a Bible passage to let them know that Erika lived with God now, and that she was happy. Shawn smoothed the back of Megan's velvet dress, to quiet her crying, and felt her drift to sleep against his shoulder. He looked at Rebecca, to see if she'd noticed, and then followed her gaze out to the stretching line of cars. His face fell. Beside him, Matt straightened up.

The priest began listing Erika's qualities: A good mother. A hard worker. A loving wife.

Rebecca leaned into Shawn and whispered, "I told you he'd come." She wasn't talking about the priest, but about the man who arrived late, a navy Windbreaker over his suit jacket. Shawn didn't answer.

Megan woke up after the ceremony and threw flowers into her mother's grave. Matt offered to take her for a walk while her brother and sister accepted condolences from the crowd, and Shawn agreed before Rebecca had a chance to open her mouth. When she saw her brother's eyes hooked on the man with the Windbreaker, she thought it best not to argue.

A light rain began to patter against the cemetery grounds. Shawn opened a black umbrella and held it between himself and his sister, silent as Rebecca spoke softly to everyone who came by. She took hugs and promises with the same earnest half smile. Shawn watched the milling crowd, gauging the time.

After fifteen minutes, Matt and Megan made their way back to the grave site and climbed inside the patrol car to wait. The headlights flipped on and the wipers began their familiar slide across the front windshield. Megan put her chin on the lip of the door, her nose squashed up against the window. Matt suggested they turn on the radio, but she said no.

She watched the man who hung around at the back of the line, letting other people join in ahead of him, and knew that he wanted something. You didn't let people cut unless you wanted something.

"Did Mommy know that man?"

Matt sighed and drummed the steering wheel with his thumbs. "Yeah, Meg. She knew everyone who came."

"Did she like him?"

Matt looked over at Megan. Her hair drifted up at the crown of her head, static charged from the rain. Her dress hovered at the bend of her knees as she knelt, pressed forward against the glass, her shoes working mud into the passenger seat.

"Sometimes, Meg," said Matt, because he wasn't sure what else he could say. He wanted to tell her all about the other times too, but knew that it wasn't his place. "Sometimes she liked him a lot."

There was quiet for a long time — just the tapping of rain on the top of the car and the slosh of tires spinning by, hurrying out of the cemetery to someplace where death could be mourned in secret.

"Should I like him?" asked Meg. She'd pulled back a little from the window, her face reflected in the glass, transparent as a ghost. Erika's ex-husband had almost reached Shawn and Rebecca. Men from the cemetery were standing by to fill in the grave.

"That's up to you, honey," said Matt. But he knew that it wasn't.

❀

Shawn and Rebecca stood side by side in the growing dark as their father stepped forward. The three of them stared at one another for a few long seconds.

At last, John Stripling cleared his throat. "I'm sorry about your mom," he said. The familiar gravel in his voice made Shawn wince. The blunt words brought back the weeks following his parents' divorce, when friends came up saying, "Hey, I'm sorry about your dad, but can't you, like, get over it or something? I mean, we don't even know you anymore," and he just wanted to tell them *No, no, no, it's not that easy.* He'd only been ten then, but the words still came to him now, and they still applied. This time they spilled out.

"No," he said, his tone flat. "It's not that easy."

He knew that Rebecca was staring at him with her mouth hanging open, and that Matt watched the three of them from his car, hoping that this reunion went as smoothly as possible. He knew that the shadows in his father's eyes came from surprise rather than regret. He knew that he should stop talking and walk away before anything else happened.

"Shawn, I'm not trying to make anything easy. I know it can't be."

"You shouldn't be here."

"You don't need to be so hard on him, Shawn," Rebecca broke in.

Shawn turned to his sister. "How can you stand there and say that, Rebecca? He made our life hell."

"He did *not.*"

"He *beat* her, Becca. He beat Mom."

"He never hit her on purpose."

Shawn's mouth went dry. His throat felt tight and stuffed inside a too-small neck.

"You believed him?" he said. "You believed what this drunk bastard said? That bullshit he sold us with bedtime stories, about loving us?"

"I did love you, Shawn," his father said. "Both of you. All of you. I still do."

Shawn glared at his father. He ignored the sun-spotted skin and the scruff of his beard and the silver creeping into his hair. "I'm going for custody, Shawn. Of you and Meg."

"No," Shawn said. "I won't go back to that, Dad, and you're crazy if you think that I'll let you get hold of Megan. I don't want to see you again, or hear from you, or hear about you." Shawn shot a look at Rebecca. "Don't try to scare me."

The comment could have been for his sister, or for their father. It didn't seem to matter. Shawn walked away from the conversation, rain spilling off his umbrella, and collected Megan from Matt's car. Rebecca had to jog to catch up with them before they left the cemetery. On the drive home, no one said a word.

The first hints of a path started out in the woods as fragments of crumbling, weathered stone. If Jeremiah hadn't been leading, Erika would have lost herself long ago. He picked his way through the forest, turning every now and then, until the cobbles began to run together and form a road. "Highway of souls," Jeremiah said, and Erika couldn't tell if he was joking. The longer they walked, the bigger the trees grew, taller and thicker than redwoods, leaves as big as place mats, and the path curved around them, or plowed straight through the arches left by rotted-out trunks. After a few hours, the straight lines of buildings could be seen through the green and brown ahead. Jeremiah took Erika's hand.

"Welcome to the city proper," he said.

"The city of what?"

"Limbo."

Jeremiah and Erika cut through the woods to make better time. They didn't even pause when they finally broke out of the forest. The city walls were fifty feet high and made of smooth, dove-colored stone. The road ran up to it and then split, making an easy circle around the perimeter. The wooden shingles of houses could be seen over the wall's crown, and the upper stories of tall, skeletal complexes with broken windows and gray laundry out to dry. In a few places, a thin, oily smoke curled and drifted, tingeing the air. In other places, towers with arched windows shot up to overlook the city. Erika couldn't make out faces in the watchtowers, but saw movement every now and then, the flicker of a silhouette making itself known.

The buildings climbed, staggering higher as they reached a craggy hill with sides so sheer and chipped they looked to be chiseled out of the granite by giant hands. The city walls twisted up the incline and disappeared into the shoulders of the hill. On the flat top of that overlook sat a palace, shining white over the city that it protected, or was protected by. It had its own gates, visible even from the road outside the city, black and impassable, to sift out the rabble.

Just ahead of Erika and Jeremiah, past a flat expanse of green, stood a massive arch that the road ran into like a tongue. To the left of this gate waited another triptych of statues. All three of them seemed to be modeled on the same woman, following the stages of her life. Maiden, mother, crone. Each sat patiently in a high-backed chair, the first with flowers in her braids, the second with flowers in her hands, the third with flowers at her feet. The maiden looked just like the statues that Jeremiah had kissed, though happy and proud, with her chin tilted up. But as she aged, her expression turned from one of expectation to one of defeat, and her back grew more crooked with time pressing down. Jeremiah went to the oldest of the statues and laid a hand on her shoulder.

"My ears, Megaera," he said gently. He put a piece of black ribbon over her knee and waited as her stiff granite fingers moved to pick it up.

With a smile, Jeremiah turned back to Erika. "All together now," he told her. "Shall we go in?"

She only shrugged, feeling worthless.

"I'm sorry, Erika," he said, taking her by the arm. "I'm sorry about what I said before. But we're almost home. My home, at least. We'll be safe soon, and then we can talk." He led her to the gate. "I'm a prince here," he added. "Of sorts."

"Jeremiah, I—" Erika broke off and looked at her arm, following Jeremiah's fingers as they slid down to her wrist, and then to her palm, and then wove themselves between her own. "I feel crazy," she said, still watching. A plea, not a statement.

He stepped back to her and tipped up her chin. Took her shoulders in his hands. "Of course you do," he said, looking sorry. "I've been a terrible guide." He cradled the back of her head, just above her neck, in his right hand, and pulled her close into a hug. He smelled the way Matt did — she'd placed it now and hated herself for not realizing before. Hated herself for barely thinking about the man who she'd left behind while she put her whole life and sanity into the hands of someone else. But she hadn't recognized it because the smell was different. Not softer or stronger; not too much sandalwood or too little orange peel. Different because he wasn't Matt. She worked two loose fists between her chest and Jeremiah's and pushed away.

"Don't," she said. "Please don't."

His hand slipped away from her hair, trailing a curl with it, which he let settle against her collarbone.

"Erika," he said, "I owe you. I owe you more than you realize right now. But if you don't come inside with me, I cannot help you."

Erika took a breath, unable to break eye contact with Jeremiah. She thought of John. Of all the men she'd ever put faith in and lost parts of herself over. Of Matt and the way he loved her kids like a dad would. He was her promise that things didn't have to turn out in shambles. She nodded and took Jeremiah's hand. He pressed it, looking relieved but not surprised. Armed with her consent, he finally led her through the arch.

Erika shivered, her body struck by the full weight of sudden winter. Jeremiah's palm, so warm, burned against her own.

"It's no longer summer in the city," he told Erika, and dropped her hand to walk on ahead. "When you leave the woods, time comes back to you."

Erika crossed her arms to hold in the escaping warmth. She looked around.

The woman at the gate was a pitiful sight. She sat off to the side, just inside the border, and waited with an empty tin can in her lap. Her hair, mussed and greasy from going unwashed, fell down a crooked back. Dirt, food, and what looked like blood stained the cloth that she used as a wrap. Beneath it, her skin stretched itself so tight over her bones that she seemed painted on. The fingertips that held her alms can were pointed, joints clearly defined. Her face and shoulders looked sharp and chipped beneath the shadows of a falling sun.

Jeremiah walked past her.

"Give her something," Erika said. "I know you have something."

Jeremiah glanced around, puzzled. "Who?"

"Her. Jeremiah, please."

His eyes found the old woman and the tension in his joints released. "Oh, Erika," he whispered. "If Earth's richest man gave half a penny to each pauper in the Middle Kingdom, he'd be a pauper himself before the line even dwindled, and no one would be the happier. They only eat to make themselves feel more alive, but one day they'll realize that their bodies are just shells. It isn't charity they need — it's courage." He tapped Erika's shoulder and motioned her forward. When he turned away, she fished through her pockets for change and dropped it into the woman's tin. The coins clattered loudly against the can, but neither the beggar nor Jeremiah acknowledged it. Erika followed him on into the city.

Limbo resembled the poor places of Manhattan, Erika thought, but without electricity or water. It smelled stale. Old food, old piss, old air. She tried to breathe as lightly as possible. Houses gaped open without window glass or curtains to line them. The streets were littered with garbage, crawling with beggars. Children ran naked, leathery skin thick on their undeveloped bodies. Babies, too young even to crawl, screamed from within the hollows of empty houses. Erika walked, hands over her mouth, as if in a trance. She stared ahead, too shocked at the poverty to register half of what she saw.

Jeremiah took to the city as if he were strolling through Central Park. Erika wondered whether all of Limbo was this destitute, or whether Jeremiah was trying to make a point — an appeal, as it were, for her gratitude. *This is how much worse off you could be, Erika Stripling.* But Erika didn't feel humbled, only terrified, and she didn't relax until they stopped at the gate of an old manor.

"A prince?" she asked quietly.

He nodded. "Of sorts."

Only in comparison with the rest of the city could you call Jeremiah's home a palace. White and double storied in the Palladian style with large windows and clean, classical lines — no amount of architectural beauty could hide the fact that it had long ago fallen into disrepair. A shell of ivy, still dead with winter, cocooned the walls and roof while the front gardens choked on weeds and stiff brown grass. The paint itself was chipping from its brick, and lines spiderwebbed the walk. Two candelabra edged out the night through the windows on either side of the front door.

"Are all the princes so Victorian?" Erika asked.

Jeremiah chuckled. "Victorian would be too peaceful," he said. "But we've been settled in the long eighteenth century since before I was born. Disease, famine, revolution everywhere. A very productive era for death." He closed the ironwork gate as they passed through. "I understand," he went on, leading Erika up the crumbling walk, "that we were quite taken with Damascus for a while. Many regret ever leaving the Crusades behind." The door creaked open before he even knocked.

"About time, then." The plump, pear-shaped housekeeper was an English maid, all powder-pale skin and tightly wrapped silver hair. A white lace cap, a straight dress cut at the ankles, and a heavily starched apron made up a uniform so hackneyed that it bordered on parody.

"Martha," Jeremiah said. "This is Erika."

"Oh?" A long silence followed, and Erika felt herself being appraised by a mother's eye. "Your mum had her hair."

Jeremiah cleared his throat. "Would you mind dressing her?"

In answer, Martha stepped back from the entryway with a half curtsey. Erika and Jeremiah stepped over the threshold together, his hand on the back of her upper arm.

The hall was papered with a curling print of gold vines and flowers. At the center of the room stood a large, round cage, as tall as Jeremiah and at least four feet across. The bird inside didn't live up to the dimensions of its home, its body white and no larger than a pigeon's, its head tucked against its breast. Erika poked a finger through the fine silver wire, but the bird just inched to one side without raising its head, plumed tail shivering as it moved.

"That's Kala," Jeremiah said.

"She doesn't like me much."

"She doesn't like anyone around here much." He nodded to the housekeeper.

"Come, miss." Martha took Erika by the hand and led her to the staircase.

"Where are we going?"

"I'll have dinner made," Jeremiah called after her. "I'm afraid that I have to work on your behalf until then. You can entertain yourself, I expect."

As she rounded the left branch of the staircase, Erika looked over her shoulder, but Jeremiah had already disappeared.

It began with a white rose, but it had never been innocent. The king would say it had been later; he would swear on it to his wife, to his children, to himself, but innocence was nothing more than a lie he began to believe. A lie he needed to believe.

Long ago, he had seen the game played by his father. He had seen the cards laid out; had seen the moves and had learned what they meant. He hated to admit now that he was thankful for knowing how to raise the stakes. He hated to admit that the quiet sorrow of his mother might prove to be the same in his own wife, and that he no longer cared.

He should have stopped.

He didn't want to.

When the king saw the roses budding out, he should have ignored them. He should have kept himself away. He should never have pointed one out to his attendant with such direct orders. He should never have waited for a reply, and should never have read it when it came.

The scrap of paper arrived small but carefully folded, the corners curling out into the petals of a lily. So flawless, so painstaking, as if she'd stayed awake all night to match the perfection of the flower that the king had never even touched. Alone in his rooms, it took him a quarter of an hour to open, because he would not let it rip.

"I've always wanted a garden," she'd written.

He should have burned it.

He should have had her banished.

He should have known better.

But it was just a flower, after all.

Martha led Erika down a dark hallway and through a door that sighed with age. The room Jeremiah had chosen for her had obviously been neglected for some time. The bottom third of the walls were plush raspberry velvet, the rest a buttercream paint that had begun to peel. Dust blanketed the tall four-poster bed and settled along the lines of the curtains, giving a fur coat to the burgundy silk. An old bureau, a wardrobe, and a mint-colored wing chair, faded and threadbare, made up the rest of the room's furniture. The door on the back wall stood open to a small bath with a tub, toilet, and single-tap sink.

"You've had a bad crack on the head, miss," Martha said. "I'll bring some bandages for that. And clean clothes for you."

"Is there warm water?"

"I could have some boiled."

"If it's no trouble."

Martha nodded.

"And a towel," said Erika.

"A towel, of course."

"And soap, please."

Martha looked her up and down. "Hm," she said, and then turned on her heel and left the bedroom.

Erika watched her leave before scanning her new haunts. She felt small and out of place in the middle of so much old-world opulence. Too much history mingled with the dust of the house, and too much pain dripped beneath the paint and the flocked wall. History and pain that she had no business seeing.

To block out these problems that didn't belong to her, she focused on her own. Now that she had some privacy, she allowed herself to begin to lay out the pieces. She didn't know how to put them together just yet, but she needed to see what her options were. Shawn, Rebecca, and Megan. She took a deep breath.

Shawn looked at his hands and saw that they were small, and tanned from summer, but, for some reason, this didn't surprise him. He was crouched beneath the hickory tree in the backyard, an old tennis ball by his knee. He picked it up and felt the summer dust rub against his palms. He remembered this afternoon. It was late July, and he was nine years old.

The screen door crashed shut as John Stripling walked down the back steps.

"She's asleep now," he told Shawn. He sounded proud.

"Why'd you hit her?"

His father's eyes clouded. "I did not *hit* her, Shawn. I never hit her. I only put her to bed. Why would I hurt your mother? I love her."

"Are you going to hurt me too?"

"Have I ever hurt you before?" He answered himself before Shawn had a chance to open his mouth: "Of course not. Your mother's so tired she doesn't know what she's saying. I only put her to bed, Shawn. Can't you see that?"

"I can see her bruises."

John Stripling jerked Shawn up by the collar of his T-shirt. "Now you listen to me," he said. A sour taste of whiskey caught far back in Shawn's mouth as the smell seeped from his father's pores. "Don't talk like that. You walk around lying like that and some cop is going to believe you. Cops like to believe little kids when they say lies like that. I don't want your mother to have any more trouble out of you."

"Yes, sir."

Shawn struggled to look innocent as his father tried to fish out the lie.

"Yes, *Dad*," John Stripling said, finally satisfied. "We're not an army family."

"We're not a family at all."

"Shawn." He yanked his son's shirt harder this time, so that the front collar made Shawn's throat flush red.

Erika came running out of the house.

"Get your hands off him!"

"Back inside, Erika," John said. "Go to bed."

"Go to bed?" she screamed. "Is that all you can ever say to me?"

"I won't speak to you like this."

"Damn you, John!" She gave him a hard slap across the face.

There was a long, dead pause. Shawn held his breath.

John dropped his son's T-shirt and grabbed his wife instead, taking both of her arms in his hands and pressing them together, so that her whole body curved in. "Get inside," he said under his breath, and pushed her up the steps.

Shawn sat down on the grass again and twirled the tennis ball on the dirt in front of him. He heard a familiar voice ask, "Was it like this every day?"

"No," he said, and then looked up.

The man named Jeremiah stood above him, with his hands in his jacket pockets.

"She stayed with him for so long," Jeremiah said. "And she hoped so much that things would change. It's a wonder she ever managed to leave."

Shawn stayed quiet.

"Do you think that he loved her?" Jeremiah asked.

"No. Yes." Shawn shrugged. "I don't know." He glanced back up. "You haven't killed me this time."

"I haven't killed you at all," Jeremiah said. "You only ever do that once."

"Who are you?"

"At this point, I'm honestly not sure how to answer that."

Shawn nodded slowly. "Tell me," he said, "am I dreaming?"

A crack, like gunfire, echoed through the house. Jeremiah patted the pockets of his slacks.

"Damn," he spat. "Your mother's a born thief, isn't she?"

"What?"

Erika ran out of the house, splattered with blood. Her right hand gripped a pearl-handled pocketknife; her chest fluttered as she tried to catch her breath. Shawn leaped to his feet and watched his mother turn her eyes on him and smile. A soft, thankful noise escaped her throat. Then her eyes skimmed past her son and her smile disappeared.

"Jeremiah."

"You don't listen, Erika. I told you not to come back." Jeremiah crossed the yard in two strides and wrestled the blade from her hands before tossing a look back at Shawn. "I'm sorry you have to see this," he said, and then plunged the knife into Erika's heart.

A scream burst from the house and Rebecca crashed through the back door. She ran out, young and scared, with a toddling Megan on her bony hip, but when she looked at her brother, an odd flash of recognition made her eyes go wide. Somewhere deep in his gut, Shawn realized that she could *see* him. She knew that he was there, beyond sleep and beyond dream. Their mother vanished with Jeremiah, leaving behind a pool of warm blood. Shawn opened his eyes and saw the speckled shadows of his bedroom's ceiling.

Jeremiah stood with his arms folded across his chest and his back to Erika. She crouched on the floor, doubled over and wheezing into the dusty carpet.

"I told you not to do that," Jeremiah said.

"You showed me how!"

"I showed you how to get in. That's not the same as getting out."

"I'm —"

"Keep your apologies, Erika. I'll see you at dinner."

Martha came in after Jeremiah left.

She carried a roll of linen bandages and a ceramic bowl, which she filled with water from the bathroom. Then she knelt on the floor, saying nothing, and cleaned the gash on Erika's left temple.

"I just wanted to check on them," Erika told her.

Martha undid the roll of linen and began to wind it around Erika's head, her movements careful and even. She knew that it ought to look like a ribbon rather than a bandage.

"I know you did, dear," she said quietly, because Erika expected it, and then turned her attention to the task at hand.

Rebecca jumped when her brother rounded the corner into the kitchen. "Shawn!" she said. "It's two o'clock, why are you up?"

Shawn sank down onto one of the wooden stools and slumped over the tiled counter.

"I had a bad dream," he said. He gave her a long, slow look from under his mop of hair.

"Oh?" She turned away to open the refrigerator.

"Becca."

"What?"

"Becca, when I sleep . . ."

"No, Shawn," she whispered.

"When I dream —"

"Don't. Please, don't." The fluorescent refrigerator light made her highlights glow amber.

"I can see things."

"Just because you *do* see things doesn't mean you *can*, Shawn. Just because you have nightmares doesn't mean any of them are real."

"You do too. You saw him."

"No." Rebecca whirled on him, slamming shut the heavy plastic door. "If you want to be crazy, then go ahead, but don't make me crazy with you. You had a nightmare and I had a nightmare and that's all natural. Our mom is *dead. Our mom is dead.*"

Shawn got up from his seat. "Calm down, Becca."

Her shoulders slumped, as if on command, and she put her hands over her mouth. "It's just . . . I saw her," she said. "I saw her on that table. She was dead. We buried her. She has to be dead. It was just a dream, Shawn. Please say it was a dream?"

Shawn put his arms around her. "You're right," he said. "She's dead and we buried her. But maybe she's —" He took a deep breath. "Maybe she's still around. Somewhere else."

"Don't," Rebecca whispered. "Please don't. It's a nightmare and I just want it to be over."

"Okay," Shawn said, rocking her a little. "Okay. We won't talk about it again."

Megan crept into the kitchen, her eyes huge and round. "You didn't come get me," she said, sounding wounded. "I called and you didn't come get me. I waited and you didn't —" Her voice caught.

Rebecca opened her arms. "It's okay, Meg," she said. "We didn't hear you. We've all been having a rough night."

Megan ran up and buried her face in Rebecca's stomach. "He killed her," she whimpered. "He killed her in the backyard and you didn't do anything."

Rebecca looked up at Shawn. Her hands were pressed against Megan's back, but Shawn could tell that they were shaking.

He reached for her. "Becca —"

"We're going to church in the morning," she said in a low voice.

"Listen —"

She held up a hand, cutting him off, and pulled Megan away to look her in the eye. "How about you come have a sleepover, Meg?" she asked. "My bed's big enough for two."

Megan nodded and Rebecca tried to smile. She ran her thumbs over Megan's cheeks, wiping off the tears. The two of them headed for the stairwell entry.

"You should get some sleep, Shawn," Rebecca said over her shoulder.

Shawn heard them pad up the stairs and across the hall. Their footsteps were punctuated by the hard *click* of the lock on Rebecca's bedroom door.

❀

Erika's whole body felt shrunken and afraid as she walked into the dining room. It was like she was sixteen again and about to face her mother at the kitchen counter, a whole nest of plastic sticks with plus signs buried in the bathroom garbage. Only tonight she was in a ball gown instead of ripped denim, her skin uncomfortably naked even under all the layers of stiff green taffeta. The dress had been chosen to match the gem around Erika's neck, a small gold and emerald teardrop that she refused to part with.

A thick white drop cloth covered most of the dining table, which looked long enough to seat thirty on either side. At the far end, the sheet had been peeled back and places set for two, a candelabra tossing its steady flames across the silverware and painted china. Jeremiah sat at the head of the table, as if holding court to a hall of ghosts. He rose and offered her a stiff bow.

"You look nice," he said. "The dress suits you."

"Thank you."

"Please. Sit."

The chair had already been drawn out for her. She took her seat.

"Bread?" He passed her a covered wicker basket.

She pulled away the cloth and felt the steam rising from each perfect little loaf.

"Hungry?"

Erika set the basket down beside her glass.

"Not especially," she said.

Jeremiah took a piece of bread for himself and broke it over his plate, the crust making a soft crackle in protest. "Have I upset you?"

"No more than I deserve." Erika glanced over at him. "I feel awful, Jeremiah. I know that I shouldn't have stolen your knife, but I just . . . I only . . . I'm worried about them." She shook her head. "I want to see my kids."

"And I told you that you would," Jeremiah said smoothly. "I don't lie, Erika. There are some things that I simply cannot tell you right now, but I would never lie."

"But you shouldn't have to chase me into their dreams. You won't get anything done for them if you do."

"Yes. Well." Jeremiah set aside his uneaten bread. Struggled for a moment to compose his thoughts. Finally, he sighed and reached for Erika's glass. The dark wine barely splashed as he poured it onto her empty porcelain dinner plate.

"Give me your earring," he said.

Erika took one of the Tahitian pearls from her ears and handed it to him. He dropped it onto the plate, the pearl's rounded edge jutting out a little above the surface. They both watched as the ripples stilled and the pear-shaped lights of the candelabra became clear in the reflection.

Jeremiah leaned in close and let a slow breath skim the wine, but it stayed blank.

"They aren't sleeping any longer," he said, drawing back to his own plate. "You can try later. But I warn you, Erika, some dreams are more true than we would like to think."

He didn't give Erika time to respond before he lifted the lid from the platter in the middle of the table, revealing a leg of lamb on a bed of greens and fruit. Jeremiah reached over and placed a sprig of grapes in Erika's empty soup bowl. "Eat something."

"I'm really not hungry."

"It'll make you feel more lively," he said.

"I don't want to feel more lively. I've had enough excitement for one day."

Jeremiah pursed his lips and moved his hands from the serving ware. "Then talk," he said. "Tell me about yourself."

"About me?"

"What else would you tell me about?"

Erika picked up her fork and nudged the pearl in circles around her plate. Wine dripped from its surface like blood as it tumbled over and over the bottom of the dish.

"The last thing I remember," she said, "were lights. Headlights. Someone hit me, didn't they? Is that why I'm here?"

Jeremiah cleared his throat and flexed his fingers, then chose a thin slice of lamb for himself. It lay folded on his plate, steaming.

"Yes," he said. "That's why you're here."

"And in the gas station. Did you know then?"

"At the end," said Jeremiah slowly. "Just as you were driving off, I realized that there would be an accident."

"Why didn't you stop it?"

Jeremiah let out a breath and looked away, down to the floor on his right. Then he looked back at his guest. "I'm not human, Erika," he said. "I think you've gathered that much."

"Don't make fun of me."

He nodded. "There are some things that I can't control. That I'm not supposed to get my hands in. I'm a guide. I teach the dead how to die, and I show them where to go. Ferry them across. That's all I'm supposed to do. It's all I'm made to do."

"So I'm dead?"

Jeremiah stopped again, then reached out and took her

hand from her fork. Held it tightly in one of his own. "I suppose," he said, "that sometimes I can make exceptions."

"But you can't make exceptions for stopping it in the first place?"

"You . . ." He wet his lips. "I'm trying to help you, Erika. But some things must be figured out first."

"What does that even mean? Please just tell me, Jeremiah. Am I alive or not?"

He pressed against the back of her hand. "You're waiting, Erika," he said. "You're waiting because someone made a mistake. But you're safe now, and we'll know something soon. I promise you that." When she finally nodded, he let go of her hand. "Tell me about yourself. About who you were before you got mixed up with me."

Erika looked down at her hand, where Jeremiah had touched her. She pulled her fingers away from the table and folded them safely in her lap. "I was born in Pennsylvania," she said. As the memories stirred in the back of her mind, she smiled to herself. "I miss it. It was a beautiful place to grow up."

"Why did you leave?"

The smiled faded. "Because I got pregnant," she said. "Things changed a lot after that. My mother disowned me, for one. My father had died by then."

"Was that Rebecca?"

Erika started. "What?"

"The baby," said Jeremiah carefully. "It was Rebecca?"

"Yes."

"What did you do?"

"I married her father. We moved back to his hometown."

"Were you happy?"

Erika shrugged. "I thought that I loved him."

"You did love him."

She gritted her teeth.

"Don't do that," said Jeremiah. "I know what I'm talking about. It *is* possible to fall out of love, you know."

"That's true, I guess."

"But you never did, did you? Fall out of love, I mean."

Erika sucked her lips into her mouth and bit down on them. "I should've left after Rebecca. I knew that it wasn't working. But I couldn't go. I couldn't —" She faltered. "And we decided to have Shawn and I thought that it would fix things, but it didn't. He was just a baby. How could he fix anything?" She kept her eyes open to hold back tears. They started to weigh on her lids and lashes, but she couldn't bring herself to let them fall. "You would've thought Megan was his farewell present. 'She's yours,' he said, and walked out of the hospital. And she *was* mine, I guess. He didn't want another one. He barely touched her when he came back." Erika pressed one hand against her mouth and closed her eyes. "He never loved Meg. Or me."

"You're wrong again," Jeremiah said gently. "He did love you, Erika. He loved you very much. He just loved himself more." He lifted her free hand from the table again. "You did the right thing, Erika, by leaving him."

"I wanted it to work."

"I know you did. You both did. But sometimes the world gets confused. I'm sorry it happened."

"I am too," she said in her smallest voice.

"And I'm sorry that this happened. You shouldn't be here."

Her eyes flashed up and now she didn't care that the tears fell, clearing themselves away.

"Of course I shouldn't be here," she said. "Do you think I wanted to get killed by a drunk on the highway?"

Jeremiah flinched and withdrew his hand. "Erika, please," he said. "Don't. I'm doing the best I can, but I don't have the same standing I once did."

"What standing?"

He shrugged. "That of a very sad bastard," he said. "My father would have me scrubbed out of the picture if he hadn't promised my mother not to touch me. He loved her. He did." He dropped his napkin on the table and got up from his chair. "You have full license of the house, Erika," he said. "No secret rooms for you, or locked doors with conspicuous keys. And you won't find a magic wardrobe or mirror. We sold that with the flying carpet."

Erika felt too tired to play along.

"I think I'll just go to bed."

They walked together down the dark stretch of the dining room, leaving the haze of candlelight behind them.

"I'll be in my study," Jeremiah said, "if you need anything." He paused as if he intended to say something more, but then he just took a step away and dipped his head in a small bow. "Good night, Erika. I'll see you in the morning."

"Good night."

"And please don't leave the grounds. I wouldn't want you getting lost."

Erika nodded and went out into the entrance hall and up the smooth marble steps. She didn't feel at all hungry or tired. She felt only hollowed out — empty. She wanted so badly to go home.

Chapter Five

When Shawn came downstairs in the morning, Rebecca sat waiting at the breakfast table with her hands around a coffee cup. She looked him over.

"It's nine o'clock," she said. "Mass starts at ten."

"You aren't serious."

"Yes, I am. Go change."

"Don't be ridiculous, Becca."

"I don't know what's going on. I just think we need some comfort right now. I'm doing this for Meg."

"Meg is *sleeping*," said Shawn. "She was up half the night crying. She needs a nap, not a sermon."

"Don't make excuses, Shawn," she said, getting to her slippered feet. "I'll wake her up. Just worry about yourself."

Shawn stood alone in the kitchen for a few minutes, debating whether or not he should just leave and come back later that afternoon. He thought better of it. After all, Rebecca had kept her word at the funeral by letting Megan stay in the car while their father said his piece. An hour at mass seemed the least that he could do.

The church delighted Megan. She tugged on Shawn's and Rebecca's shirtsleeves and pointed out the murals across the high ceiling, and the stained glass windows, and the brass organ pipes along the back wall. They nodded, smiling, and led her a little farther down the aisle. A lady stepping into a pew ahead of them smiled at Megan, and Megan smiled back at her, and then at her hat, which had a cloth rose on it and a little yellow bird.

It had been five years since Shawn had come into the Church of Saint Jerome, and he kept an eye out for anyone he might know from childhood. He wanted to avoid them.

Rebecca remembered her first Communion and the tedious confirmation classes every Sunday. She remembered the way the wafers always stuck to the roof of her mouth. The sweet taste of grape juice from a cup that everyone shared. Body and blood. Even then she stumbled after salvation.

The Stripling family had stopped coming to church after Erika's divorce. As a Catholic, she hadn't wanted to face the congregation with the news. Rebecca and Shawn soon became used to staying home on weekends. After Matt started coming over, church found itself replaced by long breakfasts and walks in the park. Erika found that her children preferred this to the rolling monotone of mass anyway.

Shawn led his sisters to a row halfway down the aisle and waited for them to be seated before he took his place beside Rebecca. The pews were made of burnished oak, cool to the touch, and the faux-leather Bibles smelled softly of myrrh.

The congregation at Saint Jerome's settled into place, pretty in their church clothes. They waited for the priest to bring them closer to God.

The room had been scrubbed free of dust by the time Erika returned, the four-poster remade with fresh linen and clean blankets. She washed her face and stripped off the borrowed gown and its soft scent of vanilla, but, after an hour of staring at the carved ceiling, felt resigned to not falling asleep. She slipped out of bed.

In the hall, Erika felt along the wall with her fingertips to avoid tripping in the dark. Feet cold on the marble staircase, eyes adjusting to the midnight shadows: She was a child waiting for Santa. A cheerleader crazy in lust and holding her breath until a set of headlights swung into view. A mother desperate for her children. Erika tried not to dwell on the repetitions of her life — she'd always been afraid to wake those who knew better.

The candelabra still burned at the end of the dining table, but the wicks had sunk into pools of melted wax and sputtered in a desperate attempt to stay lit. The dishes too were waiting to be picked up. Erika sat back down on her chair and studied the porcelain plate, where her earring lay in the pool of warm wine. She nudged it with her forefinger and watched as the reflection shuddered before growing still again. Erika sighed.

Shawn felt his eyelids grow heavy. He'd only managed to catch a few hours of sleep. He dug his thumbnail into his palm to keep himself awake and shifted in his seat. When Rebecca threw an angry look at him, he turned away and rested his chin on the back of his hand.

"Now, our Lord," said the priest, "is merciful because He knows that we make mistakes. He knows that no person is perfect because He did not make us to *be* perfect. In truth, our faults make us beautiful to Him because they show Him that we are ready to change. That we are ready to become better in His name."

Shawn drifted off to sleep.

Erika's eyes widened as she saw the gentle waves from her breath glimmer and spread out in a slow starburst. She leaned in closer. There was Shawn, standing over a slash in the ground and looking down. And then she realized that the slash was a hole, and that the hole was a grave, and that it was her body lying inside. She blinked.

When she opened her eyes, she was looking up at her son, an impossible stretch of smooth dirt keeping her away.

He knelt down. The movement knocked a trickle of dust and clay into the grave. It settled in her hair and on her dress. She rubbed soil from her eyes.

"Am I dead, Shawn?"

He stayed there, above her, his face downcast. "Yes, Mom," he said. He hesitated and then knelt down and reached deep into the grave. Erika got to her feet and stretched up on tiptoe to take his hand. She felt him shiver as he touched her bloodless skin. It broke her heart.

Her voice shook as she spoke. "Am I scaring you?"

When he didn't answer, her knees buckled under her and she fell forward.

"Mom!" Shawn leaned in to catch her but lost his own balance. He tumbled down beside her, headfirst, and landed with a heavy *crack* on the packed earth.

Erika screamed and pulled away. She plunged through a chute of rushing air, out of the dream, and back into her own body. The wooden lattice of the dining chair bit into her spine as she fell backward with it and thumped to the ground. She rolled over onto her side and pressed her chin down against her knees.

Erika's breath came shallow as she sucked thin, trembling mouthfuls of air into her throat. *Yes, Mom.* Before she realized it, she was sobbing. Hot tears slipped down her nose and cheeks. The curls of her hair grew damp and sticky as she cried, and the floor felt like a cold compress against her flushed skin.

It took Erika a few minutes to realize that she hadn't left the room because she wanted Jeremiah. It took her longer to realize that he wasn't going to come.

She lacked the energy to move. She just lay there on the unwashed tiles, her body twisted into a question mark, and shivered against the satin of her nightdress.

Shawn woke up on the floor of the church, with his head pounding. Rebecca towered above him, staring, horrified, at his limp body. Megan pressed her head against her sister's ribs.

The priest stood planted at his pulpit, a Bible and the scribbled notes of his sermon on the dais in front of him.

A few seconds went by before Shawn noticed that he had the attention of the entire congregation.

Shawn reached for Rebecca's arm, but she recoiled and he had to push himself up on his own. He pressed one hand against the back of his throbbing head and waved an embarrassed apology.

"You'll want to go to the clinic, young man," said a woman in the next pew, a book of hymns clutched against her chest. She sounded as if Shawn had personally wronged her. "You may have a concussion."

Shawn turned to Rebecca for help, but she had already sunk back into her seat, her eyes fixed on the India-paper pages of an open Bible. Her lips formed a thin, irritated line.

"I'll pick you up after the service, then," Shawn said weakly. When Rebecca didn't answer, he turned on his heel and hurried down the aisle and through the heavy front doors.

The priest looked back down at his notes as the doors swung into place.

"Luke thirteen," he said. "'He answered them: Do you imagine that, because these Galileans suffered this fate, they must have been greater sinners than anyone else in Galilee? I tell you they were not; but unless you repent, you will all of you come to the same end. Or the eighteen people who were killed when the tower fell on them at Siloam — do you imagine they were more guilty than all the other people living in Jerusalem? I tell you they were not; but unless you repent, you will all of you come to the same end.'"

Jeremiah sat on the terrace overlooking the back gardens. To the north, where the city's center crouched, buildings posed themselves at angles, forming crooked, black teeth. It was past sundown, past curfew, and Limbo held its breath, but Jeremiah wasn't listening. He had a sheet of paper pressed against his knee, and a glass of brandy in his hand.

Jegud —
I've come home, though you'll know as much by now.
There's been a mistake. I must see you.
Jeremy

Jeremiah reread the note one last time before reaching for the candlestick on the table beside him. Martha opened the door as he peeled his ring from the molten wax.

"Miss Erika is in the dining room, sir," she said.

He looked down at the sealed letter and let a small breath spill out. "I thought so," he said, passing it to Martha. "Make sure he gets this by morning."

"Yes, sir."

"And make sure he opens it."

"Of course, sir."

"That's all."

"And the miss?"

Jeremiah took a final sip of brandy and looked into the mouth of the city. It waited, hungry and all too ready to swallow them up.

"I'll take care of her," he said. "You know that."

Rebecca and Megan waited on the front steps of the church until Shawn pulled up, with the car windows rolled down. Megan gave him a peck on the cheek as they climbed in.

"Jesus loves you," she said.

"The priest talked to us after mass," Rebecca told him. "Apparently, God understands. That's more than I can say for myself."

"I'm not having the best day, Becca."

"Really?" she scoffed. "Because mine has been spectacular. My family sees dead people in their sleep and my brother collapsed in church during a sermon about infidels. I'm surprised you didn't sizzle when you hit the ground."

"It's not like I was trying."

"Weren't you? I'm impressed."

"You know, you can act like this all you want, but it won't help anything."

"I don't know what you're talking about."

"Mom's still around."

Rebecca glanced at Megan's reflection in the rearview mirror. "Don't say that, Shawn."

"Say what?"

"*That*. About *her*."

"I don't mean that she's going to pull up the driveway and ask us to help carry in groceries, Becca. But my dreams aren't random. She's watching us. I know she is." His eyes flicked from the road to Rebecca and back again. "I'm not crazy," he added.

Rebecca stiffened. "Well, I'm not, either."

"I'm glad we've cleared that up."

"I just don't find it necessary to talk about this with Meg here," Rebecca hissed. "She might get the wrong idea."

"About Mom?" Megan asked. Her head rested against the tinted glass of one of the back windows. As she talked, she kept her eyes on the houses that slid past her. "I think Shawn's right."

Rebecca let out a tired groan. "See?"

"I'm eight, Becky," Megan said. "Not stupid."

When Erika woke, she didn't know where she was. She stared at the ceiling for a few minutes, taking in the soft twist of gold fabric and trying to place it with a bedroom that she recognized. When she rolled onto her side and caught sight of the faded armchair, the heartbreak of last night came flooding back. Limbo wasn't a dream — it was silk sheets swallowing her up and keeping her from her children. And she wasn't alone.

Jeremiah turned away from the window. When he saw her awake, his face relaxed into a smile.

"How are you feeling?" he asked.

"Not well."

He looked down at her, hands clasped behind his back.

"Are you coming down for breakfast?"

She dipped her cheek against the plush of the pillows and drank in the fresh, expensive-smelling perfume they'd been sprinkled with.

"No," she said. "I'm sorry."

"I'll have something sent up."

"Don't," she said.

Jeremiah knelt on the floor by her bed and rested his chin against the mattress. The sleep-fluffed curls of his hair were a dark cinnamon in the morning sunlight. He smiled again. "You aren't going to starve yourself, are you?"

"Is that possible?" Erika asked. "I'm already dead."

Jeremiah lost his smile. He let a long breath out between his teeth.

"Who would tell you something like that?" he asked.

"Shawn."

He gave her a half laugh. "Your son? I'm sure you love him, Erika, but can you really trust him over me in a question of death?"

Erika pressed her eyes shut. "I don't know."

"Bless him," he said. "No human being knows the first thing about death."

"Except for the dead ones."

Jeremiah smirked. "No," he said. "Not even them. Especially not them."

He took Erika's hand from the pillow and pressed her fingers against his palm.

"Do you think that I could feel your heartbeat if you were dead? Do you think that I could feel your breath on my hand if your lungs had collapsed? Or hear your voice? Believe me. Trust me." He grazed her fingertips with his lips before tucking her hand back beneath the covers. "I have to go to my study," he whispered, "but let me know if there's anything you need, Erika. Anything at all." He got to his feet again and went to her door. She flexed her hand against her leg. Her fingers burned.

"You would tell me, Jeremiah," Erika said. "Wouldn't you?" Her voice came out low and sad. He nodded his head.

"I would tell you anything you asked me, Erika. It's just who I am."

She knew that he was playing her. That he was beautiful and he was playing her.

"She's causing problems," said Jeremiah as he jogged down the steps to where his brother stood, observing Kala in all of her caged glory.

"Of course she's causing problems," Jegud said. He was dressed in a trim black suit, cut just to size. Of all the king's sons, Jegud had taken to Limbo's latest dictated century with the most ease. The brothers used to joke that it had been tailored for him. "She's with you, isn't she? She must be a quick learner."

"Jegud, you have no idea —"

"I have every idea, Jeremiah. How hard this is for her. How easy it must have been for you." He shot his little brother a look to cut diamonds. "I hear you struggled with her in the Passing Woods. Rumor wants to know why it took so long for young Jeremiah to crawl through this time. Rumor says he's wounded."

"And maybe he is. I had to get back in, Jegud. Michael would've killed me."

Jegud jerked his head at the staircase. "And this was the first thing you could think of? Kidnap the nearest single mother?"

"I didn't know she had kids."

"Is that supposed to make you look better?"

"I have to fix this," Jeremiah said. "Will you help me?"

Jegud turned back to Kala, still asleep for all the bickering.

"She's going to fall in love with you," he said. "A soul shouldn't be with their guide for this long."

"I know," said Jeremiah. "But what can I do?"

"You can try not to make it worse." Jegud gave his brother a pointed look.

Jeremiah cleared his throat and clasped his hands behind his back. "Thank you for coming, Brother. You always let me feel more myself."

Jegud glanced away. "I'll find someone on staff to do your guide work. For now." He slid back into his woolen coat and ran a finger around the brim of his top hat. At the door, he paused. "Jeremy, I —"

Kala stirred and fluffed her feathers before settling back to sleep. The brothers watched her, sharing a sad smile.

"I'm glad you're home," said Jegud, and went out.

The air tasted electric, like newly struck lightning, pregnant with rain. A rush of wind swept through the city, making the stones weep against the cold. The beading water turned floors and walls to glass.

She came in, barefoot, with her curls pinned back and a fluted oil lamp in her hands. The flame burnished her skin to the color of autumn-ready leaves.

"I shouldn't be here," she said.

The king stepped away from his parlor window and tipped up her chin.

She had eyes like chips of jade, plucked from rock and polished till they blazed. If he could name her, he would; call her something precious. Instead, he kissed her cheek. Her skin went warm at his touch, and he smiled when he caught her blushing. The queen had never let herself be as delicate as this remarkable, breakable rogue. But because of that, the king believed, she had never been as strong, either. He felt himself pulled to this spirit who'd been created to serve, but who had some secret tiptoeing through those eyes; a secret but an innocence, also, that he didn't quite understand. No guile. He had never seen eyes so honest.

He dipped his head close again, sending a warm rush of air against her earlobe, along her neck. She shivered. He'd sworn never to fall as far as his father had, but now he saw that it was too late.

"I'll build a house for you," he said. "I'll give you your gardens. Better than Boboli. Better than Babylon." When she said nothing, he stepped back and took the lamp from her. Its brass base clattered against the windowsill as he set it aside.

"Are you afraid?" he asked. "Of me?"

"No," she said.

"And why not fear strangers? You don't know me."

The rogue took his hand. "I know all there is to know," she said.

The king smiled at that, and believed.

Erika stayed in bed for another hour at least, lulled by the steady *drip, drip, drip* of the bathroom faucet, which had developed a leak. Martha came in with a tray of bread and fruit and left it, without a word, on the seat of the armchair.

After Martha closed the door, Erika crawled out of bed, her skin cold on the wooden floor, and looked through the bureau for something suitable. Skirts and dresses, linen and lace; she slipped into black chiffon, the plainest piece in the wardrobe, and took her other earring out. She ran a finger down the chain of her necklace and closed her eyes. When she hooked her fingers around the emerald, Megan stood out in her memory, clear against everything else, and Shawn with her, and Rebecca looking happy, for once. The air smelled of cinnamon. Erika turned away from the dresser.

Despite her lack of hunger, she nibbled at the food for want of something to do. The grapes and peaches were unripe, the bread salty. Afraid of making Jeremiah worry, she brought the plate to her window and let her breakfast fall into the bushes.

There were two men standing outside the manor gate, both dressed in clean suits and carrying flowers that seemed out of place within the city walls. Just a few feet away, a gardener on a tall A-frame ladder battled with the dead limbs of an old oak tree, each eager *snap* of his clippers forewarning a falling branch. The men watched him intently, and he must have seen them, but neither party said a word to the other.

After a few seconds, the shorter of the men outside the gate tapped his colleague on the shoulder and whispered something without turning his head. Erika caught the unchecked glance at her window and pulled back, hiding her face behind the heavy curtains. From her viewpoint, she could see the shorter man smile as wide as the Cheshire cat before he tipped his top hat to her empty window. The two of them walked toward the gate, beyond the window's frame. Erika smoothed the skirt of her dress in one quick movement and headed out of her bedroom to find Jeremiah.

When she walked into Jeremiah's study, she was confronted with a portrait of herself. She froze. There she hung above the fireplace, dressed in a rich blue gown that clung to her shoulders. A lush garden sprouted all around her.

"My mother," said Jeremiah, and Erika started once more. She turned and found him behind a stocky rosewood desk, his expression as intent as the first time she'd met him. His study was a long, narrow room lined with glass-front shelving. Thousands of black and brown leather books waited behind the dusty panels, intermixed with brass and wood knickknacks. Jeremiah gave his mother's portrait one last glance and then set aside the book he had been reading.

"Feeling better?" he asked.

"A little."

"Good."

Jeremiah didn't get up from his seat, so Erika came forward by herself.

"I was lonely," she said.

He motioned to a pair of plush chairs across from his desk. Erika hesitated, but gave in.

"I feel like I'm in a law office," she said.

"Oh?"

"It reminds me of my divorce."

Jeremiah folded his arms and studied her.

"Can I help you with anything, Erika?"

She looked up from her hands. "I think so."

"And what would that be?"

"I . . ." She shrugged. "I need my children, Jeremiah. I need to see them. To know that they're okay."

"They're fine, Erika. You *have* seen them."

"Not really."

"You *have*. You know that they're fine."

"That's not good enough." She leaned forward in her seat, her fingers knit together in her lap. "I need you to bring them here, Jeremiah. To me."

At that, he raised his chin and sank back in his own chair. She watched him for a few long seconds, and he watched the edge of his desk where the light from the window behind him glared silver-white.

He opened his mouth. "Do you know what you're asking for?"

"I do."

"No, you don't," said Jeremiah. "But you won't give up, either, will you?"

She didn't answer.

"Are you sure about this, Erika?" She could tell from the set of his jaw that the question was merely polite and that he already knew the answer.

"I am," she said, also out of politeness.

"Then, for you, I will try."

"Do you promise?"

His eyes flicked up to her, and she felt a little prick of irritation in his glance. "I said that I would, didn't I?"

She didn't drop his gaze. "I just need to know."

Jeremiah spun in his chair to face the window. "Everything," he said quietly. "For you."

"Thank you." She got up from her seat and saw that he didn't stare at the yard, but at a bowl of flowers. Balsamine, zinnias, and eglantine roses, all twisted together with thick myrtle branches.

"Are those from the men at the gate?"

Jeremiah didn't turn, but she could feel the tension in his words: "How do you know about the men?" he asked.

"I saw them from my window," she said. "Who are they?"

"Unimportant." He seemed to think over the statement. "No," he said after a few seconds. "Very important. Just very petty as well. I'd rather not talk about it."

"Fine."

"I need you to promise *me* something now, Erika."

"What?"

Jeremiah kept his eyes on the flowers.

"That you won't try to look for your children again," he said. "Until I see whether or not I can bring them here."

"Look?" she asked. "I would never find them anyway."

His voice came cold. "You know what I mean."

"All right," Erika said. "I promise."

"And I need to know that you would do anything for them."

"Anything."

He swiveled to face her.

"Just to see them?" he asked. "You would do *anything* just to see them?" His face was so sharp, so darkly serious that Erika wavered.

"You're scaring me."

Jeremiah smiled. His shoulders relaxed and he leaned forward to pick up his book. "I'm sorry. I didn't mean to. But you should know that sacrifices will have to be made."

"I love my children," Erika said.

"I know. Of course."

"Please don't do anything stupid."

"Oh, Erika," Jeremiah said. "It's all stupid."

He took up his work again and Erika understood that she'd been dismissed.

Again, Jeremiah crossed Gabriel's retaining room. He had traded his comfortable jeans — his reaping clothes — for the starch of a three-piece suit. It was his attempt to play by the rules; all grown up and still desperate to fit in. Over the past few hours, he'd watched the light through the line of arched windows change from the bright, clean heat of midafternoon to the crystallized honey of early evening. He'd begun to wonder whether his eldest brother was even at home.

After a few more minutes of pacing, Jeremiah sank down onto the rich white velvet of one of the parlor's chaise longues and stared at the sheer curtains, gone amber with sunset. A few feet away, an old grandfather clock metered out time. Jeremiah glanced at its mother-of-pearl face and made up his mind to leave. He started to rise when the door on the far wall swung open and Gabriel appeared, with his hand on the polished knob. When he spotted Jeremiah, his face broke into a wide, honest smile.

"I didn't realize you were waiting, Brother," he said. "I'm so sorry."

Michael, the second prince, strode out of the office, top hat in hand, dark hair pushed back behind his ears. He was taller than any of his brothers and slender in his close-cut suit. He gave Jeremiah a cold look as he passed by. Jeremiah nodded but held his tongue. It had been a long time since the two of them had spoken.

Gabriel didn't miss the exchange, but he also didn't comment on it. He ran his fingers through his thick wheat gold curls and tipped his head at the open room. "Come in, come in," he said. "It's been too long."

Jeremiah followed him inside and waited until the door latched behind them both.

The crown prince still smiled — his smile always came too easily — but he looked tired. Perhaps his preparations to take the throne were finally getting to him. "What brings you home, Jeremy?" he asked.

"Michael," said Jeremiah. "He's become quite the hunter."

Gabriel said nothing as he slid behind his favorite ebony desk. He motioned to a chair but Jeremiah shook his head.

"I'll only be a moment," he said. "I have a favor to ask." He couldn't tell whether this surprised Gabriel or not, or whether it disappointed him. As the next to the throne, Gabriel had trained hard to keep his emotions in check, especially around rogues. All emotions except for his buoyancy, which Jeremiah doubted his brother would ever be able to rein in.

"I'd be happy to grant it," said Gabriel. "If I can."

Jeremiah rolled his hat slowly between gloved fingers.

"There are some children," he said. "Some human children. I need them brought into the Kingdom."

Gabriel tilted his head and leaned a little more heavily against his desk. He picked up a thick ballpoint pen and began to play with it, somersaulting it back and forth across his knuckles.

"An odd request," he said. "Whatever for?"

"A friend," said Jeremiah. "A new friend. Who deserves it."

"You know that it isn't our place to play reaper. I won't allow for anyone to lose life when it isn't their time. Especially not children."

"You misunderstand me," said Jeremiah. "I don't want them dead."

The pen stopped bouncing. Gabriel replaced it on his desk with a little too much care and concentration.

"What have you gotten yourself into, Jeremy?"

"Please, Gabriel," said Jeremiah. "I can't explain. I just need to know if you'll do it. For me."

"I can't," Gabriel said. "You know that I can't." He looked openly upset about that inability, his face pleading for his little brother to understand.

"Gabriel —"

"No, Jeremiah," said the crown prince, more firmly this time. "It's too dangerous. For them and for us."

"Just for a few days."

"Not even for a few hours. I can't condone it, Jeremiah. I'm sorry."

Jeremiah stared at the carpet under his feet. Handwoven and ocean colored, it had a delicate pattern of swirling flowers and berry-laden plants. "But you will condone Michael following me into the outer realm."

"Jeremy —"

"You'll condone him hunting me like a dog until I have nowhere to run."

"Jeremy, please —"

"He's going to kill me, Gabriel. I hope you realize that. I hope you realize that it isn't fun and games anymore, if it ever really was."

Gabriel rose sharply to his feet, but Jeremiah had already put up a hand to calm him.

"That's all, Brother," he said. "That's all. I'm sorry to have wasted your time."

He pivoted on his heel and walked through the door before Gabriel could say anything else.

Chapter Six

Shawn rinsed off his toothbrush and looked back in the mirror. His skin was swollen from lack of sleep, and his mouth was pinched thin with stress. He looked old and way too much like his father.

In the basement, the washing machine rumbled, and Shawn could hear the whir and clatter of it through the pipes along the wall. Rebecca would be down there, folding clothes and still seething over the morning slipup. She was terrible about holding grudges.

A knock rattled the door.

"Yeah?"

"Good night, Shawn."

"Night, Meg. I'll be just a minute."

"It's okay."

"No, don't worry. Find a book while you're waiting."

"Okay."

Shawn rinsed his hands and flicked the toothbrush dry before putting it away. In the basement, the washer shuddered to a stop.

"Shawn?"

"What, Becca?" He opened the door and saw his sister walking down the hall in slippers and a robe, her arms full with a basket of clean laundry.

"Will you run down and check to make sure the lights are all off?"

"Sure. Do you want me to put the wash in the dryer?"

"Yeah, thanks."

"Would you check on Meg, then?"

Rebecca pushed open Megan's door with her hip and walked inside, all smiles. It was nice not to fight, even if they were both just pretending.

Jeremiah waited patiently in the Stripling family living room, his hands in his jacket pockets, his head tipped back against the wall.

He heard Shawn coming down the steps, and glanced at the hallway when the light flipped on. Gold light spilled over the living-room carpet, just inches from his own feet. He waited for what felt like a long time before the lights went out again and Shawn's footsteps receded up the stairs. Megan's door clicked into place and then there was silence.

Jeremiah walked over to the bay windows and flipped out the blade of his pocketknife. It glinted in the moonlight as he brushed the trailing hem of the curtains. There was a space heater perched on the window seat. The report would say that it had been an accident.

How else to keep three children unconscious but safe while he granted Erika's last wish? Jeremiah hoped that she would never ask what he'd done to bring her children into Limbo, because he feared telling the truth. He feared, also, how difficult it was for him to keep things to himself while around her. Hated the armor he put on to keep her distant. There were so many things that he wanted to tell her, so many times that he wanted to comfort her. So many reasons that he knew he never could.

A stream of fire traveled up the edge of the curtains, too small to make much smoke yet. It crept along one of the pillows and then up to the wooden shutters, where it licked at the whitewash paint as if unsure of what to do next. Jeremiah turned away and tapped the knife against the knob of the front door. He waited for the *click* of the lock and then stepped out into the pitch-colored night. Behind him, the fire in the living room twinkled yellow and white, like an early-up Christmas tree.

Rebecca slipped off her earphones and sat up in bed. She reached for the cell phone on her nightstand as she sniffed the air.

The line clicked as Shawn answered. "Rebecca?"

"Hey," she said. "Do you smell smoke?"

"Why are you *calling* me? I'm twenty feet away."

"Seriously, Shawn. Did you leave something in the oven?"

"What? No."

"Go check the hall."

"I'm hanging up now."

"I'm not kidding! Shawn, go downstairs and — Shawn?" She looked at the display and frowned at the "call ended" message. "Bastard." Rebecca tucked her earbuds back into place and settled into her nest of pillows.

Her bedroom door crashed open.

"We need to get out," Shawn said, smoke curling in around his shoulders.

"What's going on?"

"There's a fire, Becca, come *on*!"

Rebecca shot out of bed and followed her brother to the stairs, Megan running along between them. The smoke smudged the hallway into a dark blur. Shawn sprinted to the front door and tried the handle. When it wouldn't open, he tugged harder, bracing his shoulder against the frame.

"It's stuck!"

They ran into the kitchen, where he tried to pry open the back door, but it also refused to budge. Megan stood hand in hand with Rebecca, but her grip began to slacken. Rebecca scooped her up and tried to keep her conscious.

"Meg, honey, please listen to me, okay? Meg? Shawn, *hurry up*."

He coughed hard into the collar of his shirt.

"Take her upstairs."

"Smoke *rises*, dipshit!"

"Then why are you *fucking holding her*?"

She dropped to her knees, pressing Megan's face against her chest. *"Break a window."*

He grabbed a lamp from the sitting room and hurled it at the window over the breakfast table. The ceramic base shattered against the glass pane. Shawn stared at the pieces for a moment, speechless and horrified.

"Dammit, Shawn, can't you do *anything*?" Rebecca lay Megan on the floor and jumped up. She lifted one of the chairs and slammed its legs into the glass. Nothing happened. She thrust it again. Nothing. The chair spun and crashed into the refrigerator as Rebecca flung it aside.

Shawn grabbed her arm. "Don't panic," he said, sounding panicked himself. "Call Matt."

"I don't have my phone."

"Well, *get* it."

Rebecca skidded down the tile of the hallway and almost slammed into the banister when she turned and headed up the stairs. Her throat burned as she took a breath. She winced with each dragging cough and her eyes, stinging with smoke, squeezed out fresh tears. She found her cell phone and squinted down at the blue-white screen as her list of contacts scrolled past. A crash rocked up from downstairs as something heavy struck the back window, then a clatter as it hit the floor. Shawn let out a frustrated yell.

Then Rebecca heard Megan's voice, weak but high-pitched, from the front hall. "It's on the stairs, Becky! On the carpet!"

Rebecca stumbled out of her room. The hallway glowed orange and gray.

"Becky! Come back!"

She tried to yell for Shawn to grab Megan, but when she opened her mouth, a massive cough ripped through her. She doubled over.

Shawn's voice flew up the stairs. "Megan, *no.* Megan, come *back.*"

"But, Becky —"

Then soft, almost a whisper: "Beck?"

Rebecca looked down, half surprised to see her cell phone clutched in her hand. She brought it to her mouth, but no words came out. She could only cough.

Matt's voice drifted through the speaker. "Beck, are you there?" He sounded frightened and very far away.

Rebecca took a step back and tripped. The phone bounced out of her hand.

Beneath the hungry crackle of the fire, the house fell silent.

Jeremiah waited for the children's voices to fade away before he broke the seal and walked off down the street. He needed to hail a cab and get to the nearest hospital. Soon the boys would be picking up his trail.

Chapter Seven

Erika sat chewing her thumbnails on the bottom steps of the grand staircase. She'd started to regret asking Jeremiah to do anything. The longer he was gone, the less she trusted him.

Kala perched in her cage a few feet away, perfectly silent and perfectly still, more like a toy than a real bird. Her beak was settled against her breast, as usual, so that Erika saw only a hunched back and a silver tail.

There were noises outside from the gardener packing away his tools for the night. Dusk drifted through the city, and Erika, for some reason, kept expecting the call of nightingales. Instead, she heard the awkward trudge of the gardener's boots, and then other, cleaner footsteps coming up the walk. A cold breeze hissed through the open windows.

Erika got to her feet and walked to the front door, trying to step lightly on the cold marble floor. Her breath caught high in her throat as she pressed her ear against the heavy wood, wondering where the footsteps had gone.

"Well, are you going to let us in?"

She jumped.

"You're being rude, Uri." The second voice sounded smoother, softer. Velvet.

Erika stepped away from the door.

"Who are you?" she asked, struggling to sound poised.

"The quality," said the first voice. "Is our charming brother home?"

She opened the door a sliver.

"Your brother?"

The two men from that morning stood on the top step in their fresh-pressed suits. The shorter of the two had gray eyes and blond curls cropped close in a cap around his head. A sharpness to his jaw suggested a career military, and indeed he wore his scarlet cloak pinned at the shoulder, like a Roman commander.

The other man was tall and slim, his black hair tied out of his face.

"Little Jeremy," said the first. He looked Erika up and down in the glimmer of light that spilled through the cracked door. "I thought I felt a human," he said. "Though at least you're pretty for one."

"And you are?"

"Uriel."

"And Selaph," said the taller brother.

"Would you let us in?" Uriel asked, his voice more gentle now that he wanted something. "We have news for Jeremiah. He's been gone for so long."

"I don't think —"

"We can entertain you until he arrives, love. You must be bored to death." Uriel smirked. "You'd think Jeremiah would be more accommodating, considering his background, but he always was a poor host. Please?"

Despite her better judgment, Erika pulled open the door and showed the brothers in. Selaph hung back near the entrance. His eyes, the darkest Erika had ever seen, searched the room with a single, sweeping glance. Uriel strode over to look at Kala.

"So this is where he keeps her now, for all the world to see. Clever boy." He turned to Erika. "That's a lovely necklace."

Her hand went to her neck.

"From my kids," she said.

"How sweet." Uriel cleared his throat. "And how are you liking our brother?"

"He's been very good to me."

"Has he? That's unlike him."

"He's never mentioned you."

Uriel smiled and seemed to warm to her. "A little more expected. We aren't on the best of terms. He can be very trite. He was an accident, I'm afraid."

"That's a terrible thing to say."

"It's true. His mother was never a favorite. He's had a time of it. Hasn't he, Selaph?"

He turned to his brother, who was straightening his jacket.

"I can't blame him," Selaph said.

Uriel shrugged. "Well, *I* can," he countered. "And why not? We've never held it against him."

"Father has."

"And who is your father?" Erika asked.

Uriel's eyebrows rose. "He hasn't told you? Then we'll have to keep it confidential."

"Between blood," Selaph said thoughtfully.

"Do *you* have blood, then?"

"Oh, hell," Uriel groaned. "Don't tell me that he did that to you as well? So dramatic. He gets it from his mother." He took a silver pocket watch from his vest and checked it. "I'm very sorry, dear. I was sure that little Jeremy would be back before curfew. He's a bad example."

"Curfew?"

"To keep the city in check," Uriel said. "We wouldn't want anyone wandering about at midnight, now would we? It's the witching hour." When Erika didn't answer, he gave her a small, deprecating smile. "Tell Jeremiah that Selaph and Uri leave their love."

Selaph opened the door, signaling that they had finished.

"My name's Erika," she said, coming forward a step as the brothers headed for the porch. Uriel kept walking, but Selaph turned back, one palm on the handle, and on his face a smile small enough to get lost.

"Erika Stripling," she whispered. She didn't know why. Maybe she just wanted a place in this world that barely seemed to tolerate her.

"Nice to meet you, Erika Stripling," Selaph said, also in a hush. "Welcome to the Kingdom." He stepped out into the night and drew the door quietly after him.

Shawn came to in the soft dark of dusk with a touch of ice in his lungs and a prickle running over his arms. He sucked in a deep breath and was startled by campsite memories of wintered earth and cold air. He picked himself up, wiped off his face, and looked around.

There were trees. A low blanket of mist hung around the totem trunks, everything a wash of gray in the twilight. Shawn fell back onto his knees, his head spinning.

"Shawn?"

He saw Rebecca emerge from the bed of fog a few feet away. He lifted his hand, but couldn't bring himself to say anything.

Rebecca's voice was strained. "Where's Megan?"

An image flashed through Shawn's mind — a glimpse of his little sister stumbling toward a bonfire on the stairs. His heart thudded as he looked around.

There she lay, asleep beside the trunk of a thin aspen tree. He scooped her up and rested her cheek against his shoulder. Her skin was smudged with ashes, but he could feel her breath against his neck. He sighed, relieved.

"She's here," he said.

Rebecca came up behind him. "Where's *here*?" she hissed. "Where the hell are we?"

"I . . . don't know."

Shawn looked down at his arms, and at the back of Megan's blue pajamas. His lungs were sore from smoke and the smell of fire.

"Did we get kidnapped?" Rebecca hissed. "Dumped somewhere?"

"I don't know."

"Oh my God. We did." Rebecca dropped to her knees and covered her face with her own ash-blackened hands. "Why is all of this happening? Oh my *God*." She was breathing hard.

Megan scrunched up her nose and blinked at the dark.

"Mommy?"

"No, Meg," Shawn said. "It's just me and Becca. You want to stand?"

"Okay."

Shawn knelt down to put Megan on her feet. Once she'd moved away, he turned to grab hold of his older sister. "For God's sake, control yourself."

She gaped at him, indignant, even as she tried to brush away her tears. "Don't you tell me what to do, Shawn."

His fingers tightened around her shoulders. "Are you trying to say that this is my fault?"

"Well, it's not *mine*."

"Nothing is ever *your* fault, is it? Wake up, Becca."

"Are we dead?" Meg asked.

Shawn and Rebecca turned to look at her at the same time.

"No, Meg," said her sister. "Why would you think that?"

"The fire," Megan said simply. "Is this heaven?"

"God, I hope not," said Rebecca. Shawn threw an angry look at his older sister.

Megan looked at the two of them, expectant. "Where are we, then?"

Shawn faltered. "We're . . . We're . . ."

The look on Megan's face made Rebecca pull herself together. "We're on an adventure, honey," she said quietly, and held out her hand as she pushed herself up. Shawn watched the transformation but didn't comment.

"I don't want to go on an adventure," Megan said. "I want to know what happened." Despite herself, she had to stifle a yawn.

"I know, Meg," Rebecca told her. "So do I. But let's find a place to sleep first."

Shawn watched his sisters stumble off through the woods and resigned himself to following along behind. He too wanted to know what had happened. He noticed that Rebecca's hands trembled as she ran her fingers through her hair and looked down at their little sister, and he realized how hard she was trying — how hard they were both trying — to be calm for Megan. He took a deep breath. The air felt clean and almost astringent, but the warm musk of smoke still gripped his clothes.

Once, when he was six or seven, his mother had gotten angry enough to hurl a vase of flowers through the back window. The vase had shattered on the patio in a spray of cobalt glass and gerbera daisies, and the hole had stayed in the window for almost a month before she found the time and money to replace it. Shawn looked at Megan's and Rebecca's clasped hands, both gray with ash, and thought about the heavy clatter of the microwave as it bounced back from the window and hit the breakfast table. One metal corner had dented, as if smashed against a brick wall.

Now they were God knew where. Maybe Megan was right — maybe they *were* dead. Maybe they would find their mother, then. Shawn's mind raced and he wondered if he wasn't coming unhinged. Then his stomach dropped and he thought about his dreams, and about how desperately his mother wanted to come home. Being dead wasn't the same as being safe. He sped up to close the gap between himself and his sisters.

The king turned away from his wife, who was weeping.

"How could you?" she moaned into her hands. "How could you do this to us? To your family?"

"I don't want to hear any more of it."

"You don't want to hear?" She leaped up from her chair. "You don't want to hear? How dare you? How dare you say that to me?"

"We will say that the child is yours."

"I will not have that slut in my house!"

"Then you will go to hers," the king said smoothly. "I've ordered a new palace to be built. You will stay there through your pregnancy."

The queen gasped, flushing red. "You would banish me?" she shrieked. "You would take that whore into my bed and then send me to watch her grow fat with your bastard?"

"I'll not discuss this any longer."

"Send her to the Colonies! I order you to send her away!"

The king paused. He looked back at his wife, whose blushed cheeks smoldered as bright as her burgundy dress. He nodded.

"After the birth," he agreed. "I'll have her taken there after the birth."

He left the queen's chambers without another word.

Her stomach turning over, the queen ran to the eastern windows and pressed her face against the cold glass. Her boys were in the gardens, playing with one another. Gabriel, beautiful Gabriel, and solemn little Michael chased the three youngest through the hedges while the sun sank low behind the house. Gabriel, Michael, Uriel, Selaph, Jegud. She had always thought that they were her saving grace.

That they were enough. She turned away, dropping the curtains to hide the view. She'd never deserved them, she knew, but had always imagined that she'd at least deserved their father. Now she felt so damaged. So painfully, permanently flawed.

Erika still waited on the bottom step of the main staircase, though this time, her nerves had doubled. She smoothed the skirt of her dress, crumpled it, and smoothed it again, trying to keep her mind away from her children before the thoughts made her sick. She felt as flighty as if she'd eaten too much sugar.

When Martha passed from one side of the entry hall to another, carrying bundles of wash or dust rags for cleaning, Erika opened her mouth as if to speak, but she never built up the courage to actually do so. Instead, Martha did all the talking. "He's late, miss," she would say after one pass-through. "It's after curfew." "He'll be back soon, miss." None of it calmed Erika, though it was intended to.

When the lock of the front doors finally clicked, Erika flew up from her perch. It was Martha, however, who appeared in the blink of an eye to open the door for Jeremiah and take his coat and hat.

"Send for my brother," he said quietly as he slipped off his gloves. Martha didn't need to ask which one or why now. She could tell from his face that he had already thought it through.

Erika took a few steps forward, looking uncertain, and steadied herself on Kala's cage before Jeremiah noticed her. He faltered, and then collected himself.

"You're awake," he told her.

"I am."

He asked nothing else, but instead gave her a one-armed hug, still looking a little thrown, and led her into a parlor at the back of the house.

Erika realized that her children were not with him, and fell silent until they had stepped into the low light of the parlor.

Then Jeremiah dropped his arm and walked away from her, over to a bronze log holder beside the fireplace.

"How are they?" Erika whispered. "*Where* are they?"

The dying coals blazed as Jeremiah tossed handfuls of kindling into the hearth. When he turned around, Erika was still on her feet.

He pointed to one of the armchairs. "Sit. Please." He took a seat himself and slumped forward to stretch the tension out of his shoulders and back. When he was comfortable, he settled against the pillows of the couch and concentrated on Erika. "They've come," he said. "But that's only half the battle. There are issues with bringing them any farther than where they've ended up. There are rules to break. Rules that I have no authority over."

"You *are* trying?"

"Of course I'm trying." Jeremiah shaded his eyes against the firelight. The logs he'd added were beginning to catch. "I'd do anything for you, Erika."

"Jeremiah . . ."

"Let me finish." His legs were crossed, his left hand on one knee and his right propped on the back of the couch. He picked at the trim of one of the throw pillows. Erika thought of Matt, who sat like that after a long day and told her about a report or a case and worried over her children in a way she could never quite grasp. There were things, Matt told her, that were worse than dying. "I'd do anything," Jeremiah repeated, and Erika came back to the parlor and the smell of smoke. He looked into her eyes. "I just want to know why."

Erika's forehead creased. "Excuse me?"

"I need to hear it from your mouth. Why do you want them here?"

"They're my children."

"Is that good enough?" He studied her. "Is that really good enough, Erika?" When she didn't answer, he laughed softly to himself. "My God," he said. "Rebecca was an accident. Shawn was a mistake. *Megan* was the only one you ever really wanted." His voice dropped to a thoughtful murmur. "You were desperate for her, weren't you?"

All that Erika's horrified expression got was a sad shake of Jeremiah's head.

"You know that it's true," he said. "So tell me, Erika. Why should *I* fight for your children when you never did the same?"

Her mouth fell open. Her words came out in a hiss. "How dare you say that to me?"

Jeremiah turned away. He seemed troubled. "We're both too tired to deal with this right now," he said, his tone becoming gentler. "You're getting upset with yourself. You should leave, Erika."

"Is it because you were a whore's son?"

He sprang to his feet.

"Who told you that? Don't *talk* about my mother."

Erika's eyes narrowed.

"I'm only telling you what you already know," Jeremiah said. "Don't try to be clever when you have no idea what's going on now or what's gone on before. Get out of here."

A tap broke on the door, as soft and timid as a cat's claws against tile. A young man who looked no older than Jeremiah peered around the edge.

"Is this a bad time?"

Jeremiah's arms fell. "Yes," he said. "But come in anyway."

"Martha let me in."

Jeremiah nodded and folded his arms across the fireplace mantle. He dropped his forehead against his crossed wrists.

"I'm Jegud," the man said, offering Erika his hand. "You must be Miss Stripling."

"I am."

"Jeremiah has told me good things about you."

"I think that his opinion has since changed," Erika said with a sad smile.

"Keep your theories to yourself, Erika."

She ignored the comment. "Are you a friend of his?" she asked Jegud.

"He's my brother," Jeremiah said.

Jegud shrugged as if apologizing.

It was true that he looked like Jeremiah, or at least more so than either Uriel or Selaph had. Jegud's features were more delicate than Jeremiah's, however. He was pale, even in the firelight, and his intensely blue eyes were bright against his skin and dark hair. He dressed like an English dandy.

"You asked me to come?" he said, turning to Jeremiah again. "Please tell me that I got that right. If I came after hours for nothing, I won't be happy."

"You're right," Jeremiah said. "And I'm sorry that it's so late."

"I don't think you really are."

"No, I am." Jeremiah turned, arms dropping to his sides. "I'm exhausted."

"There are cures for that," Jegud said. "One is called *sleep*."

"Not now. I'm not myself."

Out of the corner of her eye, Erika saw Jegud glance in her direction.

"No, not *that*. I've been out and back in less than a day. I'm not used to it."

"How did you manage?"

"Cancer patient," Jeremiah said, sounding remorseful. "She was terminal, so her family was ready to let go. She seemed happy."

"Until you made it to the gate?"

"Well, yes."

"They always are."

"I shouldn't have left her so soon."

"It's not your fault."

Jeremiah grunted. "It's completely my fault," he said. "We both know that." He shook his head.

His brother shifted uncomfortably. "I'll find her tomorrow," he offered.

"That's not your job."

Jegud held his palms up. "What can I do?"

"Get me a drink."

Again, Erika noticed Jegud's eyes flick toward her.

"It doesn't matter," Jeremiah said. "I need it."

"Fine." Jegud went to a liquor cabinet at the back of the room and took out a glass and decanter.

"You won't take anything yourself?" asked Jeremiah.

"I'm smarter than you are."

"I wouldn't doubt it." Jeremiah threw back the alcohol and set down his empty glass. "Erika? Let me take you back to your room. Jegud and I have some business to discuss."

"It's boring, really," Jegud said.

"Quite." Jeremiah offered his hand as if it were an olive branch.

Erika looked at it for a moment, still hurt, before putting her fingers against his palm and letting him guide her out of the room.

They went down the hall and up the stairs in silence. It wasn't until they reached the threshold of her bedroom that Jeremiah ventured to speak.

"I *am* sorry, Erika."

She shook her head. "I needed that," she said. "I needed someone to tell me the truth for once. It's just . . . I'm so afraid."

"I know you are. And that's not necessarily a bad thing."

"No, it is," she said. "It is, it is." She rested her forehead against his chin. "I'm sorry I said that about your mother. I'm such a mess." She lifted her head to look at Jeremiah, and saw how warm his eyes were, and how worried.

"No harm done," he said. His gentleness and good intentions washed over her and her breath caught in her throat. When she leaned in, her mouth fit perfectly against his.

For a heartbeat, Jeremiah allowed himself to kiss her. Her heat filled him up, and the taste of her skin, and he wanted more. But then his eyes flew open and he jerked away. One hand flew to his lips, forcing a barrier.

"Don't, Erika," he said from behind his fingers. "Don't start. You don't know me. You'll never know me." His voice broke as he shook his head. "I'm sorry. Very sorry. Good night."

He turned away, still shielding his mouth, and hurried down the hall. Erika backed into her bedroom. With the door shut and her body safely in bed, enveloped by moonlight and feather blankets and cold midnight air, she let the humiliation swallow her whole.

❦

Shawn flailed when he woke, because he couldn't remember where he was. He stared wide-eyed at Rebecca, who sat at the base of an old poplar and looked at her brother as if he'd lost his mind.

"What time is it?"

"I don't know," Rebecca said.

"It's not any brighter out."

"Yeah, I saw."

Shawn's eyes narrowed. "Do you have to be so sarcastic?"

"No, why?"

He shook his head, stretched with a yawn, then forced himself to his knees. "Is Megan up yet?"

"She went to find someplace to use the bathroom. What are we going to do?"

"Do you really expect an answer?"

"I'm back," Meg announced, overloud.

Rebecca held out her hand and waited for Megan to come and curl up at her side. She pressed the warmth of her little sister close against her and stared through the darkness at Shawn. Her heart beat hard, and she hoped that Megan couldn't tell. *Take care of your sister*, her mother had always said, and though no one thought she listened, Megan meant more to Rebecca than anything else. She couldn't let Meg know how frightened she was, how nauseated she felt, and as she stared down Shawn, she dared him to say anything about it. But Shawn had always been a better sibling. Had always been the responsible one. Rebecca dropped a kiss into Megan's hair and tried to keep her hands from shaking. She didn't know how they'd gotten here, but she didn't want to think about it. She would put her fear into anger and her anger on someone else's shoulders. It had always worked before.

"Let's go," Shawn said.

Megan's voice came out frightened. "Go where?"

Rebecca tightened her arm around Megan and leveled another glare at Shawn, waiting for him to answer.

"Home," Shawn said. He was lying.

It was easy for Rebecca to see that he was lying. None of them knew where home was, or if they could even get there. She pushed herself to her feet, her fingers holding fast to Megan's hand. She'd pretend alongside Shawn that they knew what was going on, but only because the alternative would be too hard on Meg. *Take care of your sister*, came her mother's voice, like a mantra, from the time she was eleven and her parents had filed for divorce. *Take care of your sister.* There was no other option.

The queen was still waiting when her husband came back into the hall. The baby lay cradled in his arms, asleep.

"A girl?"

"A boy," he said.

Her hope faded. She turned away.

"You're keeping him, then."

"Yes."

"Fine." She folded her hands to stop them from shaking. "Fine, fine, fine."

"You'll learn to love him."

"I'm not your slut," the queen replied thinly. "I can't love on command."

Her husband only stared at her sharp, straight back.

"I want to leave this house in the morning," she said after a pause. "You've kept me here long enough. With her. You'll do as you promised."

"She gave me a son," the king whispered.

"She gave you a bastard. Now be a doting father and take it to the nursery."

When her husband had gone, the queen went into the bedroom and took the midwife by the arm.

"Madam?"

"Send her away. To the Colonies. Tonight."

The midwife continued to dry her hands on her apron.

"She's gone, madam," she said. "They've gathered the ash already."

The queen recoiled.

"What?"

"She broke."

The midwife said nothing else before leaving the room.

When she was alone, the queen went over to the bed and pulled back the curtains. Empty. She crawled in and pressed the sheets against her face as she sank into the soft mattress. The sticky smell of sweat lingered in the air. For the first time in nine months, the queen let her panic drain away.

They'd been walking for so long that Rebecca's calves were sore, but the woods were still steeped in the dull colors of twilight. The fog made her pajamas damp, and when she tried to wipe away the ashes, she only managed to spread them. Shawn walked beside her, Megan asleep against his shoulder. Rebecca thought that he must be following her lead, and she let it annoy her. Her stomach grumbled and her throat hurt, so she let that annoy her too. She fought hard not to wonder where they were, or how they'd gotten there. It was easier to focus on small, insignificant things. On the slow burn of her muscles or the spinning in her head. On the way Shawn refused to talk to her.

She kept replaying scenes from the last few days, and each time Shawn's words cut deeper. She hated fighting with him, and she hated when he judged her. Worse, she hated the way their arguments ran through her mind like a looped photo reel. *For God's sake, control yourself.* Again, again, again.

Still. Anything was better than reevaluating her sanity — that's why she spent so much energy in building up her shell. The party girl. The bitch. The flippant sister. She wore her masks like a second skin because she couldn't handle living in her real body. Before she'd created this exoskeleton, the whole world had judged her. Now they just judged a face that wasn't really hers.

"We should stop," Shawn said. "Megan's too heavy."

Rebecca shrugged. She was tired anyway.

Shawn laid Megan down next to a group of trees, hovering to make sure she was still asleep. Rebecca turned her back to him and peered into the woods.

"I can't believe this," she said.

Shawn got to his feet. "Can't believe what?"

The sharpness of his voice startled her. She hadn't counted on that. Now that he no longer had to worry about jostling Megan, his own train of thought from their march threatened to break the surface.

Rebecca braced herself.

"Can't believe," he went on, "that I won't click my heels together and get us home?"

"That's not —"

He grabbed Rebecca's arm and pulled her farther into the woods, out of earshot of Megan. "I'm tired too, Becca," he said, voice low. "I'm particularly tired of you expecting me to swoop in and save the day. Believe me, I wish that I could get us out of here. You think that I don't feel responsible for you and Megan?"

Rebecca stiffened. "You're not responsible for me, Shawn."

"Well," he shot back, "someone has to be."

Rebecca could tell that he'd been rehearsing this speech for a while. She held her ground and waited for an opening.

"You certainly refuse to be responsible for yourself," Shawn said. "Even now. You just keep following me like you expect us to turn the corner and see the goddamn high school. Look, I'm sorry to break it to you, but I'm not as brilliant as you think I am. I don't know where we are, I don't know why we're here, and I have no idea how to get us out. Are you happy now? I don't know. *I don't know.* For the first time in my whole life, I can't save you from something. I'm so sorry."

Rebecca scowled. "Don't be sarcastic with me."

"Don't tell me what to do, Rebecca."

"I'll tell you what to do if I feel like it, and you'd better fucking listen because I saved your ass enough times when we were kids. And stop assuming that I see you as my own personal Jesus Christ. *I haven't been following you.*"

"You know," Shawn said, "if Mom were here right now, she'd agree with me. She keeps hoping that you'll grow up someday, and you keep disappointing her."

"For the last time, Shawn, Mom's not hoping for anything right now because *she's dead.*"

"Dammit, Becca, are we back to this again? Then how do you want to explain it? How can you make yourself feel better?"

"Shut up."

"How do you want to explain it?"

"Well, then, where is she? Not here, obviously. So stop it. Stop it and help me find the way home."

Shawn's eyes widened and he let out an exasperated laugh. "Oh my God," he said. "You're insane!"

Rebecca slapped him.

They stood watching each other in the thin light, Shawn stunned, Rebecca glaring. Shawn's instinct was to touch the stinging skin of his cheek, but he refused to give his sister the satisfaction. Instead, he ran his tongue along his gums, checking for blood, and stayed quiet.

"*Never* call me that again," Rebecca said, her voice low and barely steady.

"What the hell is your problem?"

Rebecca took a step back and felt her shell begin to splinter. "Oh, right," she said with sarcasm. "I have problems. I have problems and my brother thinks that I'm a fuck-up. I'm sorry, I forgot." Her body started to tremble with the effort of keeping herself reasonable. "Don't you think that I had enough of that after the divorce, Shawn?" Her voice crept higher as she mocked her classmates: "'Oh my God, Becca Stripling had a screaming fit because some kids were teasing her brother!' 'No! You should tell the principal, because Becca's not stable and something could happen! Didn't you hear? She's seeing a shrink. She tried to run away from home. She's on *pills* so she won't kill herself.'" Rebecca looked straight into Shawn's eyes. "'Oh my God, *she's so insane*!'"

He didn't know what to say.

Hot, angry tears started to slip down Rebecca's cheeks. "I'm not going back to that. I don't know how to explain what's happened, but I do know that you're wrong. And I know that I'm not the crazy one here, because crazy people think that they can talk to their dead parents, and crazy people look at a creepy-ass forest and assume that they've found the land of the dead. I loved Mom too, Shawn, but she is gone and it's over, so just give up. I wasn't crazy back then, and I'm not crazy now, so don't you *dare* tell me that I am."

"Rebecca —"

She shook her head, turned, and stalked off.

Shawn hesitated before starting after her.

"Becca, wait. I'm sorry." He caught her by the arm. "I'm sorry."

"No, you're not."

He held her at arm's length and looked her in the eye. "You're not crazy, and I don't think that you're a fuck-up."

"Yes, you do," she said. "And stop trying to be funny." She wiped the tears from her face with the back of her hand.

"We can't be like this, Rebecca," Shawn said. "Not in front of Megan."

"Megan's asleep."

"Not while we're lost."

Rebecca shrugged. "At least this way, no one else can see what bitches we are."

"Dammit, I just don't want to fight. Is that too much to ask?"

"Well, why don't you just ask it?" Rebecca shook off Shawn's hands and stared at him. "Fine," she said. "I'm sorry too. Even though I have nothing to apologize for." She held up her palms. "Kidding."

"I didn't realize that the kids at school hurt you so much."

She gave him a look that said *Really?* but then paused and turned away. Shawn was thinking of how his own life had changed after the divorce. He'd never gone to counseling, never blamed himself for it. He'd blamed his mother for taking so long, and blamed his father for putting her through so much. Kids had teased him, true, but even back then he couldn't see why it upset Rebecca so much. The question that had haunted him then, and that still bothered him now, was a simple one: Hadn't he loved his father at all? It used to keep him up nights, and used to make him shut down in class or during lunch with his friends. It used to fill him up, demanding to know why he was so happy to have lost a piece of his family. He had always been upset about how little the divorce had cut him.

"Rebecca," Shawn began, trying to put these thoughts into words. He'd never talked about it before, to anyone. He wondered how she would react. "When it happened, I —"

"Hush."

Shawn blinked at her, wounded. "What?"

Rebecca put a hand over his mouth and tipped her head to the side. "Listen."

"I don't hear anything."

She tightened her fingers.

They saw the apparition before Shawn heard it — a swirl of blue-black smoke drifting just above the forest floor. And then the skin began to sweep over it, dripping into place like thick house paint.

"Meg," Rebecca hissed, and ran back to where their sister lay sleeping.

Shawn stood transfixed. He watched as the figure flickered. The emerging face warped, the build of the chest and arms changed like putty. The fingers flexed, sliding out and back, longer and shorter. All the while, the thing itself slid forward, edging closer.

"Shawn!"

He spun around and saw Rebecca holding Megan against her chest. A long, low growl rippled through the woods behind him, prickling the hair along the nape of his neck. Rebecca's eyes were wide, her jaw slack with shock. Shawn couldn't help it; he looked back at the figure.

It was a man with straight, dark hair and a self-satisfied grin. He brought up one hand and held his fingers together, prepared to snap. There came a *crack*, like a gunshot, and the ground shook. Shawn lost his balance. His palms dug into the bed of fallen pinecones and needles and he cursed.

A dog howled behind him, the sound deep and guttural. It was answered by a chorus of barks and growls. Shawn scrambled to his feet and ran for Rebecca. He grabbed her forearm. She stumbled.

"Megan!"

"She's awake!" Shawn yelled back. "Put her down!"

Megan staggered as she touched the ground, but then took off ahead of them. As soon as the kids started running, the pack's hesitation broke with a hungry snarl. The kids heard the eager sounds of paws hitting earth, of claws scattering topsoil, and the fear went straight to their blood.

Megan let out a whimper as she pushed herself harder. Shawn drew on his memories of track and field and forced his legs to keep pumping, but it was a joke. He'd trained for one season his freshman year and hadn't run since. Besides, he'd been used as a sprinter. Even while training, he couldn't keep going for long. He glanced over his shoulder and saw Rebecca lag. She sucked in sharp, frustrated gasps of air, one hand against her chest.

Behind her, the dogs' coats glistened silver. Mouths open, eyes gleaming. *Not dogs, surely*, Shawn thought. *Too big to be dogs. Too big to be wolves.*

"Keep going, Meg," he shouted, though he didn't need to remind her. He dropped back and snatched Rebecca's arm. "Breathe! Run!"

Rebecca looked back and shrieked. The dogs must be close, he realized, and there must be a lot of them. One of them lunged and snapped at his ankle, then pulled back, only to return for another try. Shawn leaped and ran harder. He was almost to Rebecca and Megan. They were slowing down too much. Maybe if he stopped or veered off, he could occupy the dogs long enough for his sisters to get away. But get away to where?

A yelp snapped up from behind as some of the dogs surged forward to make a wide arc around the siblings. They were circling, winding up their catch. Toying with their prey before the kill.

Megan screamed as she tripped, hands splayed in a baseball dive. There were fallen trees in front of her, making a low barrier, and she scrambled to her knees and started to drag herself over. Rebecca pushed her the rest of the way, dropping heavily to the ground beside her and wrapping her arms around her sister's thin waist. She tucked her head over Megan's shoulder and cocooned her. She'd protect her as long as she could.

Shawn stopped in front of the wall of trees and turned back to face the things that chased him. The raspy panting of the dogs was the only sound in the forest.

The figure materialized fully, a tall gentleman in a cape the color of mulberries. He came forward without a smile but with a stride that said he owned everything around him, his huge silver dogs still pacing a half-moon at his heels.

"West," he said.

Shawn stepped back, confused, and bumped into the fallen trees.

"Taking up guide work, Highness?" came a voice behind him. "Want to see how the common folk live?"

Too afraid to look over his shoulder, Shawn dug his fingertips into the woodpile and kept staring at the man and his cloak.

"Just taking the dogs out for a run," said the man. "They got carried away."

"Does Gabriel know you're here?"

He gave a tight-lipped smile. "You watch after these children, won't you, West? In the name of the Sickle." His gaze shifted to Shawn's face. "We wouldn't want them to get hurt." The dogs turned on their heels as he dissolved into nothing more than black smoke and shot away. As they all sped off into the woods, their howls echoed back, triumphant.

Chapter Eight

Erika woke to a burst of hyacinth on her pillowcase. She sat up in bed and lifted the spray of blossoms to her nose, smiling into the open petals.

"Good morning, miss," Martha called, breezing into the room. She held a stack of towels in one hand and a long brown coat in the other.

"Are you going out?" Erika asked.

"*You* are." Martha laid the coat at the foot of the bed. "The master is in his study. He told me that he's in no hurry." She set the stack of towels down on the armchair. "But I know that he is."

"Oh?"

"I should let him tell you." Martha moved around to the wardrobe and opened the doors, pulling things down and setting them, piece by piece, on the foot of the bed.

Erika watched her. "That's fine," she said. "I can wait."

"It's about your children. He's looking for a consult."

"A consult?"

"Yes." Martha looked up from her work. "You've got a touch of pollen, love. On your nose. Just there."

Erika wiped off her face.

"There's trouble in the transition. You see, you can't bring someone who —"

"Knock, knock." Jeremiah tapped on the doorframe with

his forefinger. "I hope I'm not intruding." Embarrassment flashed through Erika's eyes, forcing Jeremiah to look away. He hated himself for having hurt her, but he knew that it was for the best. Jegud was right; rogues were never intended to stay this long with their charges. They were too accommodating, too capable of building trust and of meeting expectations. There were reasons why it wasn't allowed.

Martha smiled, tight-lipped.

"I know that I told you there wasn't a rush," Jeremiah said, eyes riveted to the pattern on the wall, "but I think I may have lied. I'd forgotten about . . . well, it doesn't matter. I . . . just . . ." He nodded. "Wanted to let you know. So. I'll see you."

Martha followed him out with a sharp *rap* of high heels.

Erika dressed as quickly as she could manage and stripped off the prettiest spray of flowers for her coat buttonhole. She carried her shoes in one hand in order to make it downstairs more quickly.

"I'm sorry about this," Jeremiah said, holding the door for her. He'd composed himself and now waited as she slipped on her shoes. When she straightened up, he pointed at his lapel. "I'd take that out," he said.

Erika looked down. "What?"

"Again, I'm sorry." He plucked the hyacinth away, his skin barely touching the fabric of her coat. He looked as if he wanted to fling the blossoms aside, like hot cinders, but instead he slipped them into his pocket. "I'm glad you liked them," he said, his tone more gentle, "but if we're out too long and someone notices . . ." He paused. "Well, flowers are expensive and I might get accused of playing favorites. Souls don't like to see guides playing favorites."

"I didn't know."

"I never said that you did." Jeremiah stepped back and motioned to the threshold. "After you."

Megan brushed the dirt from her hands as she struggled to her feet. Rebecca took up her little sister's fingers and kissed the scraped palms beneath them. Blood came off on her lips.

"Meg, honey," she gasped, sandwiching her sister's hands inside her own. She looked up into her sister's frightened eyes and felt her stomach turn. "Meg, are you okay?"

Megan had begun to cry. She buried her face in Rebecca's hair, her nose skimming the curve of her sister's neck. Her body shook as she let out her panic. Shawn knelt down and wrapped both of his sisters in his arms, and Rebecca let him. She'd seen the look in his eyes just before she'd gone over the wall. The look that said he would sacrifice himself for them, if only he knew how. Rebecca moved one arm to snake around his, and bit her bottom lip to keep from crying. They had to be strong for Megan, she knew, but she was already so tired of being strong. This shouldn't be happening.

"You're welcome, by the way."

Her eyes flashed up and she saw the man who had intervened for them. He must have been edging on twenty, but the moonlight made him look younger. Under it, his straight blond hair gave off a soft silver glow.

"It's not every day that the crown dispatches a personal welcome party," he said. "You must mean an awful lot to someone if Michael meant to ransom you."

"Ransom us?" asked Shawn. He and Rebecca both hurried to their feet. Megan hung close to her sister's legs.

"The king's sons should know better. The woods are not their place, and we don't take kindly to those who don't belong. Present company excepted."

"What is that supposed to mean?" asked Rebecca.

"You're not dead." The young man extended his hand in greeting, but Rebecca and Shawn just stared at it. He tilted his arm toward Megan and she stepped forward, ignoring her sister's fingers pressing hard into her shoulder, and accepted his shake. He smiled. "I'm West," he said. "Pleased to meet you."

"Meg."

"Who brought you here, Meg?"

She glanced over her shoulder at her siblings, but they just looked frightened. "We don't know. I think my mom."

"Well then, she must love you very, very much," said West. "And must be very, very good at getting her way." He let go of Megan's hand, and she stepped back into the safety of her sister's arms.

"I have a friend on the other side of the lake," said West, straightening up and looking at Rebecca and Shawn again, "who can help you more than I can. I'll take you over, but you have to earn the oars."

For the first time, the three of them looked past West to the wall behind him, and the cabin and the statues. They could hear the sloshing of water on a low shore.

"And how do we do that?" asked Shawn.

"You feed the Furies."

Rebecca slid her hands across Megan's shoulders, to keep her close this time. "What?"

West nodded at the statues. "The maidens. Gentle as a dove if you're steady."

"And if you're not?"

"You'd better hope you are. Every flower has a bad turn; even Aphrodite had claws." When no one said anything, he turned and started walking toward the statues. "Come on," he said. "I'll walk you through."

"I'll do it," said Shawn.

"No." Rebecca tried to smile. "I've got to be the big sister sometime, right?"

"Becca, it's fine. I'll do it."

"No. I owe you one."

"For what?"

"For everything."

He shook his head. "This is a bad idea."

Rebecca took his arm and squeezed it. "You're the smart one, remember? If anything happens, I'd rather you were left with Meg."

Shawn felt his stomach drop. He thought of West saying, so casually, that they weren't dead, and wondered what it would take to get there. "Rebecca, wait —"

She shook her head and turned to follow West.

"Alecto, Megaera, and Tisiphone," he said, pointing to each statue. "Sight, hearing, speech. You have to give one up."

"For how long?" Rebecca asked.

"I don't deal with that. It depends. Until you find your way out, maybe. You're supposed to have a guide."

"It can't be too bad, can it?"

"Oh, no," West said. "It's bad. They say that you get used to it after a while. I'm not sure how."

"So what do I do?"

"Kiss one," he said. "And don't resist."

"Kiss one?"

"I don't make the rules," West said. "I only see that they're followed."

Rebecca frowned and looked up at the statues. Creepy things. Especially the one on the end, clutching her jaw like she couldn't stop herself from screaming. Rebecca tapped her own lips and tried to tune out her fear. Something inside of her twisted, making her feel sick, and she hoped that she wouldn't vomit up what was left of her stomach. In the silence, she began to assemble a new façade. *I'm dreaming*, she thought. *I must be dreaming*. It helped her take all this news in stride. She could feel her anxiety slipping away already, and she took a steadying breath and refocused on the statues.

Giving up her tongue, she knew, would turn this into an awful horror movie in which the sidekick tries to warn the hero but can only make desperate and disturbing grunting noises. She looked sideways at Shawn, picturing him as the hero of this nightmare. It didn't make her any more optimistic.

"Do I lose the sense," she asked West, "or the body part altogether?"

"The latter, I'm afraid," he said.

Rebecca's frown deepened. No good, then. Her throat would dry up or she'd get an infection. Besides, she had to eat. She wondered why Tisiphone was even an option if it was such a stupid one.

She looked at the middle statue. She'd never been good at charades because she couldn't guess what people were trying to mime, and Shawn was already so bad at making himself clear that he'd render her useless if she were deaf. Besides, she'd snuck out enough times, growing up, that hearing was her greatest asset, as their brush with the rabid ghost dogs had proven. And if she couldn't hear and Shawn yelled for her, she'd keep wandering along, oblivious, and get mauled by something.

Then again, if she gave up sight and heard him yell, she'd just run headlong into a tree, so maybe the point was moot. And if they ever got separated, she would need her eyes. Otherwise, it would be a whole different horror movie scene waiting to happen. Probably a more frightening one. At least for her.

But they wouldn't get separated — none of them would ever leave another behind — and as long as they stayed together, she needed her hearing. It couldn't be too terrible; she'd always been good at Marco Polo. She tagged Shawn every time, even when he cheated.

Rebecca touched her brother's wrist. "You'll help me out, right?" she asked. "If I choose sight, you'll help me get around?"

Shawn looked surprised. "Of course."

"Just making sure," she said. "I'll be pissed if you abandon me out here."

"Why not speech?"

"You think I could go without talking?" She smiled. "And they would've gotten us back there if I hadn't heard them first." Rebecca breezed past West, with a smile, and climbed the steps to stand level with the first statue. *It's only a dream*, she repeated to herself. *It's only a dream, so nothing bad will happen. I'll just wake up.*

West crossed his arms. "She's taking it too lightly," he whispered to Shawn. "She'll get herself hurt."

Shawn stayed quiet and kept his eyes on his sister.

A few feet away, the water lapped softly against the sides of the boat. Rebecca leaned in and touched her lips to the statue. It wasn't too bad, she thought. Cold and a little grainy. Regardless, she wouldn't make a habit of Frenching statues anytime soon. *It's only a dream.*

Then her body went rigid with pain. A pinwheel spun in front of her eyes, flashing all the colors she'd ever seen. With each new color, the sting increased, and with each new stab, her muscles grew weaker. She reached out and pushed against the arms of the statue, but she could feel them moving toward her, and she could see blood and she could feel it dripping hot down her skin, and she could taste it like iron in her mouth, and she cried blood, and drank blood, and tried so hard to get away. Behind her, through the pounding in her head, she could hear West's voice, and Shawn's, and then she felt Megan's thin arms around her legs, and she tried to pull back, or push her sister off, but she was stuck there. Glued there. Rooted to the stone, and to the earth, and to the anchor of pain that kept her conscious, and then she heard Megan screaming, and realized that she was screaming as well, and that she had been for some time because her throat rasped dry, scraped sore. *Not a dream after all*, she realized too late. Megan's screams were too real — the pain and the blood and the fear too real — and she wasn't going to wake up.

She was going to die.

The blood kept coming, in streams, in rivers, in torrents, and she felt something hard against her eyelids, and then recognized fingers. Hands. She was pushing away and shrieking, and she hurt so much that her knees were weak, but she couldn't fall.

It stopped.

Rebecca staggered back and toppled off the platform. She could feel Megan falling with her. She wanted to open her mouth and call out to her, but her throat was too raw. Megan broke free and rolled away, whimpering like a puppy.

Rebecca reached up to touch her face, but someone else had gotten there first. She was lifted up at the neck, and a knee slid under her upper back to brace her.

"You're fine," West said into her ear, and he poured a little water down her throat and wiped the sweat from her face. His hands were rough, chapped from work, but he held her lightly, as if she were a doll. Rebecca wanted to open her eyes and smile and thank him, but it seemed too hard. Then she realized that her eyes were already open, but that the whole world was empty.

Her heart burst, the beating so rapid and so hard that she was sure it would rip through her chest. She was going to die.

She gagged on her own breath. "Megan!" she gasped, and dug her nails into West's arms. She needed to feel something concrete. She needed to know that she wasn't crazy. "Is Meg okay?"

West didn't answer. He just cradled her head in the crook of his arm and laid a damp cloth across her burning, vacant eyes.

The streets were deserted. A cool sun watched from on high, sending slivers of itself down to dance on the slick cobbles of the Middle Kingdom. Erika and Jeremiah walked side by side, her hand tucked into his jacket pocket, his back as straight as a lamppost. Anyone could tell that Jeremiah was nervous. They kept quiet for lack of conversation and moved quickly for lack of time. Erika wondered how Jeremiah could have memorized the twists and curls of the city streets, when all were lined with the same low brick-and-wood buildings that were more like shacks than houses. Mud for mortar, tin for roofing tiles. The whole city was a slum.

"How much longer?" Erika asked.

"Not very."

"Where is everyone?"

"Away."

"Where are we going?"

"No place."

Every word she spoke made him wince as if there'd been a gunshot, so Erika fought her urge to ask questions and let him go on in silence.

They paused in the middle of a long road, at a cusp where the cobbles began to give way to sand. Erika's fingers were numb from the cold, but she stayed quiet while Jeremiah surveyed the buildings around them. For a moment, she thought that they must be lost, and her panic rose. Then Jeremiah pressed his fingers against her forearm and they started on again.

The sand gave way to dirt and the dirt gave way to mud. The pair sank a little deeper with each step, until Erika had hitched up her coat to keep it safe.

"It won't kill you."

She started at Jeremiah's voice, since he'd kept silent for so long. He continued along his way, unconcerned.

Erika caught up with him. "But it isn't clean, is it?"

"You're in the land of the dead, Erika Stripling," he replied. "Are you really worried about staying pretty?"

"Shouldn't I be? Your mother had quite a wardrobe for someone who didn't care about beauty."

Jeremiah frowned but didn't comment. He nodded to the building ahead of them. "We're here," he said.

"What is it?"

"A shop."

"We're shopping?"

"Far from." He took her hand from his pocket and helped her climb the steep front steps. "Don't say anything," he whispered against her temple. "Please." He turned and rapped on the door.

The procession wound its way back to the palace and brought the queen and her new son safely home. The court welcomed her with a lavishing of gifts, in spices, cashmere, and imported pets, but she walked past all of them, her baby tucked safely in her arms. Those who saw her said that she looked tired. Said that she had aged.

Later, they would say also that she had been weeping.

The baby, however, never made a noise. It was as if he knew that silence was valuable in the king's house. Here, at least, he took after the queen.

They called him Jeremiah. "God will uplift." When the king consulted his advisors, he asked for something holy, something lucky. Something that could wash away sin.

Rebecca woke with a cold compress on her forehead and someone else's hand on top of her own. She blinked a few times, realized all over again that she was blind, and jerked back with a whimper. Panic again ripped through her veins. Her throat tightened as a haze of dizziness and nausea descended. When the person beside her reached out again, she shied away.

"It's me" came Shawn's voice. "Becca, it's me."

Rebecca tried to relax, but felt electric. Every touch shocked her, every sound made her quiver. "Where's Meg?" The desperation in her voice surprised her.

"Meg's fine," Shawn said. Rebecca noticed his hesitation. He squeezed her hand. "She can't see either, Becca."

Rebecca turned her face away to hide the flush of self-hate. "Oh God," she said. It was all she *could* say. Her stomach turned over. She sat up and put a hand over her mouth, telling the bile at the back of her throat to settle. Her guilt tasted sharp and sour.

"It's not your fault," Shawn said.

"It is," she breathed through her fingers. "Oh my God."

Rebecca began shaking. Her eye sockets burned, but she couldn't cry. Shawn climbed onto the small bed and put his arms around his sister's shoulders. "I should've grabbed her," he said.

"I can't believe that I put her through that." A silence fell as Rebecca tried to process everything, to quell her nausea, but she could sense Shawn waiting to tell her something else.

"Becca —" He sounded as if he would hate himself for what came next. "We need to get moving."

Rebecca shook her head, defeated. "Where are we even going?"

"Limbo," Shawn said. "We're in the land of the dead." He paused. "And I think that Mom's there. I know that Mom's there."

"So we *are* dead."

Shawn got to his feet and made Rebecca lie back down. He rearranged her compress. "West doesn't think so," he said. "But would it be better than being crazy?"

Rebecca gave him a weak smile and fought down the ache in her stomach. "If I hadn't just lost my eyes to a moving statue," she said, "I'd kick your ass for that."

She jerked at the sound of wood scraping stone.

"It's West," said Shawn. He brushed her hair away from her face. She could hear shifting fabric and felt a bundle unfold itself beside her on the bed.

"Here's your sister," said West, and brought their hands together.

Both totally blind, they fumbled to hold on to each other's fingers. Rebecca felt a sob seize her chest. "Meg," she whispered. "Meg, I'm so sorry."

Megan kissed the back of her sister's hand, and Rebecca knew that all was forgiven.

Erika sat quietly in a corner and listened to Jeremiah barter with the shopkeeper, a crookbacked woman who sat on a stool by her cash box and never lifted her fingers from her knitting needles. She tucked and tugged diligently against her roll of black yarn while muttering and shaking her head.

Erika began to wonder why Jeremiah had brought her there at all, as she'd said nothing since entering the shop. After Jeremiah had introduced her and shown her to the only other chair, Erika's name had been dropped. They were talking history. Law. Rules that Erika didn't understand, even when she could make out their whispered conversation. She started to doze.

Jeremiah slammed his fist on the countertop. Erika jerked to attention. For the first time, the old shopkeeper lifted her eyes from her work. She swiveled to the bookshelf behind her.

"See?" she snapped, dropping her knitting in her lap and dragging a thin book from the shelf. "See?" She flipped through the pages and then set it on the counter, jabbing a ragged fingernail at the margin. "It's written."

"It *is* written," Jeremiah agreed. "But not in stone."

"Your loss," she said, and took back up her work.

"Maybe," Jeremiah said. "Maybe so. But then, maybe not."

She kept her lips pinched shut, but tapped an old, shivering clock with the back of one of her needles.

"I know, I know." He laid his hands flat against the countertop. Jeremiah's voice fell to a murmur. "There used to be whispers, Sara."

The shopkeeper said nothing.

"They said that you broke through. They said that you learned how. Because of—"

"I don't know what you're talking about, child," she said, but she picked up the clock and slammed it down at his fingertips.

Jeremiah looked at the crooked arrows, both inching toward the twelve. "Fine," he said, and waved Erika over. "We have to go."

The shopkeeper eyed Erika without dropping a stitch. "That's her?"

"I told you so," Jeremiah said. "I told you when we came in."

"You're no liar," Sara said. "That's certainly the face that destroyed my sister." She shifted her eyes back to the scarf. "But he won't stand for it. Not from you."

"Better from me than from Michael."

"The second son?"

"He knows that Michael is selfish."

"And he knows that you are desperate," Sara said. "So go. Make your rules and break his. It's your head on the platter."

"Thank you, Sara," Jeremiah said, "for your time."

"I don't want your thanks," she said. "I just want you gone."

Jeremiah took Erika's hand. As he opened the door, Sara spoke one last time: "They say that only one woman can read the future, Jeremiah." He glanced back and saw her staring at him. Her needles, again, were still. "You came to the wrong sort of doorstep."

Jeremiah gave her a curt nod and led Erika out.

"Was that necessary?" she asked as he closed the door behind them.

"Yes," he said. "But not as fruitful as we might've hoped." He stepped off the porch and helped her down. "We came too late and stayed too long. We have to hurry back now."

"Or what?"

He buttoned his jacket as he walked. "Or they'll catch us," he said, "and it really will be my head on a platter."

"Whose platter?"

"Probably my brother's good china."

West stuck an oar into the soft bottom of the lake to keep them steady, while Shawn helped Megan and Rebecca into the rowboat.

Each time someone climbed in, the lake would rush up

toward the lip of the hull. Shawn said nothing, but found a seat and fought back the memories of fishing with his father. He kept thinking about the first dream after his mother's death, when he'd drowned in the cold, open waters of a summer lake without even trying to save himself.

Rebecca sat at the back of the boat, Megan on the floor beside her. As they set out, the two sisters held tightly on to each other's hands. Rebecca's eyes were squeezed shut, her forehead creased as if in pain, but Shawn knew that it was for her sister and not for herself. Megan leaned against Rebecca's knee and turned her head every few seconds as she caught new sounds of wind or leaves or water. Shawn didn't want to admit it, but watching her frightened him. She kept her eyes open, but they were empty sockets, cleaned and soothed by West's careful fingers, but horrific nevertheless. Shawn's stomach turned when he looked at her, and that reaction made him feel even worse.

West rowed them out to the middle of the lake, without talking. Water dripped from the oars each time they surfaced, leaving rippling trails in their wake. He kept his eyes on the bottom of the boat as he paddled, and took slow, deep breaths through his nose. Maybe that was why Shawn saw her first.

She was mostly submerged, but her arms and chin were propped against one of the rocks that stuck out above the water's surface. Her skin was dirty gray and dead-looking, her hair a dark seaweed knotted through with moldering leaves. Her eyes were closed when Shawn spotted her, but at his glance, they popped open, yellow with fever. She parted her lips in a slick snake's smile and slipped from her rock, hardly making a ripple as she sank into the lake.

Shawn cleared his throat.

He was debating whether or not to say anything when the boat began to rock. The swells were low at first, hardly noticeable since they were still moving forward. Shawn glanced at West, but he didn't seem to be paying much attention. He pulled the oars from the water and tapped them off, one at a time, with a measured patience. Then he put the pillow of his left thumb, where there was a raised callus, against his teeth and began to nibble at the thick skin. The waves, meanwhile, were growing, and Shawn was getting nervous. The boat tipped from side to side, nearly capsizing several times. When West succeeded in popping his callus, he held his hand over the water and pressed against the base of his thumb, squeezing a few drops of blood into the lake. The water stilled. West picked the oars back up and began to force them round and round once more.

Shawn cleared his throat again.

"I'd offer you some water," West said calmly, "but we forgot it onshore."

"Don't worry about me," Shawn replied.

Rebecca and Megan were nestled together at the back of the boat. If they'd noticed anything, they didn't show it.

The clip of Jeremiah's footsteps against cobblestones grew faster as more and more of Limbo's lost souls appeared in the streets. It was past noon, according to the sun. Services had just let out. They were running out of time.

Erika followed close behind as Jeremiah struggled to walk faster while appearing nonchalant.

"Pick up the pace, Jeremiah."

At the sound of Uriel's voice, Jeremiah grabbed Erika's hand and spun around.

"Up here."

Uriel and Selaph were perched on the mud-brick rooftop of a two-story house. A basket of apples sat between them, and they each had one of the blood-skinned fruits in hand. Uriel chewed slowly, smirking a salute.

Erika felt Jeremiah tense, like a shock of static through her skin.

"You're just a scared little fox, aren't you, Jeremy?" Uriel chided. "With all the dogs bearing down."

Selaph slipped from the roof and turned into a cloud of black smoke that drifted, swirling, to the ground. His skin reraveled as he touched the cobbles.

"Hello, Erika Stripling," he said quietly.

Jeremiah turned on her. "You know him?"

Uriel laughed from his place on the roof. "My God! You didn't tell him."

"Tell me what?" Erika felt his grip tighten around her fingers. "Erika, tell me what?"

"We dropped by yesterday, Jeremy," Uriel said. "She's a sweet little hostess. A better one than you," he added.

"Erika . . ." Jeremiah dropped her hand.

"I didn't know," she whispered. "They said that they were your brothers."

"Why didn't you tell me?"

"It didn't come up."

"Oh, Jeremy," Uriel pleaded with a mock whine, "don't disown us!"

Jeremiah looked back at his blond brother. "What do you want?"

"I think you know."

"I know that I've been away for a few years," Jeremiah said, "but when exactly were you demoted to page boys? Was it before or after your mother fell from the High Kingdom?"

Selaph stiffened.

"Calm down," Uriel said, and his eyes flicked back to Jeremiah. "It was after," he said, and stepped lightly from the roof. The tips of his feet turned to smoke and re-formed as he landed on the street with a soft patter. Ignoring the fashions set by the council wasn't allowed, but as a prince, Uriel was also one of the few who might be allowed certain indulgences. As always, he had his cloak pinned at the shoulder with a polished crossbow fibula. "But at least our mother didn't kill herself."

"My mother did not kill herself," Jeremiah growled.

Uriel smiled. "Oh, that's right," he said. "*You* killed her."

Jeremiah shook his head, disappointed. "Remember when we lived in the same house, Uri?" he asked. "And we used to play pranks on Michael and Gabriel? We had our lessons in the courtyard. And the tutors wanted so badly to please us because of what our father could do."

Uriel laughed. "I do remember," he said, a sweetness creeping into his voice with the memories. "And we were top in scores, but they always gave Gabriel higher marks because he was the eldest."

Jeremiah felt himself relaxing. He dredged up another memory. "And the walnut tree?"

"How could I forget the walnut tree?" Uriel turned to Selaph. "Remember that? We would climb up and throw shells at the maids, but they still loved us because we were only boys." He smiled. "Oh, and I'd almost forgotten." He looked back at Jeremiah. "Remember —" He touched his forehead with the backs of his knuckles as he laughed. "Remember how Father called us into court that afternoon and we were so excited because we thought he was going to give us a holiday? And remember how he told us . . ." He snorted. "How he told us that you were a bastard?"

Jeremiah's face fell.

"No, no, listen," Uriel said, still laughing. "Remember how he tried to tell us about your mummy, but he couldn't because he was so upset? And how *my* mother looked like she wanted to tear out his throat? Remember that? And we finally realized that all those years were lies, and that she really *had* hated you, but was too afraid of Father to say it?" He wiped dry the corners of his eyes. "And remember how he said that he loved you? And then he turned you out of the house anyway?" Now Uriel's smile was fading too. "And remember how you still tried to come home, Jeremiah, but no one let you in? How you tried to follow us to services, but the guards wouldn't let you through? Gabriel was your last ally, but he gave up too, didn't he?" Uriel shook his head. "You can't win, Jeremiah," he said. "So don't try. It only makes you seem more pathetic than you really are."

"Then why not finish me?" Jeremiah asked. "Now? Here?"

Uriel's voice dropped to a whisper. "You know why not. You know very well why not." He sighed. "But you can't stay in Limbo forever. We almost had you last time and then, well." He nodded at Erika. "You're lucky, Jeremiah. That's all. That's the only thing your mother gave you, because she was awfully lucky too. Until she died." He leaned in, bringing his lips right up to Jeremiah's ear. "What does that mean for you, Jeremy?" Then he straightened up and tugged at the cuffs of his sleeves. "Give him the papers, Selaph."

Selaph pulled a sealed letter from his pocket and held it out to Jeremiah, who accepted it without a word. He turned the envelope over in his thin fingers, picking at the red wax seal and the pale satin ribbon.

"It's from Daddy dearest," Uriel said. "We would've given it to you yesterday, but you never came home. Where were you, I wonder?"

"I'm sure you've heard."

"You're right. It's not so bad being the messenger, you know. We hear all the gossip, hardly ever get shot, and it's a shoo-in for Gabriel's cabinet later on, which is more than I can say for you." He took a step back to end the conversation. "Love to chat, but we've got too much to do. I'll put in a word to Gabriel if you'll do the same to Jegud. We miss him on the hill. Tell him that our hearts are always open as long as he keeps his shut. Tell him that Father still doesn't know. Good afternoon, Jeremy. And you, Miss Stripling. I think that we'll be seeing both of you again quite soon."

Selaph and Uriel floated off under the afternoon sky, their cloaks trembling in the wind.

Jeremiah turned away and headed back for his own house once more, Erika trailing behind. "Always," he hissed under his breath. "Uri *always* makes me argue with him."

"Are you sure you didn't want to all on your own?" asked Erika.

Jeremiah cut her an angry look and lifted his hand to quiet her. The stamped seal, against its bed of white, flashed bloody between the two of them. The rest of the way home, Jeremiah kept his mouth closed and his eyes on the ground, but all the time he measured the weight of his father's letter. The crisp, expensive paper rustled as he slipped it into the breast pocket of his jacket. Around it hung a dark, sweet smell of incense.

Chapter Nine

Jeremiah dismissed Erika as soon as they made it through the door.

"I need to be alone right now," he told her, and left the hall before she could protest. Erika watched him stalk off, her heart sinking. When she turned to go up the stairs, she saw Kala sitting in the cage, preening her feathers, the morning hyacinth wilting in one of her claws. Erika poked a finger through the silver bars.

"Does anyone ever watch after you?" she whispered.

The bird twittered softly in her throat and dropped the flower as she tucked her beak under one wing and closed her eyes.

Erika went on up the stairs and locked herself in her room, where she took off her filthy clothes and stepped into the bathroom, bracing for a shower cold enough to numb away the guilt.

After a few minutes longer on the lake, Shawn noticed the spread of light creeping down the prow of the boat, but he didn't know what to make of it. Then a burst of summer sun forced Shawn to close his eyes. Spots danced inside his eyelids. When he opened them again, the twilight had vanished, leaving the lake bathed in a silky afternoon gloss.

He looked back over his shoulder and saw that the whole world was lit — West and his crown of burning curls, and the shore they'd come from alive with green. Shawn couldn't see West's cottage through all the trees, but he did see crowds of bushes that he hadn't noticed before, their branches bowing to sip the lake water.

West dipped his head lower to shade his eyes, and kept rowing. A trickle of blood slipped down the left oar, leaving a sinking trail of cranberry red in its wake.

"What happened?" Shawn asked.

"We made it," West said easily, and continued to push the oars into the lake with smooth, even strokes. The shore, their destination, sparkled yellow-gold in the daylight, the blades of grass on the steep bank dusted with shadow. A little stone house, stitched over with ivy, perched on the top of a low hill. On this side of the lake, everything was jubilantly alive.

West stayed in the boat when they reached the beach, but helped Rebecca and Megan to shore with his uncut hand.

"The friend that I told you about lives here," West said to Shawn. "His name is Laza. He'll keep you. Give you something to eat."

"Thank you."

West shook his head. "Nothing to thank," he said. "It's my job." He pushed out with the flat of his oar. "Good luck," he called.

Shawn turned back. "With what?"

"With everything." West drifted back a few more feet and began to slip away into thin air. When the tip of the boat's prow vanished, Shawn took his sisters by their hands and led them up the hill to the little cabin, where pale curls of smoke drifted from a brick chimney.

❦

Jeremiah sliced through the wax seal with his pocketknife and unfolded the letter, pressing it flat on his desk.

In silence, he hunched over the heavy parchment. After reading it once, he picked it up and leaned back in his chair, pressing the paper against his knee and taking in each measured loop of the letterhead. Sent from a king, not a father. A god, not a man.

Regarding the Concerned:

We of the Council of the Throne, on this thirteenth day of this eleventh month in the standing and final year of our Crown, do issue a decree on behalf of the people of the Middle Kingdom:

Be it sanctioned by the progeny, and so enacted by the commonwealth, His Magnificence the Throne shall preside at the coronation of his heir, the Crown Prince Gabriel, on a date so to be debated and elected.

However:

Whereas the law of this Council does necessitate, and His Magnificence the Throne does still so seek, it has been deemed compulsory by the Council that pains be taken by the progeny to establish a consort in procession.

Whereas the law of this Council does necessitate, it is so considered requisite that all members of the progeny concur, or so render the proposition moot, on the point of coronation.

Whereas the law of this Council does necessitate, in relation to birthright, an establishment be made among the progeny due to discrepancies, as the Small Queen, mother of the Sixth Prince, was so removed from interment in the sepulcher of the Throne and thus her title has been renounced, but not that of her child and of His Magnificence the Throne.

Whereas the law of this Council does necessitate, despite the legislation proposed by the Fifth Prince, so named Prince Jegud, debate has now arisen in accordance to sections seven and thirteen regarding the legality of the sixth head of the progeny, so named

Prince Jeremiah, and it is at the request of His Magnificence the Throne that the Sixth Prince renounce his title and his standing without further concern to establishment of consort and without further concern to outside concurrence.

Whereas the law of this Council does necessitate, the renouncement of said title shall establish the progeny at five, and must therefore account for the Sixth Residence of His Magnificence the Throne, which shall be reclaimed by the Crown and the Council so standing.

Whereas the law of this Council does necessitate, the renouncement of said title shall strike the standing Sixth Prince from the record of the Council, establishing him as neither blood nor charge and so revoking his right to reside within the boundaries of the protectorate of His Magnificence the Throne.

Let it therefore be announced, as witnessed by the undersigned, that His Magnificence the Throne, and his Court, has so extended a proper and authorized request unto the Sixth Prince that shall be answered within a period of no more than fifteen days or that shall, by default, be considered a renouncement in the eyes of the Court and the Crown and the Council.

Beneath were the smooth, clear signatures that accompanied royal politics. Jeremiah recognized all the names of the men who had tutored him in his childhood, and who had brought him prizes of sweets when he studied well, and who had called him Prince. And at the very bottom, signed with an ink so fine it still looked moist, waited his father's rolling scrawl. A death sentence wrapped up in a gold-leaf box.

"So you've seen it."

Jeremiah glanced up.

"Jegud."

"I came as soon as I heard that Uriel was giving it to you."

"You knew?"

Jegud nodded. "And I'm sorry. I should have told you."

Jeremiah waved away the apology. "Not your fault. You're in enough trouble already. Have you agreed to this?"

"I had to, Jeremiah, or I would be . . ."

"In my position? I understand." He paused and looked again at the letter. "They want my name, Jegud."

"I know."

"And my mother's."

"I know."

"And my *house*."

"And they'll have it," Jegud told him. "One way or another, they'll have it."

Jeremiah rubbed his bottom lip with the back of his thumbnail. "Will they?"

"What are you planning?"

"Nothing. Not yet. Only . . ."

"What?"

Jeremiah shrugged. "I think I have a consort in procession."

"No, Jeremiah." Jegud took a step back, as if to distance himself from both the idea and his brother. "Making her a bride to an old man, just so you can get out of your own mess? You can't do that to Erika."

"It's no worse than anything else I could do. She wants her children, and I can't give them to her. But our father can."

"You don't know that."

"He has always outdone himself for love. Why else would I be here?"

Jegud turned away and paced the floor. Then he paused behind the couch, resting his fingertips on the polished wood of the mantel. He looked at the portrait of Jeremiah's mother, and at the dome of glass that sat in front of it, protecting a silver pendant, gone copper colored with age. From a length of sheer black ribbon dangled a perfect little ring, no larger than a watch face, crossed through the middle by a pair of sickles. So much trouble, Jegud thought, over something so small. He could feel his brother's eyes on him.

"She has the same hair," Jegud conceded.

Jeremiah smiled. "So I've heard. It might work."

"It won't."

"It might. And if I can make her queen, Erika can have anything she wants. She can have her children, or she can send them home. She can save them, Jegud. She won't say no to that. And I can keep my head and my house, and maybe even my name." He paused while Jegud watched him, fascinated and a little appalled. Jeremiah pretended not to notice. "Have you seen Uri's pick?" he asked. "Or Gabriel's?"

"Gabriel is refraining," said Jegud. "He finds it improper."

"Good of him. That leaves me to fight off four."

"Three."

"Michael isn't offering, either?"

"Of course he is," Jegud said. "But I'm not. I won't play politics with them, Jeremy. That's your job."

Jeremiah ran his fingers along the creases of the proclamation and reread all the names that were daggers in his back. "Then thank His Magnificence the Throne," he said, "that I'm still good at it."

It was a pretty little cabin, but in greater disrepair than West's had been. A sheaf of honeysuckle and ivy crept up the side and over the roof, and a line of bird nests clogged the gutter. Moss, like a second glue, had worked itself into the sandy mortar. A pile of firewood waited by the stoop and, on top of it, a wicker basket brimming with mulberries. Shawn looked at them with hungry eyes and realized that it had been days since they'd last eaten.

"If thinking were acting, then you would be a thief."

Shawn jerked up to see a man peering through a gap in the shuttered window near the door.

"Luckily, this is not the case. Can I help you?" The old man's eyes fell to Megan, who had turned in the direction of his voice. "A bit young, aren't you? And . . . not a man."

"Excuse me?" Rebecca's head bobbed out from around Shawn's shoulder.

"Oh, bless," the man said. "What happened to your guide?"

"We never had one," Shawn told him.

"How did you get across?"

"West brought us."

"West?" The man pushed the shutter out a little farther. "Has he gone?"

"Yes."

"Well then, what are you doing?"

"Are you Laza? He said that you would help us."

"Oh, he said so, did he?" Laza asked. "Well, fine then, but leave the berries be. The door's open."

Jeremiah made the long, slow climb up the stairway and walked down the hall with the light of the open window. The air still smelled like morning, but the sky had taken on the clear white of cloudy afternoons.

He knocked on the door.

"Yes?" Erika called.

"May I apologize?"

The lock clicked open and Erika's face appeared in the door. "If I deserve it."

"Erika," Jeremiah said, "I'm the only one here with cause to ask for second chances. You deserve so much more than my secrecy, but I stand here after having told you nothing. I haven't even told you things that you should know. That you *need* to know." He looked over her shoulder into the open room. "May I come in?"

She stepped out of the way and offered the threshold. "Please."

"Would you mind if I asked you to sit? It's a long story."

Erika sank into the wing chair and watched him. Her eyes were curious and expectant as she waited for her story. The letter in Jeremiah's breast pocket was heavy, and each careless, scribbled signature darted through his thoughts. Jeremiah shook his head to clear it and closed the door with the back of his heel. He moved to the bedroom window.

Beggars crowded the streets now, all returned from morning services. They stretched their hands out to the riders who traveled from one side of the district to the other. Jeremiah wondered how many of those dead he had brought here himself, giving them promises of peace because it was what they wanted to hear. He felt a rush of self-disgust creep up his throat.

"My mother wasn't a whore," he said.

Erika held the silence for a few seconds. "Okay," she said at last, when it became clear that he didn't want to continue.

"She wasn't." Jeremiah looked at her.

"I believe you."

"She was only unlucky." He wet his lips. "And my brother Uriel is a liar, since you're thinking about this afternoon."

"I'm not."

"You're a liar too." He picked up the edge of the silk curtains and rolled the hem between his thumb and forefinger. "I never knew her because I lost her in birth. It was out of wedlock. My father's fault." He shook his head. "And not what you think, either. It was his fault completely. He wanted another boy. He had five, but he thought that he needed one more. There's a lot of familial killings in the Middle Kingdom, ironically enough. Father didn't realize that she knew, which was stupid of him. And even so, he didn't realize that it would matter. I don't think that she did, either. She was never made to reproduce. But then, she was never made for anything. She was an accident too." He dropped the curtain and glanced over at Erika. "You don't understand a word of this, do you?"

"I'm trying."

Jeremiah left the window and settled at the foot of the four-poster.

"My father," he said, "is a seraph."

"An angel?"

"Sort of. Purebred. And yes, they breed. He is, and was, the ruler of souls. Of the Middle Kingdom."

Erika nibbled her lip. "And your mother?"

"My mother . . . was different. There are three groups here. There are the seraphs, who live like royalty; the souls of men, who live like dogs; and the rogues, who are halfway between. Rogues guide the dead along the road and try to help them transition.

"Souls are sad creatures, Erika — the only parts of humans that matter but the only parts that they don't understand. Human feelings and memories and selves are all wrapped up in their souls, but they're so afraid of letting go of their bodies. They stay here, in Limbo, eating because they think they must eat, bleeding because they think they must bleed, feeling because they think they must feel, when their skins aren't even real anymore. Not here. And when they can finally face that, they can set themselves free."

"Free into what?"

"Well, that's the problem," said Jeremiah. "To die in one of the Kingdoms is, as far as we know, to die forever. It's a thought that even frightens seraphs, so there's no reason why it shouldn't terrify humans, who come here and believe that they've found immortality." He stared at the window, out of the city so filled up with souls that he had ferried in. "That's why rogues exist. To be soulless, since the rest can't be." He smirked, and then grew serious again. "They . . . *We* are not supposed to feel. At least not for ourselves. We identify with those who *can* feel. We appear as they wish us to appear, speak as they wish us to speak. We cannot lie, but we do what we can to make our charges comfortable because *that*, above all, is what everyone wants, whether they are seraphs or souls."

"You are what you're made out to be," Erika said, her eyes darting to the pocket where he kept his pocketknife. She was thinking of the first time he'd showed it to her.

"Exactly," Jeremiah said. "And because we cannot feel, we cannot love." He glanced sideways at Erika, but she didn't seem to notice. She stared at her hands now, her bottom lip between her teeth as she concentrated on a thought that Jeremiah couldn't read. "We're made by the seraphs," he went on, "from the earth of the road and the shells left by souls who've moved on. There are only ever supposed to be male rogues," he said, "but sometimes . . . sometimes there are mistakes. Martha was a mistake. My mother was one too."

Erika pulled her feet from the floor and tucked them under her legs. Jeremiah handed her the quilt that lay folded at the foot of the bed and went on.

"They put my mother into service at the palace," he said. "As a handmaid to the queen. They shouldn't have. My father became enchanted with her. He wanted her. And what was she to do? It wasn't her choice. It wasn't even her choice to make.

"He fell in love, and because he wanted love, she gave it to him. And because he wanted a child, she gave it to him. Before that, no one knew that it was even possible. Rogues are supposed to be sterile." He clasped his hands together as he said that, and looked up and out through the bedroom window, as if he were speaking to thin air and the shattered city beyond.

"The queen wanted her gone, but the king refused. It tore my mother apart, those conflicting desires. She lost herself in childbirth. He had her entombed in the royal crypt, thinking nothing of it, and hoped that he could bring me up as his own, as a last promise to her.

"The funny thing, I guess, is that he put that promise on her lips. Because he wanted her to be able to love, even to love an unborn child. He needed to know that she could do that, and so she said that she could." Jeremiah paused, and Erika waited for him to push through that private pain.

"I lived like that," he went on, "without knowing, for a long time. Rogues don't live for long, but seraphs hardly age at all. My father wanted me to be like my brothers, so I compensated, never realizing what was happening to me. Once I looked about their age, I slowed down. Everyone noticed, but they were afraid to mention it aloud. They said that I was an early bloomer." He shook his head.

"In the end, my father was wrong about a lot of things. The queen could never love me, for one, and, for another, I didn't take it very well when they finally sent me away. How was I to take it? I still don't know what he expected.

"He gave me my mother's home, his sixth house. It was the one that he'd built for her to live in while she came to term. He gave me Martha, my mother's old maid, and Simon, the gardener. It was more than was his duty, I know, and it made the queen sick, but that was nothing, compared to her children. Boys will be boys, they say, but human children don't have the power behind the king of the dead. He had to call for legislation to protect me. I can't be killed as long as I'm in Limbo. The problem is that I'm still a rogue. I'm still a guide. I'm expected to work, and so I have to. Whenever I go back to Earth, my brothers follow me. I've been endangering more souls than I've helped. And now," Jeremiah said, taking the letter from his pocket, "they want me exiled. My father is passing his crown to my eldest brother, and it would seem that I'm a complication. They had my mother taken from the crypt, but I've always been an official heir. And, as they say," — he folded over the letter and read from the last clause — "'the renouncement of said title shall strike the standing Sixth Prince from the record of the Council, establishing him as neither blood nor charge and so revoking his right to reside within the boundaries of the protectorate.' Rogues don't live in the Kingdom if they don't serve the throne. I'll be sent to the Colonies. And then my brothers will break me." He tried to force a smile.

"But why?" Erika asked. "Why go that far? If you give up your birthright, then you give up your claim to the throne."

"If it were only Uri, it would be that easy. But to Michael, the second prince, I will always be a threat to his claim to the throne and to his family's purity. I'm still half seraph, and he's terrified that I'll have children of my own. And then what? The War of the Roses, but without British etiquette. If I were like my mother, then I suppose it wouldn't matter, but I'm not. I follow her in a lot of ways, but not in this. I'm so afraid to lose, Erika," Jeremiah said, "because I don't know what's waiting there. At least I've seen what death means."

Erika clambered out of her chair and sat down beside Jeremiah on the bed, putting a wing of blanket around his shoulders and tucking her head beneath his chin. Jeremiah wanted to resist her, but he felt too fragile and her presence was too powerful. He didn't know whether he was drawn to her because of her own wishes calling out to him, or whether there was some of his father in him, capable of loving all on its own. When he rested his cheek against Erika's hair and held her, his own body shifting with her steady breathing, he wondered whether it mattered. Humans and seraphs couldn't explain why romantic love happened the way it did, and could hardly describe what it felt like, so who was he to judge? Maybe this, whatever it was, was enough. It was probably as close as he would ever get.

"This will work out for you," Erika whispered. "I promise."

Jeremiah knew that she was only hoping, but he didn't argue. He only wished that she were right.

The young man opened the cottage door and looked at his visitor. A grin spread across his face. "Highness?" he said. "Welcome. How long has it been since you last ventured the Woods? I thought that you had given us up."

The king pulled back the hood of his cloak. "Don't chide the Sickle," he said. "They call you West?"

"They do," the young man said, amused. "West of the Woods."

"I need to speak with your sister."

West's smile faded. "Of course, Highness," he said eventually, taking a lantern from the wall. At his touch, a flame blossomed inside the glass flute.

The pair followed the stone path past a line of statues, to the black edge of the lake.

"Your knife?" West asked.

The king took a pearl-handled pocketknife from the depths of his robes. He handed it to West.

The man turned it over in his hands.

"Your crest will have to be remade."

"That is why I come."

"Then I hope you brought more than your name, Highness," West said. "It barters less credit than before."

The king turned to the lake without answering.

West held his work-worn palm over the water and flicked the knife blade across it. "Blood calls blood," he said, kneeling. He slipped his hand into the water.

They waited.

A thin line of air crept down the surface of the lake. As it funneled in, deeper and wider, water rushed to fill it.

West pulled his hand from the whirlpool and a woman

came with him, hair clinging like seaweed down her shining back. Her dress, tied around her neck and waist, was a worn and filthy gray, frayed and speckled with sticks and river beetles. Over her shoulder, the lake continued to shudder until a stairway appeared, cut in stone and painted with dark algae. She smiled, revealing rows of thin fish teeth. Air whispered through the spaces as she spoke, and to make her words clear, she said them slowly, as if puzzling out each one.

"Brother," she murmured. "Too long away." She dropped his hand, leaving a film of slime on his skin. "You never did much love the cold and hungry South. Or are you still afraid of me?"

When her brother said nothing, South turned away and took the king's arm. Down the steps they went, their footsteps heavy in the dark. West stayed behind and watched as the water tumbled in around their feet and swallowed them alive.

Baba Laza cracked his knuckles before he took the clay platter into his spotted, wrinkled hands and carried it to the table in the next room. The children were already seated, with mugs of herbal tea, and he took his place at the table's head. He watched without comment as Shawn loaded plates for Rebecca and Megan and guided their hands to the food. Laza waited for Shawn to take some for himself, but the boy only folded his hands over his wooden plate and looked down the length of the table into the old man's face.

"How can I get their eyes back?"

Laza's laugh came out sharp, like a dog's bark. "You think you can? So arrogant now. Like your mother."

Shawn hesitated, struck silent. His sisters also stopped moving; Rebecca's hand hovered in midair, a piece of flatbread halfway to her mouth.

"You know our mother?" Shawn asked.

"She came through with the Small Queen's boy. Thought she knew everything. Stole his knife while he was sleeping. It must be you who she was looking after. He forgives her. Fool of a boy. Just like his fool father and fool brothers. In that blood, I think."

"When did they come through?"

"I could never tell you. It all runs together after a while. Not too long ago."

Rebecca opened up her blank eyes and turned to Laza. "How was she?"

"Dead." He shrugged. "How is anybody who comes over the lake? You're the first three I've ever seen to cross alive, and the girls might as well be dead." Laza smiled when Shawn threw him a sharp look. "I won't lie for my benefit," he said.

"So why should I lie for yours? You aren't any better than a rogue who comes through after giving up their eyes instead of their tongues, and I certainly would not lie on their behalf. I don't know what you were thinking."

"That's enough," Shawn said.

"Snap, snap, snap. Learn better manners before you open your mouth." Laza took a piece of sesame candy from the plate and pointed at Megan. "Her," he said. "I think that I can help the little one. Alecto cannot use four eyes." At that, Rebecca perked up. "But she can use two," he said, giving her a knowing look, "so it is absolutely no go to get both pairs." He popped the candy into his mouth and shook his head, gesturing now at Rebecca. "She doesn't belong here," he said. "None of you do. You'll lose more than your eyes on your way to the Kingdom."

"We've made it this far," Shawn said.

"Barely. And if you think that this is far, then you truly will be dead before you make it out. There's only one road through here, and it is never marked."

"I'm sure we'll be fine," Shawn replied.

"You're a liar if you say you're sure of anything, but have your way about it."

"Can we sleep here for the night?"

"Sleep wherever you want," Laza said, waving his hands above his head. "But if by 'night' you mean 'dark,' then you'll have a time. The sun never sets on this side. But windows shut, and there are sheets in the cupboard. I am working outside if you need someone to bother." He pushed himself to his feet and tottered out of the house, moving on joints that seemed to have stiffened just from holding still.

The passageway led to a stone room at the heart of the lake. Shelves lined the curved walls, each stuffed with books and glass bottles. The air smelled of moldering leaves and damp parchment, and the only light seeped, cold and green, from the fishing net suspended across the ceiling. Near the far wall was a cauldron on a bed of dying coals. In the middle of the floor, a shallow silver bowl sat on a wooden podium. South brought the king to this table and let go of his hand. As she walked away, she tapped the bowl with her knuckles and turned her yellow eyes back on him.

"And what does the Reaper King come to ask of South?"

He felt his pockets for coins.

By the time he found one, South was already at one of her shelves, shuffling through the crowded vials. She paused to appraise the clatter of his offered gold.

"Shall I guess?" she asked, her voice echoing softly back against the stone. "Five sons there have always been in the house of middling kings. No inheritance, then, for the unlucky sixth?"

"No."

South slid over to the cauldron and sunk her arm, nearly to the shoulder, into the simmering broth. She came up covered in what looked like mud, thick and gray-brown, and, holding her arm away from her body, padded back to the king. When she opened her hand above his, a baby bird tumbled out, warm and shuddering; he could feel, beneath the sticky feathers, its heart pounding against its chest.

South watched it flounder against the nest of the king's palm. "A rogue must learn to see the dead for what they really are."

"A Caladrius?"

She turned away. "A promise parting," she told him, "which says that, by some, the boy will not be forgotten. In life, the eyes of death, and, in death, those of life. So tells fate."

The king tucked the bird into his pocket. "And my wife —"

South's glance cut him. The bowl clicked as he laid down another coin, and she softened.

"The slighted queen will live unhappy while her greatest shame lives at all. So it must be."

"But he —"

Another look, another coin.

Water dripped from the walls and ceiling, pattering against the shelves and floor. "Jeremiah, king's son," South cried, as if announcing the name to a full court. "Child of myth." She slit her eyes coyly at the king and dropped her voice. "The boy who never feels wanted."

She turned away, seemingly finished, and wiped the cauldron's mud onto her dress. The last of it, she licked from her fingers.

"Bitter," she whispered, and then paused again. "Your last child is stronger than you, Highness. He will fly, like his gift, until they pin him to the wall." She shook her head and turned back to the king. Looked him dead in the eyes. "But passion breeds passion," she went on, "and so your son will burn. You, great Reaper King, have condemned that boy to a life consumed by fire."

Jeremiah brushed a handful of hair out of Erika's face.

"It's your turn to purge yourself," he said.

"Oh?"

"Are you really sure you want this?"

She faltered.

"Your children," he said. "I'm talking about your children. Are you sure that you want them here?"

"Can you take me back to them?"

He clicked his teeth together in deliberation. "No," he said at last. "I can't."

"Then you have to do this. I *need* them."

"There are millions out there who would say that they need their own families."

"I know," Erika said. "And look how they're living. They're empty. Hardly human anymore. I don't want to be like that."

"Erika, your children can't help you there. Only you can."

She bit her lips. "I need them."

Jeremiah rose from the bed and stuffed his hands into the pockets of his suit jacket.

"I sometimes wish that my own mother had been more like you," he said.

Erika gave him a sad smile.

"Where's that coming from?" she asked. "The angel or the rogue?"

"I don't know," he said. "Not the rogue. My mother didn't love me because she couldn't. She didn't want me because she couldn't. I can't hate her for that, but how can I love her?"

"Maybe your father cared enough for both."

He laughed softly to himself. "Of course," he said. "And I guess that disowning me is just a birthday present. No, Erika, I've been alone for a long, long time."

He knew that she would touch him before the words left his mouth, and he hated himself for saying them anyway. Her fingertips crept up his wrist, his forearm, and jumped to the side of his face. She barely had to press to make him turn, but he focused on the soft, pale inside of her wrist. He feared looking at her face and seeing something there that he couldn't fix.

"Jeremiah."

"Erika, please."

"Jeremiah." Her voice was a whisper, pleading. "I need to know," she said, "how much of this is you, and how much of this is a lie."

He risked a glance at her eyes and saw that they were sad, scared.

"What are you talking about?"

"Are you leading me on because you can't help it, or because you want to use me?"

"Erika." Now he reached out too, cupping her face in his hands, rubbing the corners of her eyes with his thumbs. "You've been through too much to let me make you look this heartsick."

She allowed him a small laugh but didn't answer.

"I got you into this, and I'm going to get you out."

"Stop," she said. "This is not your fault."

"It is," he said. "More than you realize." He sucked in a sharp breath as the pressure of her needs crushed against his chest. "I know that you don't want to hear that," he said, "but sometimes we have to believe what hurts us."

"Am I dead, Jeremiah? Did you do this?"

He concentrated on the bedspread, because he knew that if he looked at her, she would know. She would catch the answer in his eyes, and she would fall to pieces. If he could heal her, he would much rather do that. Take this burden off both their backs.

"Do you remember what I told you before?" he asked, reining himself in enough to look her in the eyes.

"That I'm waiting," she said.

"I would never lie to you." He gave her a smile to cheer her up. "I can't, remember?"

Now it was Erika's turn to examine the coverlet. She smoothed a piece of it against her thigh, and then let her fingers run along Jeremiah's leg, tracing his knee.

"Then I don't understand," she said. "Why can't I leave? Why am I here in the first place?"

Jeremiah brushed handfuls of hair from her face and tucked them behind her ears.

"I don't always understand, either," he said. "There's no sin in that."

She studied his face, searching him out, sinking straight into his eyes.

"We can't do this, Erika."

She put her palm against the back of his neck, drew him close, and let her mouth hover there.

"Just once," she said, her words brushing hot across his lips. "If you mean it — if you aren't just reflecting for me — prove it just once."

Jeremiah looked at the face that he'd stared at for so long the day he killed her. At the person whose soul he'd lifted up, careful as if afraid of waking her, from a crash that he'd orchestrated. He hadn't even noticed her smile until later, and the way it rose a little higher on one side of her mouth, or the way she rubbed her hands when she got nervous, or laughed when determined not to cry. He hadn't even noticed the way she said his name, so smooth it polished him, or the way she pulled her sleeves down to cover her palms, like a girl wearing clothes too big for her.

He slipped one hand around to cradle her head, as he had that night in the rain, and he kissed her, deep, vowing that he never would again.

Chapter Ten

Shawn woke up with a stream of sunlight across his face, let in through a crack in the wooden shutters. He wiped his mouth and ruffled out his hair as he got to his feet. His eyes scanned the room with the same unfamiliarity that was fast becoming custom. He kept replaying the timeline since the fire, but nothing could make this feel less like a dream. A ridiculous dream that made him sick and frightened and excited, but a dream nonetheless.

A canvas shoulder bag sat just inside the door, and with it a white blindfold rolled up alongside a tiny bird's nest. Inside the nest waited two glass beads, each the size of a hummingbird egg. On top of them lay a note, rolled up and tied with string. *Swallow.* Shawn looked at his sisters, arms wrapped together in sleep, and silently thanked Laza.

He knelt down beside Rebecca and nudged her. She gave a half scream that woke Megan.

"I didn't mean to!" Shawn said.

Rebecca pressed a hand against her chest. "Scare me to death."

"I'm *sorry.*"

"What d'you want?"

"I'm supposed to blindfold you," he said.

"Right," Rebecca scoffed. "Because I can see so well. Just be sure to make the knot tight enough so it doesn't slip off and show me everything."

"Laza got Meg's eyes for us. I don't want you to scare her."

Rebecca closed her mouth. Her fingertips traveled up to the bridge of her nose and paused, hovering over the blank sockets of her eyes. When she finally found her voice again, it came out rough.

"Fine," she said. "Do it."

Shawn wrapped the cloth around her face and tied it at the back with a sharp tug. Rebecca's hands drifted up again, feeling the span of fabric that went from her brow bone to the tip of her nose.

"Is it too tight?"

She shook her head. "It's fine."

"I'm sorry about this."

"Help Meg."

Shawn picked up the nest and went to kneel across from his little sister.

"It's me, Meg," he said, taking her hand. "I'm going to help you, okay? If you swallow these, you'll be able to see again." He dropped the glass beads into her palm.

"Okay."

"It's like a vitamin, okay?"

"Can I drink something with it?"

"Right." He crawled back to the satchel and flipped it open. There was a wool blanket packed inside, two loaves of bread wrapped in cloth, and a few animal-skin flasks of water. He brought one back to Megan and unscrewed the lid.

"Here."

Her hands shook a little as she took the flask, but she put the beads onto her tongue, one by one, and then tipped her head back and drank the water. She opened her lips when she finished, showing off an empty mouth as her mother had taught her to do.

"Good job, Megan," Shawn said.

Megan fluttered her lashes, as if testing the air. Then her lids flew open and she grinned, flashing rows of clean white teeth.

Shawn threw his arms around her. He'd never been so happy to see that smile in his life — the wrinkles around her eyes that made her look older, the color that rushed into her cheeks, and her black lashes that fanned out as she tipped up her head, laughing.

Rebecca stumbled over and joined in on the hug, smiling with her little sister.

"Why are you wearing that, Becky?" Megan asked, reaching for the mask.

Rebecca quickly brushed her hand away. "Don't worry about it, Meg," she said, and pulled her sister against her chest. "It doesn't matter now. It doesn't matter."

Jeremiah stood in his study, hands clasped behind his back. He stared through the eastern window, at the light that spilled down over the bowl of wilting flowers.

Either way, he was lost; it was now just a matter of how soon and how painful the going would be. Jeremiah wasn't even sure that the call was still his to make.

He held his pocketknife in his left hand, running his thumb down the side where the family crest had been carved into the handle all those years ago.

A trumpet for the first son, a sword for the second, a scepter for the third, a quill for the fourth, a chalice for the fifth, and a sickle for the father. Relics of the old Kingdom, the king and his five princes. It was how it had always been. But with Jeremiah had come a bird, for the sixth son.

Jeremiah knew that his father held the blame for all of this, and if the king of souls had made war on history's legends, then who was he, a runaway prince, to preserve them now?

He flipped out the knife blade and held it up to the light of the window. The sun played against the worn edges, growing brighter as he took his father's letter from the desk beside him. He touched the tip of the knife against the paper, and waited. The lick of fire searched its way along the decree, the flames making the stiff line of Jeremiah's jaw glow faintly. He held the paper until the fire licked his fingers and then let the last scrap drift down to float alongside his brothers' thirsty bouquet.

"Et factum est proelium in caelo," Jeremiah whispered, conjuring up the verses that he'd memorized while guided by the great masters. "And there was war in heaven."

The scattered keys of the Kingdom. The last blood of the monarchy. The laws set in broken stone. Who was he to preserve them now?

The children found an empty house when they finally decided to leave. Dust stirred and settled as motes in sunlight, tripping on table legs and skimming the tops of kitchen counters.

They stepped into the front yard and were greeted with the smell of jasmine and a shock of color — a tropical garden in the middle of the woods. It would have been impossible to miss the day before, but somehow they must have, because no plants grew that quickly. The lush blanket of ferns was spattered with dahlia and rainbowed gladiola spears. Diving anthurium hearts poked through tangles of snapdragons and birds of paradise. Nearby, trees were choked with bougainvillea and honeysuckle, whose flowers dripped into the blazing mouths of amaryllis blossoms. Shawn wanted a moment to appreciate the color before they headed back into the slate green and gray of the woods, but he knew that they should move on. He walked with the satchel over one shoulder, while Megan trailed behind, guiding Rebecca with a quick and unrelenting commentary.

Shawn found the forest pretty, at first, and a welcome change from the dark woods that he was now used to. The light and warmth chased away the fear that they'd suffered through before. The fact that they now had a destination, whether or not they knew where it lay, was also comforting.

But then a few hours passed, and doubt began to creep back into their footsteps. Shawn broke off tree limbs, trying to mark their way. He began to worry that he was leading them in long, pointless circles. The sun never wavered, but only gave off the same warm, high-noon light. Time had stopped, and they were the last ones left alive, left moving, left guessing.

Shawn gave up. He found a fallen tree and sat down. He gave Megan and Rebecca some of the bread, but took none for himself. He was desperate to remember which direction they'd come from. His headache grew.

When a bird twittered nearby, Shawn froze. As the first sound since the lake and Baba Laza's cottage, it split the air like gunfire.

"Shawn?"

He glanced at Megan, who was staring into the woods.

"What, Meg?"

"Who's that?"

"Who?" He followed her eyes.

A man stood a dozen yards off, dressed in a dark brown trench coat. A light shadow of stubble dusted his jaw and his hair settled, curly and dark against his temples. He had an arm propped up against one of the low limbs of a poplar tree, and a white bird bobbed its way along the length of the branch, from the slim trunk to his waiting fingers and back again.

Shawn staggered to his feet.

"What is it, Shawn?" Rebecca, who looked ready to bolt, held on to Megan with one hand.

"I'm not sure."

The man raised his arm in greeting.

"Don't be afraid," he said. "I won't hurt you."

Shawn tried to place the voice.

"Who are you?"

"Jeremiah," the man said. "Would you mind if I came closer?" When he moved, the bird he carried bobbed its neck to match his footsteps.

Megan finally recognized him and gave a muffled cry.

"Oh, I'm sorry, darling," Jeremiah said. "You're thinking about that dream, aren't you? Your mother's fine. She isn't even angry with me." He held the bird at arm's length. "Would you like to hold Kala for a little while? She's a very good pet." He offered his hand and waited as the Caladrius minced her way onto Megan's fingers. Kala looked at him with her shining black eyes before burying her face deep beneath her wing. He folded his arms and measured up Erika's youngest child. "No," he said, puzzled.

"What are you doing here?"

Jeremiah glanced back at Shawn. "Pardon?"

"Are you going to help us?"

He opened his mouth, and then shut it again. "Hardly," he said at last. "Not that I haven't been trying. I just needed to know . . . but I was wrong. So." He pressed his lips together and then started pacing. "I won't be able to come back again."

"Why not?"

"Because someone is trying to kill me."

Shawn looked at Megan but didn't say anything. She was too busy trying to coax away Kala's fear. She kissed the bird's small white head and stroked the long feathers of her back and tail. Kala cooed and shivered into her own little breast.

Jeremiah reached up to massage his neck and felt a two-day growth of beard. He stopped pacing, hand poised just an inch away from his face, and glanced back at Shawn, and then Rebecca.

"Someone has a strong personality," he said.

"Excuse me?" said Rebecca, offended.

"And knows it," said Jeremiah under his breath. He dropped his hand and gestured at the elder Striplings. "Can I talk to you two for a minute?"

Shawn took Rebecca by the hand and led her away. Jeremiah smiled at Megan before following them.

When they were far enough away for a private conversation, Jeremiah stopped walking. "You're here because of your mother," he said flatly. "She wants you to be with her. Personally, I think that it's a terrible idea, but it doesn't seem to matter. And after what I've done, how can I refuse her?"

"What exactly have you done?"

"To the point, Rebecca," he replied. "Unfortunately, I haven't finished doing it, so it would be preemptive for me to say. But it started with a mishap." His voice dropped. "Actually, it started with coffee."

"Excuse me?"

"Never mind," he said. "Listen. I have a brother who might be able to help."

"I need my eyes," said Rebecca.

"Your . . . Oh." Jeremiah touched the side of his head. "I'll try," he said. "I *will* try. But I'm afraid that some things are more pressing. I need my head, for example, and I'm very close to losing it right now."

"You said that someone wanted you dead?"

"Not just dead." Jeremiah wet his lips. "I don't think you'd understand."

"They're after us too," Shawn said.

Jeremiah sighed. "That's not possible."

"They wear black," Shawn said.

"Around here, a lot of people do."

"They're made of smoke."

Jeremiah raised an eyebrow. "Oh?"

"They have dogs."

"The hounds? I can't believe . . ." He shook his head. "They went for fireworks, did they? Well, then yes, you're right." Again, Jeremiah sighed. "Don't talk to them. Can you do that for me?"

Shawn let a disgusted grunt escape his throat.

"It's the best I can do," Jeremiah said. "They shouldn't be here. I could have them *charged* for being here." He clicked his tongue against the roof of his mouth. "Actually, that's not a bad idea. But look, I'm trying. I haven't slept for trying. I haven't eaten. It's complicated. I can't exactly waltz you through the gates."

"Then what *can* you do?"

"Give you a little hope," Jeremiah said. "You're human, so that should mean something to you. I won't give up and you shouldn't, either."

"But what are we doing?" Shawn asked.

"Keeping on the move," said Jeremiah. "You have to, since they're following. I'll send in the cavalry as soon as I figure out how, but now I have to go. I'm putting you at risk by standing here."

Rebecca looked annoyed. "Then why don't you just *leave*?"

"I will," Jeremiah said, "before you make me say something stupid." He pricked a finger with the tip of his pocketknife and then whistled at Kala, who fluttered out of Megan's hands and latched on to his wrist. She opened her beak to the rising mist and, with a dry hiss of shifting leaves, they both vanished.

It was late summer and the gardens were golden with afternoon sun.

There were five boys sitting on the west patio, books open in their laps. Behind them went the *tap-tap-tap* of their tutor's cane. The youngest of the boys, a slim child with a nest of curling brown hair, picked a pebble loose from the patio stones and flicked it at one of his brothers. The second prince, and the eldest there among them, smirked and scratched another line onto the count. Jegud picked up the stone and rolled it between his thumb and forefinger, his eyes on their tutor, before he tossed it back at his little brother. Another smirk. Another tally mark.

Across the lawn, in a wooden gazebo, the queen sat sipping weak tea with her sister, the Lady Sara. They were watching the children because conversation had failed them, as conversation often did.

"He's grown," Sara said.

"Hmm?"

"Jeremiah. He's grown."

"He has, hasn't he?"

Sara set down her teacup. "Dramatically," she said. "Is that rogue of yours his nursemaid now? I haven't seen her in so long."

"She was dismissed," the queen said, her voice stretched thin.

"I've never heard of a rogue failing their job."

"She didn't fail," the queen told her sister. "She worked too well. It distressed the other help."

Sara nodded slowly before risking her next move. "Tell me the truth, Sister," she said. "I've heard such —"

"I would expect you to ignore the gossip, Sara," the queen cut in. "We both know how badly hearsay damaged you in the past."

Sara closed her mouth and tilted her head away, as if she hadn't heard.

The queen, of course, had also caught the rumors as they flew past her windows:

The sixth prince had aged so quickly.

The sixth prince looked nothing like his mother.

The sixth prince made his father so sad. So distant.

And, most curious of all, part of the royal crypt had been closed to the public. The queens' tombs only. It was as if the palace mourned.

Holding back her temper, the queen calmly poured out another cup of tea.

The sun set long before Jeremiah finally made it back to Limbo, so when he saw lights glimmering over the city wall, they surprised him. He slipped through the gate and peered down the main street into the square.

A figure in white stood on a makeshift stage. He gripped a spitting torch in one hand, his other fist raised above his head. Jeremiah recognized him as a councilman and a friend to his brother Michael.

A crowd, made up of the city's charges, pressed close. At first glance, Jeremiah thought that it may have been a few dozen people, but then he saw a glitter in the dark, and realized that it was the flame of the man's torch reflecting in the eyes of a hundred hungry souls. Of a thousand. They faded into the blackness of the night, snaking into the alleys between buildings, perched like gargoyles on the eaves of tenements, hanging out of windows to catch the angry words that this courtier shouted.

"But he does not only claim rights to the throne! No! He takes in a human soul! Never has this been done in all the millennia of the three Kingdoms! Why that one over you, I ask? Why that one over any of you here?" The councilman's voice dropped, and the crowd huddled forward with anticipation. "The balance, then, is broken forever by these rash actions," the man said. "By his stupid self-importance!" The mob leaned back out and hummed to itself, thinking. Believing.

Jeremiah shivered.

Then he saw the horses.

Michael's train appeared at the top of the northern hill and started down, his black carriage surrounded by low-cut chariots of gold. A flag, emblazoned with the original five-part crest, flew at the back of each. As the procession neared the stage, a hand darted out from the prince's coach, and the speaker caught the cloth thrown at him.

"Look now!" he cried. "The second prince offers a gift to you!" He unfurled the cloth and held it up at arm's length; the six-part crest hung limply from his fingers. "What shall we do to the sign of the traitor?"

The crowd hesitated as it turned over his question. Since entering the Kingdom, it had never been asked to form an opinion. Then one man leaned out of an upper-story window and called out the answer: "Burn it!"

The councilman pointed at the window and held the flag higher. *"What shall we do?"*

The crowd answered, eager: *"Burn it!"*

"For Jeremiah!" he screamed. "The boy who wants to steal the crown!" He brought the torch to the heart of the flag and held it there until the center had burned away and the flames were beginning to lick his fingers. "Will he ever steal it?" he yelled, throwing down the last scraps.

"No!"

"Will you ever call him king?"

"No!"

Jeremiah turned and fled, clutching Kala safely against his chest.

When her master came in, Martha continued to refill the water dish in Kala's cage. Her eyes flicked up to him, but she didn't smile.

"Erika is in the study," she said.

"Why did you let her in there?"

"Because you did. You said that she had range of the house. I knew that it was a bad idea."

"No, *I* did."

Martha's eyebrows drew up to the lace of her cap. "Sir?" she asked.

"That was rude."

"Indeed, sir."

"I know it was."

"Apparently."

Jeremiah held Kala out to Martha.

"Put her away, please," he said.

"Of course." Martha took the bird in her wrinkled hands and gently smoothed the white feathers.

"Did Jegud come by?"

"No, sir."

"Did Uri?"

"Only if Erika let him in."

Jeremiah hissed and clamped a hand over his own mouth.

"You're having a bad day, sir," Martha said quietly.

"I know."

"Apparently."

He groaned and left the room, tearing off his scarf as he went. Martha returned to her work without a word, her transition as tactful as a housemaid and as blind as a rogue.

When Erika ran her forefinger over the mantelpiece, she came away with a thick pillow of dust. The hearth looked too clean for anything to ever have been burned on its polished black stones, but a pretty rack of cast-iron shovels and pokers stood ready, just in case. Erika wiped the dust from her hands and stepped back for another look at the portrait that hung over the mantel.

The woman, dressed in dark blue, her hair twisted up and held with gold-and-amber netting, sat perched on a patio wall that overlooked an expanse of gardens. She held her right hand posed in midair, but the trinket she dangled had been painted over since the original commission. Her thin white fingers were smudged from the poor touch-up job and detracted from the beauty of the painting as a whole. A lovely piece, but not a happy one. The gentle smile on the woman's lips never reached her eyes. Erika thought that the painter must have been very brave to have captured the emptiness there.

Behind her, the study door clattered open.

"Leave, Erika," Jeremiah said, tramping in. He had a black scarf balled up in one fist and tossed it to the side as he struggled to pull off his jacket.

"Excuse me?"

"Leave," he repeated. "Go to your room. I've had a bad day."

"You sound like my husband."

"Your ex-husband. You shouldn't have divorced him if you didn't want him to leave."

Erika's mouth flew open.

"I'm not my mother's son today, and you've had enough of my brothers to know that the alternative isn't lovely."

"What are you saying?"

"That you, as I have now mentioned twice, need to leave."

"This morning —"

"We cannot talk about this morning, Erika. Not now. I should never have let that happen, and it will not happen again."

She squared her jaw, stood up straighter. "I stayed up to talk to you. You don't understand —"

"No, Erika, I understand perfectly," Jeremiah said. "I wished before that my mother had been like you, but I take it back. It isn't love that's driving you, it's selfishness, and your selfishness is oppressive. Overwhelming. You're in a house full of slaves who would read your mind and do whatever you asked before thinking twice, and you still aren't satisfied. I've pampered you like a queen and you haven't even married my father yet. I've given you everything and you've never thanked me." He threw his coat down on the back of the sofa. "All you can think about is your children, and all they want is to move on. God, the Striplings are a stubborn family. I don't know who's worse, but it *must* be you because at least *they* listened when I said no. You certainly haven't shown the courage to do that. I'd even say that —"

"Yet?"

Jeremiah planted his palms on the couch back and let his shoulders slump.

"I haven't married your father *yet*?" Erika clenched her jaw. "You make it sound like I'm going to, Jeremiah."

He glanced from Erika to the portrait on the wall. After a silence, he risked the question.

"And?"

Erika paled. "What have you done?"

"I haven't done anything, Erika," he said. "I haven't done anything at all, except what you asked. You wanted your children, so I nearly killed them."

"What?"

"*Nearly*," Jeremiah barked. "I said '*nearly*.' If you're going to pick words to overanalyze, you might as well choose important ones. You wanted me to make sure they were all right, so I risked my head and theirs to see them. I've spent half of my day wandering to cover my trail, and then I come back to the city and you know what I see? I see my big brother in full regalia on the streets, trying to rally the entire Kingdom against me. I'm a traitor now, or didn't you realize? And I'm housing *you*, which makes things unfair and unholy and unprecedented and every other damning 'un' that the court can think of." He waved a finger at her. "And then I come home, and I find you, here, in my study, touching my things, and wondering where your children are. Well, I don't know, Erika, and I'm sorry. Sorry because I know that that's going to piss you off, and sorry because it makes my own job a damn sight harder. So please, in honor of everything good left, just go to your room and leave me be."

"I need to know what you mean about your father."

"No," Jeremiah answered, "you don't. If you *needed* to know, then *I* would know, but I don't. You can't see, can you? I don't have all the answers. I don't have *half* the answers. Maybe you shouldn't ask for things if you won't accept the consequences. There are things that I'd like to have happen too, you know. I'd like to have a biologically stable mother, for one. I'd like to have a dad who actually acknowledges me, for another, and I'd maybe even like to have a family that doesn't want me spitted and charred. But I don't ask for any of that, because I know that everything has consequences. It's cause and effect and it always has been, even on Earth. I know that you died young, but for God's sake, you'd think you would've learned a few things. Like how having sex gets you pregnant and running off with an alcoholic gets you disowned."

Erika had gone red faced, half shocked and half enraged. She spun out of the room and into the hall, slamming the door behind her so that the bookcases rattled. She wasn't there, then, to see Jeremiah collapse onto the sofa with his hands over his face. He felt sucked dry.

Shawn spread out the blanket that Baba Laza had given them and lay down beside Megan. It felt awkward, sleeping so exposed in the woods during midday, but he was too exhausted to care. They'd taken Jeremiah's advice and walked as long as their legs let them. It was rough going, since they were barefoot.

The forest had changed. A bed of underbrush crept in, and the canopy thickened out. Brambles and sticker weeds lay buried in the carpet of dead leaves. Shawn carried Megan on his shoulders when she became too afraid to walk.

"My feet hurt," Megan whimpered against his ear.

"My skin hurts," Rebecca said. She reached over and squeezed her brother's shoulder and then pulled Megan to her in a hug. "You've been a good brother, Shawn," Rebecca said. "And you've been good too, Meg," she added before being prompted.

Shawn covered his face with the crook of his arm.

"And you've been good too, Becky," Megan whispered.

Rebecca and Megan giggled together for a little while, their voices low and strained. As Shawn drifted off to sleep, he wondered how much longer the water would last.

Erika knelt on the floor in the middle of her bedroom, hunched over a white porcelain bowl. She dipped cupped hands into the cold water and dampened her bandages until the edges started to come loose.

When she found the end of the wrapping, she peeled it back, following the trail in circles around her head, unraveling the clean cloth gauze. Finished, she gathered the long rope of it into a pile beside her.

Her fingers shook as she dipped them back into the water and touched the side of her head, where her hairline turned down toward her left ear. Her curls were knotted there, but she wanted to credit that to the baby-fine texture her mother had given her. She pressed through the knots and felt where the blood had clotted and dried. The black dust that came away on her fingers touched the water and melted, swirling down to the bottom of the bowl, trailing red.

She bit her bottom lip as she felt along her scalp one last time, and now she found the paper-dry edge where skin met bone. She sucked in a tight breath.

Erika realized that the cut didn't hurt at all. That it would never hurt again. That she belonged on those streets with rags and filth and an empty tin cup, begging for money that she didn't really need, eating food to make her feel less hollow, sleeping in rooms to make her feel more human. Hopeless with fear either way, because the fear she ran from was folded deep inside.

Erika came back into the study, with her bandages trailing from one hand. Jeremiah sat on the sofa, with his head in his palms, staring at the fire that crackled in the hearth. He looked up when she opened the door, and then turned back to his own thoughts. She walked over to him, stone-faced, and dropped the long string of linen at his feet.

"You lied to me."

He wanted to say that he had not lied, because bending the truth was not the same as breaking it. He wanted to say that, of the two of them, only he knew what the limits of reality were. He thought better of it. He could tell that she was too upset to listen, and since he was too tired to argue, he only hoped that, eventually, she would see this all on her own. Instead, he said, "I hoped that I could send you back. But I can't."

Erika took this without comment. She wasn't thinking about herself right now. "Is that why my kids can't come through?" she asked. "Because they're still alive?"

"Yes," Jeremiah said. "And I would send them back, but it's too late now. I thought that I could change things, but I can't. It's not my place."

"Whose place is it, then?"

"I don't know."

"You *do* know," Erika said. "It's your father's, isn't it?"

"I suppose."

"Don't *suppose*, Jeremiah. Not now."

He looked up from the floor and took in her face, so thin and worried, and her long, swirling hair. His mother's portrait smiled coolly over Erika's shoulder: navy dress against alabaster skin and a piled cap of copper hair. The hair that was her trademark. They said that it used to burn in the sunshine. They said that the king kept a lock of it in his bedroom, tucked away in a small wooden box.

"It's my father's place," he said. "He's king of the dead, and if anyone can get your children home safely, it's him. But he doesn't make allowances for anyone but family."

Erika squared her jaw. "Well then," she said. "What do I have to do?"

In spite of himself, Jeremiah smiled.

Chapter Eleven

"Good morning, glories."

Shawn blinked against the sunlight and saw a blond man smiling down at them.

"I am speaking, of course, to the ladies. To you, sir, I'll leave it at 'good morning.'"

"Are you Jeremiah's brother?"

The man looked a little surprised. "I am, yes. And he told you about me?"

"He said that you could help us."

"Excellent. But I'm afraid, actually, that he must have been talking about young Jegud. I'm an older of the set. Uriel, the third prince, entirely at your service." He swept them a deep bow.

Megan was sitting by this time, and Rebecca had propped herself up with an elbow. Uriel twirled his cap between his fingers and studied them.

"How can I help you?" he asked.

"You could get us out," Shawn said.

Uriel's eyes slit at the sarcasm, but he waved off the annoyance with a flip of his hand.

"That, unfortunately, is not my department," he said. "I have no idea what brilliance Jeremiah has planned for that, since all of you seem to be very much alive, but I'm sure that it will be well worth watching. Can I find anything to make you more comfortable? The young miss may want her vision, for one? And shoes all 'round, perhaps?"

"That would be helpful, yes."

"My pleasure." He smirked. "I only ask for something small in exchange."

At that, Shawn jerked his chin. "And what would that be?"

Uriel's smirk broadened into a grin. "It's a bit complicated, I'm afraid, but you'll have to trust me. A test, of sorts. Now, are we agreed?"

"Not without knowing what we're expected to do."

He laughed. "Well, that's part of the test, isn't it? Listen, just don't say a word to my brothers. My father is overseeing them. Quality control, as you might say. I only need to know, from time to time, how they've been doing."

"That's all?"

"Cover to cover."

"Fine, then."

"Excellent." Uriel smiled again, a flash that came smooth and debonair to his mouth. A politician's grin. "You're in angel country now," he said, offering his hand. "You *must* shake."

Uriel let his smile linger as Shawn held out his arm.

Static crackled between their palms when their skin touched.

"Have an excellent day, Master Stripling," Uriel said. "I'll be back with bells on."

He straightened up and disappeared into the woods, the edges of his cloak flapping around his ankles.

Jegud arrived in the morning and showed himself into Jeremiah's study. He noticed the pile of bandages near the sofa but said nothing.

"She found out," Jeremiah said.

Jegud turned, startled, and found his brother considering a row of books on one of the tall glass-front shelves.

"I told you that she would."

"I never said you were wrong."

"Yes, you did," Jegud said. "You said exactly that."

"I said 'you may be right, but I think not.' I'm entitled to an opinion, aren't I?"

"Certainly. For now."

"Maybe not *just* for now." Jeremiah pulled out a set of law books and swept the dust from their spines. "If I give the king his new queen, I'll be as good as an advisor."

Jegud's eyes widened. "She didn't," he gasped.

"She doesn't have another option, Jegud."

"You didn't tell her that, did you?"

"No. She saw it for herself."

"But she doesn't have to do this."

"Just like you don't have to accept Gabriel's succession. But what would happen to you if you didn't? The same thing that will happen to me if she doesn't sacrifice. The same thing that will happen to her children."

Jegud followed Jeremiah as he brought the books back to his desk.

"You can tell me that you don't agree," Jeremiah said. "You're entitled to your opinion too, after all."

"I'd rather not cause trouble," Jegud said. "What did you want from me?"

"The Stripling children need a guide."

Jegud scoffed. "Fine plan, Jeremiah," he said. "Except that, first of all, I'm not one, and second of all, they're not dead."

Jeremiah winced.

"What was that for?" Jegud asked, straightening.

"Nothing."

"Liar. What do you know?"

Jeremiah started slowly. "On my last visit," he said, "Kala was a bit shy."

Jegud reached out, then let his arm drop, defeated.

"Don't look so troubled, Brother," Jeremiah said. "I think I'm mistaken. We weren't there long. But check on them, at least. They've seen the hounds."

Jegud's face grew more troubled. "That's impossible."

"That's what I thought."

"Michael has plenty to do without borrowing Gabriel's dogs to chase children."

"Michael will do anything to get to me."

Jegud sighed, looked away, through the window and out into a city that he wished he too could leave. "Fine, then," he said. "I'll go. But I'm warning you about Erika: She's not what Father's looking for. She's not what anyone is looking for."

Jeremiah laid down his books and came back around to the front of the desk. He draped an arm over his brother's shoulders.

"Look at my mother's portrait, Jegud," he said, "and tell me that she doesn't look like Erika."

"She has her hair, but that's all."

"And her eyes. And she has the same nose, the same cheekbones. The same everything. She's the same. *They're* the same."

Jegud smirked. "Such a close study. Are you sure you're not the one attracted to her, Brother?"

The comment stung more than Jegud intended, or realized.

Jeremiah took a step away and cleared his throat. "You know very well," he said, "that it can't be like that."

"And you know very well that remaking souls is just a myth."

"What else is myth, Jegud? Female rogues."

"Not myth, just unusual."

"Childbearing rogues?"

"It can't be a myth if no one ever talks about it."

"A king loving a commoner?"

"You're reaching too far," Jegud said. "Looking for things that aren't there." He noticed Jeremiah's shoulders, slumped and beaten, and he felt sorry for him. "Your life isn't a storybook, Jeremy. Don't try to make it one just for a happily-ever-after."

"You will have her moved," the queen said simply. "You will have that dust of hers taken from the crypt and mixed with the dirt that she came from."

The king ignored his wife's order.

"You promised me," she whispered. "You promised to send her away."

"I did not think that she would die."

"It was the only honorable thing she ever did. And now it is your turn to be honorable. You will take back your family and you will put your whore in the ground."

"I will not."

The queen bit the insides of her lips to keep her emotions in check.

"Then I can no longer stay here."

"Don't be stupid."

"You've put your queen in her tomb already, and her baby in my nursery."

"Stop it."

"I can't live like this anymore." The queen's voice faltered as she went on. "I can't listen to the gossip and pretend that I don't hear it. I can't ignore the court. I can't take the ridicule. The pity. I don't know which is worse." She shook her head. "I loved you. I loved you for so long. You were my god."

"I've never wanted you to see me as a god," the king said. "You, of all people. You promised me that you never would."

"You were hers. How can I blame her? She had no other choice: I'm a seraph and even I couldn't choose. You broke her." The queen turned to leave.

"She loved him. Jeremiah. She told me so."

“She was a rogue, dear,” the queen replied. She sounded like an exhausted mother speaking to her child. “She told us all a lot of things. You know that none of it was true.”

She opened the door and walked away. Her husband watched her go.

Shawn let Megan ride piggyback because they'd found themselves in a thicket of nettles and she was nearly crying from all the stings. Rebecca held on to Shawn's sleeve, cursing quietly under her breath with each step.

"Let's turn back," she hissed.

"We're halfway through already," he said. "It's easier just to go on."

"I don't know why we had to go anywhere in the first place. Uriel said he'd be back soon."

"Jeremiah told us to keep moving."

"Jeremiah was an ass."

"Gently now, he *is* my brother."

Uriel strode up behind them. His clothing slipped easily over the underbrush, whispering over the thorns as if they were meadow flowers. He seemed as polished as that morning, except for a shadow that disappeared into his shirt collar — a light burn down his neck and shoulder.

"Your shoes," he said, holding up three pairs of leather sandals that were tied together with black ribbon. "And your lovely eyes." He put the beads into one of Rebecca's hands and folded her fingers over them as he stepped back. "I would stay to see the unveiling, but I'm afraid that other duties call. I'll come to you again as soon as I have time. Good luck."

Rebecca slipped the glass pearls into her mouth and swallowed them dry. She fought to untie her blindfold while her brother and sister watched, Megan's pointed chin resting in a bed of Shawn's hair.

The fabric left lines on Rebecca's cheeks and forehead, and as she blinked, she rubbed the marks with her palms.

"They itch," she said in a small voice. "I bet I look awful.

And I can't believe that you . . ." she trailed off, sniffing, and then threw her arms around Shawn's neck. Megan petted her hair and Shawn patted her back until she'd finished drying her eyes on his shirt.

"I missed you," Rebecca said, struggling to explain herself. She snatched the bundle of shoes from Shawn, still wiping her nose against her wrist, and began to undo the tight double bow.

Erika came down the stairs as Jegud opened the door. He touched the brim of his top hat in salute and gave a final nod to Jeremiah before setting out.

"Where's he going?" Erika asked.

Jeremiah locked the door against the morning chill.

"To check on your children."

"Is something wrong?"

"Not that I know of," Jeremiah said. "Things are looking up, actually."

"Oh, are they?"

Jeremiah felt the edge to her voice and dropped a bow.

"You're right, Erika," he said. "I apologize."

Erika lifted her chin in a way that reminded him of his mother, or rather — Jeremiah checked himself — his stepmother, and he allowed that motion to distance him. Erika would be the next queen, he told himself, if he had anything to do with it. And he must have everything to do with it.

"Are you going out too?" she asked, noticing his coat and freshly polished shoes.

"Indeed," Jeremiah said. "There's a great amount of work to

be done before services dismiss. Courtiers to be flattered. Arrangements to be made." He shrugged.

"What are you planning?"

"A party, it would seem. Only I'm not planning it. *That* is totally up to the council, and they'd better hurry because it's set for tonight. Your invitation just arrived by word of mouth. Jegud's mouth, to be precise, though he seems far from happy about it."

"A party for what?"

"For introductions. The princes are bringing choices for the king's new bride. It is to be a royal ball in the traditional style. Pomp, circumstance, and courtly love." He tipped his head to the side in mock feminine flirtation and covered the top half of his face with a gloved hand. "And masks, dear Erika," he said, with a chuckle. "Just think of it — how fitting, how fortunate, and how perfectly ironic."

Rebecca gloried in the return of her vision. She grew more and more thankful each time she avoided a root or low-growing tree branch. Shawn was relieved to see her happy again, even if it made her unusually chatty, and Megan was thrilled at how quickly tensions had disappeared since Uriel had come and gone. As far as Megan was concerned, Uriel was their new savior.

When the man appeared a few yards ahead of them, leaning casually against an old birch tree, Megan squeaked with excitement and dashed toward him. Taken aback, he staggered away from her out-flung arms. She froze, realizing her mistake, and pulled herself together to stand stick-straight in front of him.

"Who're you?" she asked.

His gaze drifted to her brother and sister, who were jogging to catch up with her.

"My name is Jegud," he told her. "But who did you think I was?"

Hand pressed against her chest, Rebecca stopped short of Megan and tried to catch her breath.

"Who's been here?" Jegud asked.

"Nobody."

"Jeremiah," Shawn said. His eyes flicked to his older sister. He prayed that she followed his lead; they owed more to Uriel than Jeremiah.

"Jeremiah," Rebecca agreed. "God, I'm out of shape."

"You haven't seen *anybody* else?" Jegud pressed.

"Nope." Shawn put his hand on the crown of Megan's head. "Should we have?"

Jegud hesitated. "No . . ."

Shawn tried to relax, but his palms were damp from nerves. "Then everything's fine," he said, forcing a smile.

"It took me forever to find you," Jegud said with a frown.

"Jeremiah told us to keep moving."

The prince made a scoffing sound in the back of his throat. "That would be his advice, wouldn't it?" Then he focused in on the three siblings again. "Look," he said, "do you really want to see your mother?"

Now Shawn frowned, and Rebecca beside him. Megan just stared at Jegud with her guiltless child eyes.

"What kind of a question is that?" Shawn asked.

"A pretty straightforward one, I thought. How much do you really care to see her?"

"She's our mother," Rebecca said with disbelief. "Of course we want to see her."

"Then why are you lying to me?" Jegud asked. "I'm the only one who can help you except Death himself. Tell me who's been here."

"*We've* been here," Shawn insisted. "The three of us. And, once, Jeremiah. That's all."

"That's *all*?"

"I just told you so, didn't I?"

"So it would seem. Is there anything I can get for you?"

"No," Megan said. "Because —"

Shawn cupped a hand beneath her chin. "Because Laza gave us some supplies before we set out," he finished. "But water would be good, I guess."

"Water," Jegud repeated.

"Yeah."

He gave them one last long look, waiting for them to break down and offer him the truth. "All right, then," he said at last. His skin blurred, as if they were watching him through a camera lens slipping out of focus, and then he dissolved into a white mist that fanned out and faded into thin air.

Megan tipped her head back to look into Shawn's face. "We're really bad liars, aren't we?"

He grinned and ruffled her hair.

"Yeah," he said. "Looks like it."

"Ah." South looked up from her reading, a finger still pinned to the last word. "Jeremiah, king's son. I nearly had you, there at the last. You would do well to choose a more careful listener when you next forfeit your ears. But how come you now without my brother's blood?"

Jeremiah opened the side of his black coat to reveal Kala, perched lightly on his wrist.

"I come with hers," he said.

"A gift to keep you unforgotten," said South. "But that was many years ago. Tell me, has she done as bidden?"

"She has. My family can never forget me," Jeremiah said, "because they can never ignore her place on the crest."

South ran her tongue over her teeth. "Then what do you seek from water that you cannot find in her?"

"I need to know —" Jeremiah hesitated. "I need to know the truth."

"Mm."

"They say that you can see everything," he said. "They say that you know how the world ends."

"It ends with me," South said. "Just as yours will end with you." Her eyes grew sad as she studied him through the half-light. "Poor whipping boy," she murmured. "You've inherited much, haven't you? Your father's curse as well as your mother's. But I can promise, for what it's worth, that your battle is nearly over."

At that, Jeremiah felt the trembling of hope. "And do I win? Tell me; in the end, do I win?"

"My dear child," she said. "You, I fear, have gambled all without ever learning the only rule that matters."

"And what rule is that?"

South yawned and went back to her reading. "No one ever wins."

The room trembled, and from the door came the awful groan of rock breaking rock.

South closed her book with an irritated grunt and pushed herself to her feet.

"I must go," she said. "And so must you, Jeremiah, king's son. I leave you with a warning — you have a brother with a curse upon his head."

"Which brother?"

"The one who found the Furies' nest."

"The Furies? Then they do exist?"

"You would question that, Jeremiah?" South asked, amused. "You who have spent a lifetime giving them sacrifice?"

"But why? I don't understand."

She paused at the door, one gleaming hand pressed against the wall. "When everything is dark," she told him, "the sisters still see all."

Simon let Jegud in, and said that the rest of the household was upstairs with Martha.

The prince walked up to the southern wing and along the hall to the first bedroom. A jet of light spilled through the open door and onto the carpet. He knocked on the wall.

"Jeremiah?"

"Yes? Jegud!" Jeremiah crossed the room and clapped his brother on the shoulder. "Isn't she beautiful?"

Jegud looked at Erika, who sat on a low stool near the wardrobe.

She wore a dress of black brocade, gathered at the waist and spread in heavy skirts around her feet. Diamonds, likely borrowed, glittered in her hair and all down her neck.

But despite glowing in the lamplight, Erika's face looked far from happy.

"Quite," Jegud said, and then, deciding that would not do, he cast around for something else. "You look lovely, Erika."

"She's stunning," Jeremiah said. Jegud glanced at him and wondered what his brother's tone brought back to him. There was pride there, and physical pain, and a hint of something darker.

Jegud looked back at Erika and forced a smile. "They will love you," he agreed. "All of them."

Color rushed into Erika's cheeks as she smiled and dropped her lashes. Jegud decided that all women, human or seraph, were endearingly vain.

Jeremiah squeezed his brother's shoulder. *It's nearly like a thank-you*, Jegud thought, and when Jeremiah smiled, this time he seemed to have recovered. "And you aren't bad yourself, Jegud," he said. "You'll make a very smart couple. In fact, you may both fall madly for each other and leave me without an escape. What will I do then, Brother?"

"You underestimate our sincerity," Jegud replied. "May I have a word with you before we go?"

"Certainly."

They went down the hall to where the stair lamps splattered gold across the floor and walls. Jegud ran his heel along the line where light met shadow and rolled the brim of his hat between his fingers. Jeremiah folded his own hands behind his back and waited patiently for his brother to compose himself.

At last, Jegud stopped his fidgeting and looked his little brother in the eye. "Her children are all liars," he said flatly.

"What are you talking about?"

"I went out there, and I asked if anyone else had spoken to them since you did, and they told me no. They were lying through their teeth, Jeremy. Every one of them."

"Every tooth or every child?"

Jegud let his arms drop to his sides. "I'm not trying to humor you," he said. "For once in your life, please just try and pay attention. Do you honestly not realize how serious this could be? I think that Michael may be trying to win them."

"He could hardly do that after letting the hounds snap at their heels."

"Uriel, then," Jegud said. "Or Selaph. I don't know, and I'm not saying that I do, but you need to consider the consequences of this. Those children could do more damage to us than Erika ever could, and you're drunk on your own self-importance if you won't hear me out. Think: If we tried to bring three living children into Limbo, and they died on the streets — I can't even begin to imagine the fallout of that. You would be worse than exiled, Jeremy. You would be worse than dead, even."

"Jeremiah?"

Both men spun around at the voice. Erika peered around her bedroom door with a silk fan in one hand and a mask in the other.

"Please," Jegud said. "Allow me." He hurried down the hall and took the black glazed porcelain from her.

"Actually, I was just going to ask whether or not you were ready."

"I am, yes," he said, helping her to tie on the mask anyway. "Shall we be off, then?"

"I guess."

"Don't be nervous, Erika," he said, smoothing the ribbon over the waves of her hair. "Doesn't every child want to be a princess?"

"I suppose," she said, playing with the swivel of her fan, "but I'm not a child anymore."

He took her hand and draped it over his arm. "I know," he said. "None of us are. And it's true that this is looking like Russian roulette, but there is a bright side."

"And what's that?"

"The gun isn't loaded. Not yet, anyway."

"Cupid is ruining my plans already," Jeremiah said from the end of the hall. "You aren't even alone and the confirmed bachelor is losing his principles. Perhaps the chaperone needs a chaperone?"

"If you can find a ticket, then you are certainly invited," Jegud said, turning on his heel.

"And that is precisely where I may surprise you."

"Oh?"

"I'll leave it at that."

Jegud smiled at his brother. "Afraid of looking the fool when you're still here at midnight?"

"You know me far too well."

The three of them walked together to the door and out to where the gate stood open to the road. With Erika safely in the waiting carriage, Jeremiah caught his brother by the sleeve.

"Don't tell her anything," he whispered. "Please."

"About the children?"

"About anything. I don't want her to worry through the entire ball."

"For what end? You can't think that she'll actually enjoy herself?"

Jeremiah said nothing.

"Have you told her," Jegud went on, "anything about Father?"

"I thought that she would find out soon enough."

"Jeremiah —"

"He's not a bad man, Jegud. She would be lucky."

"*You* would be lucky, you mean. She's doing this for your sake."

Jeremiah felt his jaw tense. "She's doing this for her children."

Jegud shook his head. "We *will* be talking about this later," he said.

"Have it your way."

"It's healthier than yours." Jegud opened the door again and swung into the empty seat.

Jeremiah nodded to the driver and heard the familiar slap of a whip against a horse's flank. It reminded him of early mornings from when he was young and still in favor, and of the procession that his family had made on their way to the common for daily blessings.

He watched the black carriage roll on down the street, pulled by its matching hackney horses, and then disappear into the closeness of the night. When they had gone, Jeremiah turned to his house, hands still clasped behind his back, and nudged the gate shut with the toe of his polished leather shoe.

"The Brigham, sir?" Simon asked without being prompted.

Jeremiah started, a little surprised by his voice in the dark. "Yes, Simon," he said. "Thank you."

"With the gray Arabian, sir?"

"Precisely the one." Jeremiah hurried up the front steps and closed the door behind him.

The public common was a large, round building at the heart of the city, made entirely of white marble. Every morning, lines gathered in the arched hallway that circled it, and would wait for guards to let them enter. Then they would walk in file to the main floor, their way marked by high, polished walls, before dispersing, a little disoriented, to find their way to empty seats. The common had no roof, and, as the sun rose higher, shadows threw themselves over the benches, draped like expensive gray silk.

The royal box perched across from the entrance, its footing level with the tops of the highest steps. A wall had been built from the floor to the edge of that gallery, so that no one but the royal family would sit behind the king while services were in session.

It was early yet.

The king waited in the royal box, watching the common fill. He saw the seraphim glide to the western half, holding their clothing close about them. He saw, in the east, the souls of men pressed close together. They covered their faces and did not look up from their laps, where their hands were tucked like seashells. A few of them thumbed rosary beads. The king smiled.

Rules did not call for the seraphim to be segregated from the men, but a split was obvious. The entrance hall served as a line between the two groups, and neither moved to sit near the other half. The king found it sad that even here, at the very edge, they were so divided.

His sons were beside him, drowsy and solemn in the dawning morning. Jeremiah had nodded off, his cheek on Michael's shoulder, his curls nestled sweetly against his brother's neck.

Today the king would tell them about their mother. Tell them why she had not come. Tell them why she had locked herself in her chambers with heavy trunks, as if she were readying for a long trip. Today he would send Jeremiah away and strike his mother's name from the crypt. He would win back his wife's love, and stop her from leaving. He would make her break the promises she had spat last night, out of anger and out of pain. Today he would mend things, as he should have done long ago.

In the east, the sun crept higher.

The crowd fell silent as the king got to his feet and descended the shallow staircase. His footsteps echoed against the marble.

When he reached the main floor, he stood behind the stone podium, his back to the wall and to the royal box. His sons would be watching. He had taught them not to be afraid.

A knife lay on the podium. Its long, thin blade fit into a bone handle that looked creamy in the morning blush. Rites of passage were cut into the bone, the symbols dove gray with shadow. This was why the Middle Kingdom needed its throne. Souls could not be judged until they felt themselves prepared, and it was a seraph's job to allow them their last rites. The king had been raised as he now raised his sons — to be the hand that cut away sin and left these souls as untouched as the day they were created. To be the hand that finally saved them from their bodily pain and poverty, as soon as they were ready to leave those bodies behind.

A woman came forward, from the east, taking slow, hesitant steps. The king waited patiently. He had seen her before, watching and praying, while she tried to make up her mind.

She went to the altar bed and lay down, closing her eyes as she did. Her long hair fanned out around her face and draped over the edges of the altar. She kept her eyes shut tight. Her hands lay empty at her sides, free of her beads.

The king took the knife from the podium and walked over to her side. He studied the woman, noting the bruises on her neck. She had been pretty, once. She was still young.

He lifted the knife above his head and felt the power twist through his body like a jolt of electricity, familiar. He would save her. He would set her free.

The blade flashed down in a clean arc and split through her chest. She didn't scream. She didn't even open her eyes.

Her soul seeped out, its edges honey colored. He waited, wanting to make sure that he was right. The first was always the hardest to tell. He could feel the air sway as the seraphim to his left leaned forward and the souls to his right pulled away.

He opened his lips and felt the soul drift closer. It slid into his mouth and down his throat, tingling like warm cider.

The guards came to take the woman's shell away.

The king watched them leave, and waited for the next.

The king's palace sat on a hill at the outskirts of Limbo, close enough to overlook the city, but far enough away to spare the royals a view of the poverty. When the halls were lit, as they were tonight, the residence looked like a jack-o'-lantern perched on the shoulders of a giant. The souls of Limbo were drawn to that glow, but were too afraid to leave the city limits. On nights that the court gathered, millions of other faces also showed themselves to the moon, their shoulders pressed so closely together on the roofs of Limbo's buildings that the skyline looked gnawed on and rumpled.

The road to the king's estate started at the base of the hill and wound up in one long gravel drive. At the gates, palace guards stood in traditional white, with long bronze-tipped spears in hand. They saluted Jegud's carriage as it trundled past.

As they entered the grounds, Erika brushed aside the curtains for a better view. A lake sprawled to the left, its surface aglow with lanterns. An army of black swans skimmed through the glittering field, curved necks bobbing. Beyond the lake, an orchard grew in a web of hanging lights. The silhouettes of strolling couples signaled that the ball had begun.

Jegud's driver tugged the horses to a stop at the palace's front steps and jumped down to hold the door for his passengers. Jegud climbed out first and took Erika's hand to help her down. He surveyed the front walk and the light that came from the palace's frosted windows, looking underwhelmed.

"I hate parties," he said under his breath.

"So do I."

Jegud tipped his head toward Erika and smiled. "I think my brother would call you out on that," he said. "You're a rose, love, but we aren't here for you to charm *me*. I don't think you could if you wanted to."

"Am I not your type?"

"You could put it that way."

"Jegud!"

The young prince sighed. "Oh God."

Erika flapped out her fan at the sight of Uriel, who turned on his way up the steps and glided over to meet them, his hand flat against the back of a girl who dripped with pearls and peach batiste.

"Good evening, Uri."

"Good evening! And it's been such a long time." His eyes flickered over Erika. "You don't think you can hide, do you, darling? I see that there's been some double-dipping of the ostracized princes. Is little Jeremy actually staying away, then?"

"I hope I'm not yet ostracized, Uri," Jegud said. "And as for Jeremiah, it would seem that the council neglected to invite him."

"Blast the council," Uriel said. "They never think about the principle of the thing, do they? It would've been a stunning send-off. I'm sure you've seen the decree?" He flashed a smile. "Though you must have. I noticed you signed it."

"I signed for Gabriel's succession," Jegud said stiffly.

"Yes. Good of them to put both birds in a basket, hmm? One little paper to give Gabriel his wings and take away Jeremiah's."

Jegud tucked Erika's hand around his elbow and glanced toward the open palace doors. "You should know by now that Jeremiah always has an escape route."

"Yes," said Uriel, "but you two are here with us. Who does he have left?" He bowed to Erika and turned away with his guest.

The queen sent away her entire train. She didn't turn when her bedroom door opened, but she knew who had come in. She recognized his footsteps and hated herself for it.

"What is it?" she snapped.

The king hesitated. "I thought . . ."

"You thought what, exactly?" She tossed a handful of pearls into the wooden chest that sat open on her bed. "You thought that would be good enough? That little show? Well, it wasn't."

"But —"

"You put her in the crypt," the queen said with careful enunciation.

"She —"

"You gave her the Sickle!" she screamed, spinning on her heel. Her skirts flew out in a wide bell around her legs. For the first time, the king heard desperation shoot through her voice, and his mother's selfsame pain. It shamed him. "Not even your own father was that stupid!"

"It's nothing," he whispered. "It's only a trinket."

"A trinket?" The queen's hand flew to her neck, where her own medallion gleamed; a ring of silver crossed by a pair of sickles. "Then why did I throw my life away for it?" She ripped the necklace off and cast it at her husband's feet. A pink welt sprung up along the skin of her throat, following the line where the ribbon had lain. "Well, I'll waste myself no longer," she spat, "on your little trinket."

The first room of the king's palace resembled a stadium, with a thin line of marble leading to steps that descended to a low-level floor. There, lines of couples waltzed to the vibrato of a string quartet. On the other side of the hall, across from the doors, a platform supported a pair of thrones whose gilded backs reached the skirts of the domed ceiling.

"The king hasn't arrived yet," Jegud said into Erika's ear. "But keep an eye on Uri and you'll know exactly when he's due."

Erika had already lost sight of the third prince. He'd vanished into the swirling, dipping crowd of silk, velvet, and organza. The opulence of the hall, radiant with white marble and gold relief, made her head swim, and she stumbled on her way down the steps. Jegud caught her by the waist and waited as she steadied herself against his arm.

"Too much?" he asked.

"A bit."

He sank down on one of the steps, offering Erika the place beside him. A scatter of other guests were doing the same, putting the staircase to practical use. Erika covered her flushed cheeks as she sank gratefully to the marble.

"We are the bourgeoisie of the underworld," Jegud said, a light apology in his voice. "It's a caste system that Earth's socialites would kill for. In fact, most of them have." He smirked. "Only they all end up on the wrong side of the gate."

A sharp clap of laughter came from behind them.

"If it isn't the fifth son."

Jegud turned to his right, where a tall man stood, arms linked with a girl in copper satin.

"Peter."

"My wife."

Jegud gave her a flickering smile.

"You've done well, Peter," he said. "For a roguemaker's son."

"I have," Peter said. "And is this . . . ?"

"*My* wife? No. This is Erika." Jegud touched her chin. "This is the reason you all are here."

"Then I am honored to meet you, Erika," Peter said, doffing his top hat. His wife dropped a low curtsey.

"Well, *you* at least are convinced, darling," Jegud laughed. "And I hope that you won't be the only one. But now that I've said it, where *is* my father?"

Peter checked the empty throne.

"I couldn't say," he admitted. "Fashionably late, I suppose. You'd better hope so, at least."

"And why is that?"

"I've heard that Prince Michael brought his own guest early," Peter said. "A lovely angel from the High Kingdom." He raised an eyebrow at Erika. "She isn't . . . ?"

"No," Jegud said. "Not quite."

"Not that there's anything . . ." His voice died in his throat. "Nevertheless, if the contract is being drawn with Michael's name on the header, then Jeremiah can forget his pardon."

Jegud coughed quietly into his fist and Peter's young bride turned wide-eyed to her husband.

"Oh, come now," Peter said. "Everyone knows that you aren't one for social gallantry, Jegud. You wouldn't be here at all if Jeremiah hadn't asked." He turned away. "But just the same, for your sake and his, I hope that your offer's face is as pretty as her hair."

Jegud glanced at Erika as Peter walked away.

"Maybe Jeremiah was right," he said to himself.

"Right about what?"

"Oh, nothing. He just said that you reminded him of someone, is all."

A yelp came from the yard — high-pitched, miserable, animal, and cut short with a resounding whip crack.

"Gabriel's living trumpet," Jegud muttered, getting to his feet.

The quartet stopped halfway through its waltz, bows clicking against music stands. The rush of guests found itself greeted by the baying of hunting dogs. Erika let Jegud lead her to the front doors, holding on to his hand as if it were a lifeline.

For a heartbeat, she thought that she had lost him in the swelling crowd, but then she felt his fingers tighten around her wrist and let herself be sucked out of the throng, vacuumed through like a champagne cork. She took a breath of the crisp night air and smoothed her dress.

The coach glistened bone white, accented by cream, and drawn by a double line of silver hounds. A handsome gift from the High Kingdom, to serve the needs of the future Middle throne. They were huge, stocky, with dinner-plate paws and long teeth that dripped saliva.

A procession of black carriages trundled past, serving as a backdrop, matte boxes pulled by high-stepping ponies. Jegud took special note of the last driver, who had forgotten his cap. When the steps of Gabriel's carriage clattered into place, Jegud's attention turned back to the prince's coach.

A footman leaped from the rear of the carriage and took the curved handles of the cabin door. A break followed, like a slip in time. The air of the courtyard felt alive with the static hum of expectation.

Gabriel stepped out.

He had his hat in one hand, and accepted with the other a plain porcelain mask from the footman. He returned the favor with a quick nod and an underbreath whisper. The soft laugh that followed prickled the ears of his neglected audience.

Then Gabriel turned, his hat and mask still in his gloved hands, and his hair, smooth, freshly clipped, and shining in the candlelight, was a streaked blond that reminded Erika of sun-blanched beach walkers. Gabriel let his eyes wander across the breathless faces, his interest subdued. His own expression was perfectly composed and perfectly patient.

"Am I late?"

His audience exploded, applauding, laughing, crowing, glowing, as if a dam had broken and left a rush of water thundering down the king's front steps. He could have said anything. He could have asked for the jewels from their necks and fingers and hair and they would have stumbled over one another to drop them into his gloved hands. There was rapture in the mob, and, for one glittering moment, it was not the crown or the throne or the Sickle that mattered, but the cradle it had built.

The curtains flapped against the open window, drawing themselves taut against the wooden sill and then fluttering back into the room as the Middle Kingdom breathed in and out. A cloud, the deep silver-gray of charcoal, slipped over the sill with a gust of wind that smelled of the city below. The specter hovered over the carpet, uncertain, and then a pair of heavy boots lowered themselves from the swirl of smoke. Michael walked across the bedroom, hardly making a sound, and looked at the bureau. There were paint pots of makeup and pretty blown-glass bottles of perfume. Combs and pins and clean strips of dark linen. There was, also, a single pearl earring and an emerald necklace.

The second prince smiled.

Jegud brought Erika to the front of the spectators, but the couple was among the last to seek out the crown prince's audience for themselves. Jegud leaned against one of the lawn's marble statues, feigning conversation to keep others away, and kept an eye on his eldest brother.

"Gabriel's far from the worst of the family," he admitted. "I do think he would try for change."

"Change in what?"

Jegud rubbed his forehead. "I couldn't say. He *is* a traditional, but underneath all the spit and polish, he has a good heart." He took her by the arm. "Come on."

They walked across the gravel drive to where Gabriel stood, wrapping up a conversation with a High Kingdom ambassador and his two daughters. When the group moved on, Gabriel finally smiled at his brother.

"Am I seeing ghosts?" he asked, tugging off his glove before he accepted Jegud's hand. "My father's favorite son back from a decade's worth of pilgrimage!"

"You flatter, Gabriel," Jegud said. "But I think we all know that the throne's affections are played by number."

If the crown prince felt the sting of those words, he did not affect to show it.

"Then you will be *my* favorite, Jegud," he said. "I would repeat all of this grand entrance nonsense just to see you here, and happy."

"Here, in any case," Jegud said.

"And with a proposal? The throne *will* be pleased." Gabriel bowed to give Erika's hand a kiss. "You're an ice princess, milady, with a discourteous chaperone to keep you in the cold. Or is that my fault?" He offered his arm and led her back toward the house. "Your name?"

"Erika."

"Charming. And what brings you and Jegud together, Erika?"

"Well, I . . ." She glanced over her shoulder and faltered.

"Has he gone already?" Gabriel asked. "I would have given him ten minutes more. He's a matchmaker, Erika — don't worry. We'll be seeing him again before long." He leaned in close to her ear. "Between the two of us, I would say that he's looking for your *actual* chaperone."

Erika's heart jumped to her throat. "I don't understand," she said. Pounding. Pounding.

"Don't be coy, Miss Stripling," Gabriel murmured. "What kind of an heir would I be if I had fewer eyes than the king himself?" He led her up the stair, taking short steps for her benefit. Her skirts rustled over the gleaming marble. "I find it admirable, but I think my brother hopes too much."

"You won't say anything?"

"Why should I? I grew up with Jeremiah. I won't forget that. Right now," Gabriel said, "it is the king's business, not mine. Speaking of which, is it too bold to ask for a first waltz with my stepmother-to-be?"

He hardly waited for an answer. The court could watch, and they could whisper, and Gabriel would never mind, just as long as all the secrets managed to wind their way back into his own pockets.

Two hours into midday, and the tops of Jeremiah's shoes were already scuffed. Black leather gone dull from running through sand and gravel, but he knew that his mother wouldn't care. After all, she wasn't his mother anymore. Or that's what Michael said.

Jeremiah pounded the wall in front of him with one fist, the brick hot against his skin. His stomach flipped at the sound of other shoes behind him — the firm, confident knock of Michael's heels, the eagerness of Uri's. They ran because it was more fun than flying; more of a game than snaking their way, dark and smoky, through streets and over buildings. So Jeremiah gathered; he had not been invited to play with them since the queen left, veiled and silent in the night.

"Jeremy," came Jegud's voice above him, hissing down from the rooftops. "Jeremy, hide."

Instead of looking up for his brother, Jeremiah spun on his heel and thrust out his chest; he had often been teased for being so small. Michael came around the corner. Jegud cursed.

"Stop following me!" Jeremiah shouted. His voice flew too fast and high-pitched through the humid air, the only thing in the city not rolled in sweat and dust. Michael still came forward, but he slowed, shoving a handful of dark hair out of his face. The grease of Limbo stood out on his skin, dark smudges across his nose and cheekbones. His smile sparked with August sun.

"If you weren't pressing your dirty nose against my windows," he said, "I wouldn't follow."

Jeremiah gritted his teeth. "Stop it. Stop saying that. You can't scare me."

"You can't scare me," Michael parroted, voice shot to a trembling falsetto. "Thou shalt not lie, Jeremy."

Uriel shot past the alleyway and then backtracked, panting. He flashed to smoke and sped up to Michael's side, then changed again. He glanced at his big brother to gauge the situation.

"I told you not to cheat, Uri," Michael said. "It sets a bad example."

Jeremiah looked up, careful to move his eyes but not his chin, gauging the distance to the top of the building. To Jegud. To someplace out of the streets and back to the big empty house that his father said was safe.

Michael's fist closed around his neck and slammed him backward into the wall.

"You said not to shift," said Uriel, running forward, his edges blurring like he thought he should change too. "You cheated."

"He's getting ideas," said Michael, words sticky against Jeremiah's ear. "Aren't you, little Jeremy?"

Then Jegud was with them, feet puffing up dust as they touched step-smoothed cobbles. His fist connected with Michael's jaw and propelled him back, mouth frothing spit and curses. Jegud's face had gone red, his skin as rosy as it was the afternoon Jeremy had found him in the woods with the son of a courtier and his laces undone. Embarrassment then, but anger now, and maybe fear caught up between them both.

"He's still our brother," Jegud shouted. Michael wiped away saliva with the back of his hand.

"He's a halfie," Michael said. "A whore's son."

Jegud punched him again and then looked at Jeremiah.

"Go, you idiot!"

The three of them shifted at once. Clouds of black and gray

smoke tumbled over one another until one dove-colored blur shot up and disappeared over a lip of brick rooftop. Jeremiah re-formed and peered over the ledge, hair falling in his face, his face gone pale. He heard a flutter behind him and spun to catch Selaph staring, arms hanging at his sides, his expression thoughtful.

Sharp sun licked them both, burning the bricks beneath their feet, sucking the color from their clothes. Selaph tilted his head, barely enough to notice, off in the direction of Jeremiah's new home. Then he shifted into smoke, clean white as milk, and flew past his little brother, plunging off the rooftop.

"He's gone," Selaph said, voice calm in the alley. "Follow me."

Jeremiah dropped to his knees and hid behind the searing bricks as he watched his brothers shoot off down the alley. He shifted to smoke himself and streaked away, back to the place he had been told to call home.

Jegud walked into the stables just as Jeremiah came down the aisle to leave.

"My God," Jegud hissed. "How brash can you be?"

"Plenty, thank you."

"In Gabriel's own *train*?"

"He didn't say anything, did he?"

"No." Jegud's face clouded. "Jeremiah, don't tell me that he saw you!"

"I'm sure he did."

Jegud leaned against one of the stall doors and let out a long, wandering sigh.

"Gabriel never misses much," Jeremiah said. "But how else was I supposed to get in?"

"You *weren't*. That's why *I* came in the first place."

"I had to see how things went."

"You couldn't wait to hear?"

"Storytelling doesn't have the flavor of the moment."

Jegud grabbed Jeremiah by his lapels and shoved him against the wall.

"Don't you understand?" he spat. "Don't you see at all? You think that you can do anything, because you've always gotten away with it, but that won't work anymore! They want you *gone*, Jeremiah. You're so afraid of Father, but it's Michael who wants to bury you. Michael and trigger-happy Uriel, who can't quite believe that this is no longer a game. *Open your eyes, Jeremiah.*"

"What do you want me to see?"

"The *truth*," Jegud snapped. "Michael knows that he's second for the throne, and wants his own children there after that. He wants that crown on his *own* head, and he'll kill for it. He'll kill Gabriel and he'll kill me and he'll certainly kill you. You think of that as brotherly love? To hell with you, then! This isn't family, Jeremiah, this is politics." Jegud let go of his brother's jacket and turned away. "You've been fighting to get in all this time, when you should have been begging to get as far away as possible."

"Like you?"

"Yes, like me," Jegud said, unaffected by the snub.

"If you've finished, then I'd like a breath of air."

"You've used us, Jeremiah," Jegud said, sounding tired. "You've used all of us. Anyone who ever tried to help you. Gabriel may not care that you've come, but there are other people in the audience and you're throwing yourself on full display. What do you think the council will make of this?"

"You're overreacting," Jeremiah said. "I'm not as stupid as you make me out to be, Jegud. I won't be killed over this."

"And if you are?"

"No one will blame you."

"I'm not worried about the blame."

"Then don't act like it," Jeremiah said, and headed out into the night.

A rumor of the king's arrival and disguise began to circulate; Erika overheard the warnings that were offered in the strictest confidence to Gabriel. He listened to each with a feigned gravity, as if this or that mention was the first he had heard.

By the end of the half hour, it became common knowledge that His Magnificence was either in the orchard, the courtyard, or the hall, wearing red, or perhaps gray or dark blue, and a matching, or contrasting, mask that definitely covered his eyes and may or may not have been made of velvet. At a pause in the dance, a young noble came to whisper, with poise, that the servants were rushing blankets up the stairs and that His Magnificence might well be dying. Gabriel thanked him and led Erika away from the floor.

"How can you listen to all that without worrying?" she asked.

"Because," Gabriel said, "His Magnificence the Throne is in a black waistcoat near the door with a glass of champagne."

Erika smiled. "And what color is his mask?"

"His mask?" Gabriel shook his head. "No different than usual."

Jegud came up behind them. "You've taken my guest," he said.

"And you, your time," said Gabriel.

Jegud smiled. "I thought you might appreciate the company."

"I did," Gabriel replied. "You wouldn't know how much I did. This has been the first time I've ever entertained a beautiful woman without considerable implications." He bowed to Erika. "I would say good night, but I expect to see you later. I hope that you're radiant for my father, and lovely to him. For Jeremiah's soul, your well-being, and my crown." He kissed her hand. "No pressure."

"Never."

Jegud led Erika outside as quickly as he could. "Not too much trouble, I hope?" he asked.

"I'm fine."

"Good, good," he said without looking at her. "You told him about Jeremiah, then?"

He had meant for it to prick, not cut, but when Erika stopped in her tracks, halfway to the door, he realized that he'd gone too far.

"He *knew*," Erika hissed. "How could you think that I would tell him anything? How *dare* you think that?"

"You're making a scene."

"Don't tell me what I'm *making*."

"Erika." Jegud took a few steps back down to her side and pretended to fix the tie of her mask. "I know that you're falling in love with Jeremiah," he said. He didn't mention his suspicions of Jeremiah's own feelings. It would be too much for Erika right now. It was too much even for him.

"I never —"

Jegud shook his head. "You can't allow it," he told her. "You're here to catch his father. *My* father." He tipped up her chin and looked past her mask, into the cool green of her eyes. "And *I'm* here to make sure that happens. Do you understand?"

"But I —"

"Yes or no, Erika? Because if you can't do this, I'll know why. I might be the only one in this entire room who would know why. And if you can't do this, then I need to know right now, before I walk you up these stairs and introduce you to my father. I won't say that he'll save your children, because I'm not sure that he can. I won't even say that he'll save Jeremiah. Knowing that, and knowing everything else, are you ready to listen to me?"

She opened her mouth and he shook his head again.

"I want to help you," he said. "But if you won't let me — if you won't follow me in lockstep — then this room full of piranhas will eat you up without even thinking about it. It's just a game to them, Erika, and I need to know exactly what you'll risk in order to play."

Erika stood frozen, her jaw stiff as she puzzled through silent thought and half-formed sentences. At last, she brushed them all off with a jerky nod.

"I'll play," she said. "I'll play everything."

"Even yourself?"

"Yes."

"Even Jeremiah?"

She bit her lip.

"Yes."

"Then we can go." Jegud took her hand and led her past a group of chattering women. The front doors appeared before the couple like holy gates. Erika softened at the cool air that drifted in.

"Are you ready?" Jegud whispered. She only nodded.

The king stood in the courtyard, wearing neither hat nor mask, and sipping a flute of champagne. Beside him stood one of the few people who knew him well enough to recognize his face.

"I don't think that you've yet met my brother Michael," Jegud said gently, and propelled Erika a few steps ahead of him.

She was a peace offering, and he felt better for knowing that she understood. In the eyes of the court, she was nothing more than a beautiful, empty olive branch.

The king was a man softened by age. The skin of his eyes was lightly swollen, likely helped along by liquor. Time had left notes across his body, the years scribbling their due into each wrinkle, leaving hollow thanks in every brown sunspot and every risen vein of his hands, writing damages into the silver-gray of his hair. He was more grandfather than king of the dead, and in one sweeping glance, Erika fell to feeling very sorry for him. He had held on to his perfect posture, but youth was no longer there to support it. The king did not seem to be a very happy man.

"Jegud?" His eyebrows rose as he took in his son. "I wasn't expecting you to come."

"I know my duty, Father," Jegud replied with a bow. Beside him, Erika dipped in a low curtsey.

Michael cleared his throat. "I should hope you would."

The challenge that flashed between the two brothers either went unnoticed or unacknowledged by their father.

"I should always hope that everyone would know their duty," he said.

The silence went on painfully. Erika was trapped between the two scowling princes.

"Your palace is beautiful, Highness," she said, praying that was neutral enough.

Michael shot her an acidic look. "Is that what you're after?"

"I didn't —"

"Your grand entrance is being missed, Father," Jegud cut in.

"Is it?" The king smiled. "Well, the people will always pine for what they do not have. I don't much care to put myself on show. There at least you and I are not so different."

Michael kept his face expressionless and folded his hands behind his back. "Tell me, Brother," he said, "where would one go to find such a delightful girl?"

"Not as far as you would think. Erika is one of ours."

"Well, I would hope you wouldn't involve the Low Kingdom," Michael said dryly.

"No, Brother. I mean that she is one of our charges."

Erika felt Michael's eyes running over her again, and nearly shivered.

"Isn't that a little inappropriate?" he said quietly.

"Not at all," Jegud said. "The council has always held that the people are equal to the throne. Isn't that right, Father?"

"Certainly," the king replied, but he was looking off in the direction of the lake. "Our lights are fading," he said. "Should we add more?"

"That is an excellent idea, Father," Michael answered.

The king held on to that same distracted but reasonable tone. "I was asking Jegud."

"I don't see how it would hurt," Jegud said slowly.

"See?" A wistful smile broke the king's face, but his eyes lingered on the faraway lake. "We *can* all agree on something."

Jegud, looking concerned, turned to his brother. Michael only frowned at him and glanced back at the manor.

"I'll go see about the lights, shall I?" Jegud asked.

"That would be good of you," the king murmured, as if to himself. "And thank you for coming, Son. I should have known. After all, you've always done as you were asked."

"I do try."

"Mm."

Jegud bowed to his father and threw a careless half bow

at his brother, before taking Erika by the arm and rushing her away.

"Father's fine," he whispered to her. "I promise."

"He didn't even look at me."

Jegud pursed his lips, worried. "I know," he said.

"Boo."

Jeremiah popped his head into the space between Jegud and Erika and draped his arms over their shoulders.

"And how did the introductions go?" he asked.

"I'm not sure," Jegud admitted.

"Don't lie, Jegud," said Erika. "He overlooked me."

"He was dumbstruck," Jeremiah said.

"He was more struck by the *lake* than by me," she said. "I tried, Jeremiah. I swear I did. I'm sorry."

Jeremiah took off his mask and ran the cuff of his sleeve over his forehead. A gurgle of laughter rippled from the building, followed by scattered applause.

"Never fear," he told Erika, but his tone had lost the cheerful lilt. "Magic will prevail."

"And if it doesn't?" she asked.

"Then I'll no longer believe in miracles."

When the angel came, the children were asleep.

It brought no slow creep of brilliance — just a blast of cold, white light that drained the color from their skin, like a flashbulb overexposing film. It made all of the forest look dark.

They woke at the same time, and their hands and arms went up to shield themselves from the supernova. When they squinted, they could just make out a slim figure in the mist. Then, as it raised its arms, they saw each pointed finger, and when it tipped its head, they saw the gently sloping nose. Its yellow-white robes were cinched at the waist, the pleated shadows running in long sunsets of copper and rust.

It held out a hand and let the long chain of a necklace slip through its fingers, catching against its thumb with a jerk. The children crept forward, afraid and in awe, and saw a smudge of olive through the light. An emerald birthstone. They thought of Christmas two years ago, and the blush on their mother's face. They thought of how she'd clipped it around her neck, and fluffed out her hair, looking so much younger. Looking so much happier. They thought of how she swore to never take it off.

"Are you quite all right, Father?"

The king shook off his reverie.

"Yes, of course," he said. "I'm sorry. I was only . . . But it doesn't matter. What did your brother call that young lady?"

Michael shrugged. "Erika, I think. I could ask Uriel for you. It's his girl."

"Oh? But I thought —"

"Uri asked Jegud to amuse her while he handled some business. You know how dedicated Uri is to the council."

"Of course."

"Why, Father," Michael began, stifling a laugh, "you didn't actually think that Jegud would find a consort for you? He hasn't done anything but blunder away his life since Mother died."

The king blinked, and a sharpness that had not been there before slipped into his eyes. "*Your* mother is not the one who died, Michael," he said. "I have not *quite* forgotten everything yet."

"I'm sorry, Father," Michael stammered. "I didn't mean —"

"You don't mean to do much at all anymore, do you? Or so you say, but that's not really the case, is it?"

His son paled. "I'm not sure what you're talking about, Father."

"Come. You know very well what I'm talking about. We can both see that. And there is no need to call me Father at every opportunity. I've not forgotten who *I* am, at least, and I can't imagine the uproar to follow if we tried to renounce *you* as well as Jeremiah. *That* certainly wouldn't be worth it."

"I . . ."

The king handed his empty glass to a passing servant and took the path that ran down to the lake, leaving Michael dumbstruck behind him.

But the spell did not last more than a few minutes. Somewhere, a roulette pistol was being loaded.

The angel held its glowing hand out to Megan. She drew forward slowly, hesitantly, but there was so much patience in the moment that her doubt did not at all matter. It waited without moving, palm open with a pillow of the clearest light she had ever seen. It saw through her. Saw her fear. Saw her mind. It understood. It could wait. It had all the time in the world.

❦

"I'm sorry, Brother. I hadn't heard that you were coming!"

The cry sliced open the night. Uriel stood at the top of the terrace, arms open, backlit by the manor. He took a few swaggering steps forward.

"In fact, Jeremiah," he went on, "I was under the impression that you hadn't even been invited."

Jegud covered his eyes, guarding the flash of pain that shot through them. Jeremiah, meanwhile, made motions to replace his mask, before realizing that it no longer mattered.

Instead, he straightened up, hat and mask in hand, and forced an amiable smile.

"Good evening, Uri," he called. "It's been too long."

"Not so long," Uriel replied. "Did you appreciate the letter?"

"An engaging read."

"Eternally optimistic." Uriel smiled. "But then I guess that you couldn't survive, otherwise. Jegud and I were just discussing it: That safe spot is always around the next corner, isn't it, Jeremiah? That escape hatch is always over the next hill. But what happens when the road runs flat? Does your mother's magical luck disappear for good?"

Protected by the folds of Erika's dress, Jeremiah's hand felt for hers.

"Now isn't the time, Uriel." The gathering crowd turned to Michael, who stood in the courtyard alone. "You've been drinking."

"But that makes it all the sweeter," Uriel said. "Your problem, dear Michael, is that you never *do* know the time. It's after midnight now, and the day is already warming somewhere just below the horizon. It's always been your intention to meet the sun, hasn't it? And yet you always let the moment pass. Why not tonight, then? I think the dogs are ready for a little run, don't you?"

Jeremiah bolted, dragging Erika by the wrist. A courtier had arrived late, and was stepping from a dark, little calash. Jeremiah shoved Erika inside and leaped into the driver's box, snatching up the whip and reins. The stallion leaped forward with a jolt, and they were off.

Wind lashed at the fabric hood and sung along the lines of each slender wooden spoke. It wasn't long before the howls of Gabriel's hounds rolled down the drive, so painfully, fatally close. A staccato *crack, crack, crack* of the whip punctuated the screams of passing guests as Jeremiah tried to break the stallion from its panic. They were at a full gallop, and Jeremiah could see the horse struggling against the harness.

He saw the line of the gates ahead. The guards were panicked, torn between safety and duty, and Jeremiah felt the familiar rush of stolen freedom, sweet and heady, rising in his chest. *Crack. Crack. Crack.* And then his eyes widened when the gates, slowly, inevitably, began to swing shut. *Crack! Crack! Crack!* He felt blood from the horse's shoulders spatter his face. They could make it. They had to make it.

The gates clattered shut with a sound that trembled in Jeremiah's veins and made his heart skip. He dragged hard against the reins. The stallion reared, frantic. It was too late. Jeremiah leaped from the driver's seat before they hit the ground. He tumbled, skin scraping gravel, to the side of the drive.

The lead dogs slammed him down with their wide, sandpaper paws. Together, they lowered their muzzles and panted against the soft line of his neck.

Uriel jumped down from the box of Gabriel's carriage. Jeremiah could hear him crunching down the road with measured steps, taking his time. When Uriel reached the head of the line, he knelt down beside one of the dogs and tucked his fingers into its silver coat.

"Pinned," he said. "I could kill you." He sounded reasonable. Affable, even.

Hot saliva dripped onto Jeremiah's throat.

"Let him go." The king materialized from the direction of the lake with a paper lantern cradled in his hands.

Uriel's eyes never left his brother.

"It wouldn't take much," he whispered.

Another carriage trundled up, with Michael and Gabriel side by side on the driver's bench.

"Let him go," the king repeated in an undertone.

A crowd began to swell, but Uriel kept watching a limp and haggard Jeremiah, and the king kept watching them both.

A line of flushed cheeks filled the distance from gates to manor as every courtier, masked and beautiful, rushed down to see the dead bastard brother. Rumors flew down the road. There was a duel. There was a bloodbath. There was an arrest.

The assembly that made it to the gates found a different story altogether.

At the gates, the hush fell thick and heavy.

At the gates, there reigned a morbid, dignified horror.

At the gates, no one moved.

The seconds stretched on, and as the crowd grew, the tension mounted. The outcome, whatever the outcome, would be on every lip come morning.

"He's still your brother," Gabriel said at last, in the same soft voice his father had used.

"By half," Michael whispered beside him. Gabriel looked at him, surprised, and saw that his brother's eyes were bright, and that he leaned ever so slightly forward.

"He lost," Uriel shouted. All the attention snapped back to him. "What due have we been taught to pay losers, Gabriel?" When he received no answer, Uriel closed his eyes, let himself unravel into vapor, and faded away.

Gabriel clicked his tongue at the dogs. As they drew back, the horses began to shift restlessly.

"Go home, Jeremiah," Gabriel said. "Sign the council's order and renounce yourself. I promise you asylum in my court."

Jeremiah got to his feet and brushed himself off. He helped Erika out of the overturned calash and gave a parting bow, first to his father and then to his eldest brother.

"Thank you for your promise, Gabriel," he said. "But it was never your court I doubted."

Gabriel looked at his father, whose hands and chest were still lit by the flickering lantern.

The king's gaze traveled across his line of sons: Jeremiah, Gabriel, Michael. Then he turned and walked away, an orb bobbing slowly in the dark. By the time Gabriel looked back at the carriage, the cast-iron gates were standing open and both his brother and the girl had faded into shadow.

When Megan put her hand into the angel's palm, she felt the warmth of pure light spread all through her body, like sunbeams under her skin. She tipped up her chin, meaning to search out its eyes, and saw that it was bringing her mother's necklace up to her face. She blinked at the glittering pinprick of color.

The angel drew back its other hand and undid the delicate clasp. Megan held stock still as the chain settled down around her neck, dipping over the hollow of her clavicle. She felt those clean, glowing hands on the backs of her shoulders and she relaxed, happy to be safe.

Shawn and Rebecca watched in a state of wonder so complete it shut out everything else. Only the angel existed, and their little sister, and their mother's necklace.

Then came a flash of silver and Megan drew back, her movements stiff and heavy. The spell broke.

"Meg!" Rebecca dropped to her knees and barely caught her little sister's falling body. Megan made a soft noise, almost a whine, as her head settled against Rebecca's chest. Shawn dropped down beside them and pushed the hair out of Megan's face. Beads of sweat appeared on her upper lip, and he wiped them away as well. Each trembling breath felt hot on his hands.

"Megan," Rebecca whispered. "Megan, honey, stay with us. Listen to my voice. Megan. *Meg.*"

Megan gasped. Black eyelashes quivered against her pale cheeks. Rebecca adjusted her weight, though it was slight, and pulled her hand out from under Megan's back. Her breath caught in her throat as she tried to fight back a scream. Blood. Slick and brilliant down her fingers, over her palm, streaked across her wrist. Her little sister's blood.

Shawn caught her arm before she could move it into Megan's field of vision. He gave her a hard look and shoved her hand down to the forest floor.

"Meg," he said gently. "Meg, can you hear me?" He was very much aware of the steady white light coming from the angel, but he refused to look up and distract himself. He thought that he saw Megan nod.

"Good, good," he said, forcing himself to stay steady. "Hold on to my voice, okay?"

In answer, Megan reached up and pressed her fingers lightly over Shawn's lips. She managed a smile, and, as she did, a bubble of saliva escaped her own mouth, trapping her last breath against her skin. When Megan's pale hand slipped and settled on Shawn's knee, Rebecca broke down. Then, with her brother frozen and her sister crying hard into her hair, Megan Stripling died.

Chapter Twelve

Jeremiah and Erika were silent as they made their way back through the starving city. They passed blocks of crumbling apartments that sat like hunkered stone giants in the cool moonlight, and by alleyways lined with the blank, gaping faces of squatters' hovels. They crossed plank bridges, the make-do shortcuts that spanned open-air sewers, and ducked under the reaching fingers of dead trees. They kept their heads down when the stutter of crying children reached their ears. They picked up their pace when doors opened and closed behind them, or when an echo of footsteps tripped over the cobbles.

Jeremiah dug a key from his pocket when he reached the manor and took the padlock from the gate. He said nothing to Erika while he opened the front door, or while he let her in, or while he locked it. He said nothing to her when he struck a match to light one of the lamps in the entrance hall, and he gave it to her, still speechless, before turning away to fumble through the dark on his own. Erika watched him go. He headed down the hall and to the left, where his study waited, smelling of books and dipped in memory. On her way up the steps, she imagined him striking another match, lighting a fire, watching his mother's portrait. Waiting. Wondering.

He did none of these things.

Erika took off her gown, washed away her makeup, and let

down her hair. The wound on her forehead, the wound that had killed her, now paper dry and ugly, would be visible, she knew, but she didn't care. She found the clothes that she had died in and put them on. She looked for her jewelry but could only find one earring, and she didn't need to be reminded of Matt right now. She went into the study instead and approached the mantel and its painting of her twin. Then she slipped out of the house, and because she did not want Martha to catch her, her escape went without a hitch.

Erika walked through the city of Limbo, alone but only a little bit afraid. She didn't talk to the faces that peered through cracked windows, and didn't listen to the wailing of babies kept too long dead. She didn't know how to get where she was going, except that the many eyes of the palace glowed bright on the hill ahead of her, and she knew that if she walked long enough, she would find what she was looking for.

The Colonies lay in the Low Kingdom on the wastes of a desert plateau, and were populated by rogues who had outlasted their usefulness, and by those seraphim who had fallen out of favor. When famine came to the bottomlands, as it often did, and the beasts of the Low Kingdom began to roam for food, the Colonies became favored hunting grounds.

So it was that the buildings were made of mud brick, with the hope that they might blend into the earth and be hidden from view. The summer sun did its part by baking them hard as rock, and by winter, when the rains came, there was nothing soft left to wash away.

To the west of the Colonies ran the Devil's Teeth, a mountain range that stretched to both sides of the horizon. When the sun began to set, the barren face of the Teeth threw shadow over the valley like a blanket, giving the only respite from the heat that ever came. The highest of the Teeth was called the Arrowhead because it stretched far above the rest, its summit providing a view of the entire Kingdom. A platform, just wide enough for a man to lie on, jutted out of the side of the mountain, two hundred feet away from the peak. A rope ladder spanned the rest of the way to the Arrowhead's crest. At the top waited a plain rock cave with a wide mouth. It was there, they said, that the Furies lived.

When Rome named them, the sisters were already old, and their stories had already been played, but they took the honor as a token forewarning their return. The Winged Women of the Mountain, part human, part eagle, made a bitter, selfish sisterhood. Their history was so winding and steeped in myth that the Kingdoms had largely forgotten them. They had become monsters for children's stories and old wives' tales. But this had not always been the case.

In the old days, under kings and queens long past, the Furies had sought out the masters and learned from them, dreaming to one day serve as a single council for all three Kingdoms.

As their vanity consumed them, however, their vision came and went, until, ever self-indulgent, each sister promised herself an empire. After a painful war, the queen of the High Kingdom bound the Furies to the Arrowhead and cursed them to share their wisdom with those who made it into the upper cave. They asked only for the power to defend themselves, and this she gave them in pity: Two hundred feet from the crown of the mountain was a shelf, and between that shelf and the top she placed a ladder. Anyone who wished to seek the Furies' counsel would have to weather the climb, and anyone who fell on the ascent would die before he or she touched the ground. In exchange for this concession, the queen took the eyes from the first sister, the ears from the second, and the mouth from the third, and ruled that each time a rogue offered his or her own in sacrifice, the sisters would be forced to pass judgment on the soul of a human charge. In this way, the Furies became council to the dead, their original wish, but they were slaves to their duty: never sleeping, never living, and always hoping for someone to venture up their mountain that they might dash him to pieces and win back some of their stolen dignity.

The last of the king's guests were leaving for the night. Their laughter spilled loud and tipsy out of their carriages as they trundled down the curve of the mountain. Erika climbed and climbed and never hurt because she didn't want to. Because she was dead and she knew it. Accepted it. Used it. She reached the front gates and looked through the cast-iron bars at the warm and happy-looking palace. *Behind closed doors*, her mother always said. Only now Erika knew what was going on. What had gone on.

She took an unsteady breath and walked up to one of the seraph guards.

"I want to talk to the king," she said.

The guard did not smile, or laugh at her, but his eyes lingered on the gash across her forehead.

"The palace is closed," he said.

She reached up to her neck and fumbled with the ribbon tied there, then held the necklace out for both of the guards to see. They exchanged glances before the first guard unlocked the gates and held them open. Erika refastened the Sickle and stepped through.

The sun had drowned in the west, and the Devil's Teeth had vanished into the night, black stone against an empty, starless sky, when a cloud of silver-gray smoke flew, quick as lightning, up the side of the Arrowhead. As it neared the climber's ledge, it slowed, and then stopped to hover next to the ladder. Jeremiah flexed backward as his body re-formed. He took a few moments to gather his thoughts, and then grabbed a rope in each hand and threw himself into the climb.

Halfway up, he heard the first gasps of air from beating wings. He kept his eyes firmly set on the rock wall in front of him.

"The sixth son," hissed a voice against the back of his neck. "Has your luck run so dry?"

Jeremiah said nothing. The palms of his hands had begun to ache.

He felt the hair on his neck rise as the Fury put her lips against his ear. "Poor child," she cooed. "Wouldn't you rather fly? Reach out and take my wing."

He ignored her and heaved himself up another step.

The Fury drew back and clicked her tongue. "Clever, clever boy. I wonder why your father let you go."

Jeremiah clenched his teeth.

"Or are you still hoping that he hasn't? That he'll change his mind? Oh, Jeremiah. The time is past for dreaming. Why, your own blood brothers already signed away your soul."

He paused.

The Fury crept close again.

"Aren't you tired, Jeremiah?" she murmured. "You've been so strong, I know, but you must be exhausted by now."

A thin breath of air slipped around the Arrowhead, gently rocking the ladder.

"Let it end, Jeremiah," hummed the Fury. "Let it go."

Jeremiah pressed his eyes shut and heaved himself up another step.

"Let it go."

He paused, shook his head to clear it, and reached up again.

"Let go."

He slipped.

He knew that he was sliding down, but he couldn't make himself stop.

He wanted to listen.

He wanted to fall.

His arm caught against one of the knotted rungs and he screamed, slamming back into himself. As the ladder smacked against the side of the cliff, he heard the Fury's wings again, as she plunged down to finish him.

Jeremiah wrapped his forearms around the coarse rope and regained his footing before starting over.

The Fury shrieked, her shrill eagle's voice echoing up and down the Devil's Teeth.

"Fool! Weak fool! You can't even end it! Weak like your mother! Weak like your sniveling, sneaking mother!"

Jeremiah grunted but kept going. Hand over hand. Step by step. He tried to concentrate on the pain in his arms rather than on the voice at his back.

"She left you, Jeremiah! They all left you! None of them wanted the little bastard boy too feeble to speak up for himself!"

"I tried!" Jeremiah hadn't meant to say anything aloud, but the words slipped out anyway. He dragged himself up another few feet as the Fury made an angry swoop above his head, the wind from her wings rocking the ladder.

"You never tried!" she yelled. "Not hard enough, Jeremiah! Not enough to matter!" She hovered behind him, her wings beating the air into a whirlwind. The ladder danced. "Not hard enough then, and not hard enough now!"

"Leave me!"

"Like everyone else? Is that what you want, then? You want to be alone?"

"Yes!"

"Then take yourself away!"

He needed to stop and regain his composure, but he knew that wasn't possible. He sucked in a lungful of thin mountain air.

"I thought that rogues did as they were told!"

"I'm not a rogue!"

"Then are you a prince?" The Fury let out another screech as she did somersaults behind him, throwing him and the ropes against the mountain. "They won't have you!" she screamed. "No one will have you after what you've done!"

"I haven't done anything!"

"It's not so easy to leave your past behind you. There's only one way to make them all forget."

He felt the edge of the cliff above him and scrabbled at it. At last, he pulled himself up, moaning and too worn out to do anything but crawl away from the overhang and collapse against the sandy rock.

The Fury alighted behind him. She flapped out her wings one last time, to settle the feathers, and then walked on, stepping delicately over Jeremiah's body.

"I beat you," he groaned, not yet ready to raise his head.

"Yes," she admitted, unperturbed, and went on into the cave to tell her sisters.

When he felt well enough, Jeremiah pushed himself up and brushed the dust from his clothes. A light flickered ahead of him, a flame burning just inside the lip of the cave: He walked toward it, trying to look more confident than he felt.

The guard left Erika in the dark hallway outside the king's quarters. She rapped lightly on the wooden door before nudging it open, a little bit surprised to find it unlocked. The king looked up from his reading and his face flashed recognition before he composed himself and set the leather-bound book aside. He wore silk pajamas, one ankle resting on the opposite knee, a fire burning happy in the giant hearth beside him. The winged armchair that he sat in was high and plush, cream colored with patterns of pale blue flowers. It reminded Erika of a summer dress she used to love.

"You'll have me thinking that I can see ghosts," said the king. He smiled a little, which gave Erika courage. She stepped into the parlor and shut the door behind her.

"I'm sorry to bother you," she said. The king shook his head, still smiling, and motioned to the chair across from him.

"Sit, Miss Stripling," he said. "Tell me why you're here."

"I'm here for my children," said Erika.

"Yes," he said quietly. "That always makes us a little bit braver, doesn't it?"

Erika sank into the armchair, elbows on her knees, back sloped forward. The firelight danced on her face and hair.

"Do I look like her?" she whispered.

The king paused, sighed, straightened up. "You've seen the portrait, I'm sure. What do you think?"

Erika stared at her fingertips. "I think that we see people differently when we love them."

In the fireplace, a pine log snapped, beads of sap exploding as they warmed. The sound swallowed up the silence, like hunger, because air will always let itself be burned.

"Who have you lost, Miss Stripling?"

She glanced up and caught the king's concerned eyes.

"A lot of people," she said. "And I don't want to lose any more. My kids —"

The king shook his head to silence her. "I know about your children," he said. "I may be declining into senility, but I haven't reached it yet." He lowered his eyelids, dropping into his own private thoughts. Erika watched him, lip gripped between her teeth. She was scared. She'd never been so scared.

"I would die for my kids," Erika said, a last plea, but she knew that there was another side to that promise. She would kill for them, also. And maybe she was sitting here because she wanted to be forgiven; because she'd tried to make them die for her.

"And I suppose," said the king, "that you've come here to tell me that you would marry for them, as well as die."

Erika bit back tears as she reached up and untied the Sickle one last time. She turned the pendant over and over in her fingers, the tarnished metal glinting in the half-light.

"I understand you," the king said, his voice kinder this time. He waited until she looked into his eyes, the blue of his irises gone thin and watery with age. "And I hope that *you* will understand that sometimes we do things that we're not proud of. Sometimes, we do things selfishly, even when those choices are made for the ones we love."

Erika ground the silver into her palm to keep herself from crying over her own selfishness. She finally understood why souls found it hard to let go of their bodies, since things like mourning and tears always came in pairs. And, if she were honest, she didn't want to lose that. The world was borne more easily when your body bore it too.

The king watched her grief for a long time before intervening. "Do you love my son?"

A little laugh burst from Erika's lips as she sniffed and tried to calm herself. "I don't know," she said. "I hope not. It would be much easier if I didn't."

"But if you did," he said, "would it be because he takes after his mother?"

Erika stared at the rug beneath her feet and thought of her

own mother and how she always said that you couldn't change a man. She thought of Jeremiah and how wrong he made her look. And she thought of all the changes he couldn't help, all the accommodations he made without thinking. How much she hated to watch him struggle over balancing her wants and his own, and how much she hated it when he lied to protect her.

"It would be because he won't give up," she said. "Because he knows what's right, even when I don't. Because he tells me when I'm wrong, even when it hurts us both. So no," she said, "if I love him, it's not because of his mother and what she was."

"You care about Jeremiah most when he's honest?"

Erika ran her thumb around the Sickle and nodded. Her eyes burned.

"Then, regardless of what he is, your love for him *is* because of his mother."

Erika gave him a weak smile and took a breath to steady herself before rising from her chair. She crossed the rug and knelt down at the king's feet.

"This belongs to you," she said, offering him the Sickle.

He hesitated before reaching out, but when he finally did, his skin felt warm against her own, and soft with the wear of old age. He took the pendant and clasped it tightly in his fist.

Erika looked up at his face, cheeks slack and weighted, slipping from the bone.

"The first time you saw her," she said, "did you know?"

"That I would love her?" His lips pouted as he shook his head, still examining the Sickle. Round and round it went, spinning slow between his fingertips. "I have never believed in love at first sight, but yes, she was beautiful. One of the most beautiful women I have ever seen." He closed his eyes again.

"Whether she was more beautiful than my own wife, I cannot say. I never had enough distance. They were very different, the two of them." He looked up again, at the small paintings that hung near his fireplace — all of his sons, even Jeremiah, small and smiling.

"Whatever anyone may think," he said, "my wife, my sons, my entire council — I did not fall in love with Jeremiah's mother because of her face, or hair, or voice. And that may be the hardest thing for anyone but myself to understand or accept. That I only came to love those things because they were a part of her. I have been a lot of things, Miss Stripling, but I have never been vain enough to love a mask."

"And when did you stop loving your wife?"

"Never," he said. "I lost respect for her, but not love. It's not until it happens to you that you realize exactly what the difference is."

"I think I understand," said Erika. She thought about John, and the way his breath felt on the nape of her neck. The way he woke her up with biscuits and fresh jam when she was pregnant, just because he could. The way he played with Rebecca on her toddling legs, running and running and scooping her up in the yard, clutching her like a football through the sprinklers, his clothes getting wet but his laughter getting louder. No matter what he turned into when he drank, and no matter how Shawn remembered him, Erika would never stop loving those things.

The king called her back from her thoughts by cupping his right hand against her cheek. The thickness of her hair kept their skin from touching this time, but she could feel his warmth even through her curls, and could see it in his face as he took in every line, every spot, every crease on her own. "You could be her twin," he said, almost wistful. "Jeremiah was not wrong about that. But you could never be her." He brushed his fingers down her hair again, from crown to chin, before pulling back his hand. "And maybe that's for the best, because I don't think that my heart could withstand loving her again."

Erika nodded slowly, and he watched as she pushed herself up.

"Good night, Highness," she said, not knowing whether she should bow or curtsey or kiss his hand.

"Thank you for coming, Erika," he said. "You've helped an old man reach peace with his decisions."

She wanted to ask him, just to clarify for the sake of her nerves, what those decisions were, but she held her tongue. Instead, she looked at the wall above the fireplace and the paintings of his boys. A fluted oil lamp perched on the corner of the mantel, looking too inexpensive for the private rooms of a palace. Beside it, a thin, black box inlaid with mother-of-pearl cuttings hovered open, by just a crack. Erika looked back at the aging king. He smiled and gave her a small nod, the tarnished Sickle still cradled in his closed hand. They said nothing else before Erika let herself out, taking the scent of roses with her.

The insides of the cave were scraped smooth, with pillars jutting up at intervals and a mural engraved all the way around. The Teeth and Arrowhead rose proud against the back wall, defended by the sisters, while the Colonies huddled, frightened, in one dark corner. Any unlucky seraph etched into the walls was being hunted down and devoured by hoofed animals with two faces, one human, one hyena, or by small, naked dogs with quills down their backs.

Jeremiah drew forward, to a space where the carved floor was badly scuffed and scratched. For the first time in his life, after offering sacrifices to them for centuries, Jeremiah laid eyes on the Furies.

The sisters lounged near the far wall of the cave, about forty feet from the entrance. They were lit by a bed of coals, twenty feet across and four feet deep, which distanced them from any visitors. Their women's torsos slipped into the scaled legs of eagles, claws glinting copper in the firelight. Their bodies curled like panthers', tails flicking lazy behind them, but were feathered, as were the cuffs on their forelegs, shafts sweeping up like bracers, and the crowns that grew in headdresses around their faces, fending off locks of long, thick hair.

The first sister was Alecto, the Sunset. Her hair and feathers were ocher, as were her eyes, when she had them. Legend said that Helen herself had taught Alecto how to splinter men with one glance.

The second sister was Megaera, the Twilight. She was the vainest of all the Furies, and so proud of her silver feathers and pale skin that she never left the cave while the sun burned. She wore thick ropes of pearls around her head, to hide the ears that the high queen had taken.

The last sister was Tisiphone, the Night. She was the wisest, because her temper bubbled quick and violent and had won her the most knowledge when the sisters first began their hunt for power. Her curse left her in silent disdain, hearing all, seeing all, but unable to speak her own mind.

"Jeremiah," Alecto whispered. "The boy unwanted. What secrets do you hope the devil might tell you?"

"I come to take the eyes of Alecto," Jeremiah said, "that I might do one last decent thing."

Megaera hummed and tipped her head to the side. Jeremiah saw that she had her ears, and knew that there was a guide wandering the Woods. "Then you do plan to break soon," Megaera said. "You couldn't, I suppose, have done it here for my sake."

Alecto interrupted her sister's complaint. "Who is this rogue who cannot collect his own eyes," she growled, "and how many princes does it take to bring them back?"

Jeremiah faltered. "What?"

Alecto drew herself up on her taloned feet and leaned over the coals. "Does it look, child, as if I have my eyes?" She opened her lids to show that her thick black lashes framed empty sockets.

Jeremiah, devastated, barely managed to open his mouth. "Who came?"

"The boy who oversteps his place," Alecto said, settling back down. "We were bidden to give knowledge, not donations."

"I don't understand."

"He stole them," Megaera hissed, and then groaned. A trickle of blood slid down her jaw and throat and dripped like oil onto the stones in front of her.

"Yes," Alecto said. "He stole them. But he will suffer much for it." She smiled. "I am not quick to forgive."

Tisiphone gave a guttural sigh and arched her back as if just waking. She stretched her jaw wide and then cut her eyes at Jeremiah, still licking her lips with a newly formed tongue.

"What else, then, do you want to know, young prince?" she asked, savoring the words and her ability to speak them. "Would you like to hear about your mother? Would you like to learn what she really said before you lost her?"

"No."

Tisiphone chuckled. "Quick to the answer. Tell me, Jeremiah: Why are you so terrified?"

"Does Michael mean to kill the children?" he asked instead.

"The children . . ." For the first time, Tisiphone seemed at a loss. "I do not understand." She leaned forward and looked down the line at Alecto. "What children are these?"

"Then you don't know everything," Jeremiah mused.

"Or you guess at questions to wound us," Tisiphone said, but panic soured her voice.

"No matter," Alecto yawned. "If it is worth knowing, then the winds will tell us, in time."

"There is no time," Jeremiah said.

Tisiphone squinted at him through the semidark. She seemed to have gotten control of herself. "Of course there is, young prince," she said. "There is nothing *but* time." She moaned and sank back into the shadows, silent again.

"I have to go," Jeremiah told them.

"Then go," said Alecto.

But Jeremiah hesitated, watched by the large almond eyes of Alecto's sisters. "What did she say?" he asked, finally.

Alecto wet her lips. "Who, child?"

"My mother," Jeremiah said. His voice barely rose above a whisper. "Before she broke. My father said —"

Alecto chuckled, cutting him off. The sound rolled so deep in her throat that it came out as a purr. "Your father was desperate," she said. "Now not even he can separate his fictions and truths." She reached up and wiped the corners of her eyes, where blood was beginning to fall like tears. "Do you know what your father asked your mother?"

"He asked her if she loved me," Jeremiah said.

Alecto nodded and opened her huge cat eyes. The firelight made them glow like orange citrine, and at last Jeremiah understood why they were so dangerous. They were eyes to lure you into the dark. Eyes to tempt and tear you slowly. "She said 'I can't,'" Alecto told him. "So simple, isn't it? The one thing that he never wanted her to say. The one real thought she ever had."

Jeremiah walked from the cave to the brink of the cliff and jumped.

When he passed the magic of the climber's ledge, his body faded into smoke and was folded into the night.

To *the* Fifty-*seventh* Council *of* His Magnificence *the* Throne:

Though I *feel that your conclusions have been gratuitously callous on my part,* I *recognize the obligations ascribed to me, and to all recognized sons of the* Throne, *and know them to be irrefutable. Therefore it is with great sorrow that* I *move to accept your request. In full understanding of the consequences of this declaration,* I *hereby renounce my title of* Sixth Prince *of the* Middle Kingdom *and dissolve all relation with the current and reigning* Throne, *and therein all relation with any of its descendants.*

It is my intention to emigrate from the Kingdom's *protectorate within a period of no more than five days, and I request transitory papers to be delivered before this time.*

With this so stated, I give my complete goodwill to His Magnificence the Throne and to His Majesty the Crown Prince, and beg pardon for any wrongs done to either of their houses.

With constant loyalty,

Your humble subject,

Jeremiah of the Lowland Colonies

Erika woke to a room filled with sunlight, and the quiet trundle of a carriage in the street. Martha stood at the window, pinning back the curtains with her careful hands.

"Is Jeremiah awake yet?" Erika asked.

"He never slept, miss."

"Is he indisposed?"

"He's not at all disposed," Martha replied, smoothing the wrinkles of her apron. "He's locked himself away, in fact. He had a letter for the post this morning, for the first time in his life. For the council."

Erika gaped. "He hasn't renounced himself?"

"He has. I think it's broken his heart."

When the door flew open, the handle hit the wall so hard it chipped the paint. Both Erika and Martha let out little screams of surprise.

Jeremiah rushed into the room, a smile splitting his face, and his eyes shut tight.

"We've won!" He threw his arms around Martha and spun with her, the toes of her shoes skimming the floor. When he let her go, she tottered and fell back against the wall, bracing herself on the windowsill. Then he turned to Erika, scooped her up from the bed as if she were a child, and pressed his forehead against her cheek. His dark hair brushed her skin, tinged with the scent of chocolate and black coffee.

The smell of fresh cotton clung to Erika's nightclothes, and the soft perfume of sleep hung across her neck. Jeremiah had to put her down before he forgot himself. He took a step away before carrying his hand up to her chin and opening it to reveal his miracle.

"The Sickle," he said, his voice low.

There it lay, knotted to a piece of black silk, the pendant itself, so thin and delicate. Polished to a high shine, it kicked light across the room like a mirror. Erika took the ribbon from his palm and let the Sickle twirl slowly in midair.

"What does it mean?"

"It means that you've done it, Erika," he said. "It means that you've won the throne."

Erika closed her fingers around the pendant and pressed it against her chest.

"Then help my kids," she said.

Jeremiah's smile vanished. He looked at her, small and vulnerable, and felt his stomach lurch. Before he could stop himself, he'd wrapped her close to his chest and tucked her head under his chin. *Your father's chosen bride*, his mind screamed. *Your father's new queen.* He closed his eyes to shut out the thoughts and rocked Erika slowly back and forth. "I assumed that you'd be happy, Erika," he said. "I didn't know —"

He expected to feel the warmth of tears against his neck, but he never did, and the lack of it worried him more than the tremble in her voice.

"Help them, Jeremiah."

"I will," he whispered.

The words felt more like a deathbed promise than a wedding gift. Jeremiah let the weight of them settle on his shoulders, even as Erika turned away. Jegud stepped into the room.

"I don't mean to interrupt," he said.

Jeremiah waved off the apology.

"I need to speak with you for a moment," Jegud ventured. "Alone."

"Say whatever you have to say."

"Are you sure?"

Jeremiah looked meaningfully at Erika. "No more secrets."

"Are you *sure*?"

"Just *say it*."

Jegud pursed his lips. "Erika's children are missing," he said.

"What?" Erika spun out from her place at the window.

"Dammit, Jegud." Jeremiah crossed the room in a stride and grabbed his brother's arm. "It's a misunderstanding," he said to Erika. "I'll take care of this."

As the brothers left the room, Martha led Erika to the chair.

"Don't look so distressed, miss. This will turn out."

Erika could do nothing more than shake her head, her face buried in her hands.

The brothers took Jegud's carriage. Jeremiah glowered at the floor as they clipped along, flashes of the city peeping through the open windows.

"I looked everywhere," Jegud repeated.

"Why would they do this?"

"You told me yourself that Erika got the Sickle. Can you imagine Uriel standing for that, after what happened last night?"

"Oh, yes, and thank you for defending me there, by the way."

"What could I have done against them that Gabriel couldn't do? He's a better man than you give him credit for; more noble and far more courageous than you, Jeremiah. He even took care of that horse that you almost flogged to pieces."

"I was only trying to —"

"Run away? I hope so. Because if the word 'help' was about to leave your mouth, then I would have to be even more disgusted with you than I already am. You haven't tried to help anybody but yourself, Jeremiah, for a very long time."

"I'm out of practice," Jeremiah said. "I haven't *had* anybody but myself to take care of for a very long time."

"Admirable of you to bring Erika, though. Even if you *did* nearly crush her in the earl's calash."

"I wouldn't guess she's thinking much about that right now." He looked at his brother. "Can I fix this?"

"To be honest?" Jegud shrugged. "I doubt it."

"I promised her."

"You've made a lot of promises, Jeremiah. You're too easy with them, I've always said. If you'd ever think about the words coming out of your mouth, you might live a better life."

Jeremiah no longer listened. "Kala knew," he said. "She saw it."

Jegud thought about that for a silent moment. "I thought you weren't sure."

"I thought I could change it. She was so young."

"You should have known better."

Jeremiah's brow wrinkled. "You can't ever be helpful, can you, Jegud? You can't ever just say that everything will be fine." He leaned his weary head against the side of the carriage. "You couldn't just say that we don't know yet. You couldn't just say that there's still a chance."

"A chance of what?" Jegud let out a hollow laugh. "If you want me to lie to you, then I will, but what would be the point? You know that the predictions of a Caladrius aren't governed by hope or luck or chance. Know it better than anybody, I'd wager. Why do you have to keep pretending that life is easy? Is Uriel right after all?"

"About what?"

"About the fact that you'd die without your silver lining. You're a rogue and a seraph, but you act more like living man."

"Is that so wrong?"

Jegud shook his head. "I think that it might be, Jeremiah," he admitted. "And I'm sorry that you can't see it too."

The carriage rolled to a stop.

"Since you agree on so much," Jeremiah said, "I'm sure that you and Uri will have a spectacular talk. But please try and save it until *after* I waste my own time. I'd hate to think of either of you as rude."

Jeremiah jumped from the carriage and followed the paved walk to the king's third house. He walked alone, hands deep in his pockets, and cast an appraising eye over the front of the manor. He had always been proud that his own house was larger than Uriel's. Since it had been built specifically for his mother, this fact had been a mark of honor for him. It proved that she *had* been loved once. That house had given her dignity.

Standing. While she lived in the king's sixth house, Jeremiah's mother could not be a whore.

A maid answered at Jeremiah's knock.

"The master's out."

"Tell him who it is."

"I can't, sir," she said, "as he's out. If you'd —" She stopped herself and stepped aside. Uriel had changed his mind, then.

"I'll take it," the third prince said, turning into the hallway from one of the far rooms. "I owe him something, after all." He shuffled through one of the inside pockets of his jacket. "Whose wagon did you steal to get here? I heard that your own was detained." He spotted the black coach in the circle and broke into a wide grin. "Joined at the hip, are you?"

"And how *is* Michael?"

Uriel's face hardened. "Fine, I should think," he said stiffly. "He won the Sickle, but I suppose you've heard. If you'd take that as a cue to leave forever and give up your stake in the throne, we'd all be much obliged."

Jeremiah gave an uneasy laugh. "You're mistaken," he said. "Erika had the Sickle as a gift this morning."

"Don't add lying to your list of sins, Jeremiah. It doesn't suit a rogue."

Jeremiah tilted his head. "I don't think that anything can quite measure up to kidnapping."

"What are you talking about?"

"Where are the children?"

"What children?"

"The Striplings."

"Erika has *children*? I'm sure the crown would love that. Bouncing human brats popping in for the holidays."

"I know that you spoke to them," Jeremiah said with impatience. "Now tell me."

Uriel faltered. His forehead wrinkled as he finally pulled an envelope from his pocket. "It's not my fault you've lost them, Jeremiah. Take your travel papers and stop twittering around my house." He slapped the letter against Jeremiah's chest.

"I mean it, Uri. I need to know where they are."

"And *I* mean it when I tell you that I haven't a clue." Uriel stared at his little brother as if trying to read the joke. "Don't tell me that you're trying to pull your mother's magic on me. There's no amount you can change to make me love you." When Jeremiah said nothing, Uriel sighed. "Well, go ahead, then. The last I saw of those monsters, they were still walking a pointless circle through the woods under your direction. Really, Jeremiah, I don't know whether you were trying to drive them insane or ragged, but it borders on heartless."

"I was *trying* to keep them safe."

Uriel gave him a dagger smile. "Well, it didn't help much, then, did it?"

Jeremiah stared at the oak door as it clapped shut in his face.

He marched back to the carriage, the traveling license crumpled in his fist.

"Well?"

Jeremiah threw himself onto the bench.

"He said he doesn't know."

"And?"

He jerked his head back at the window. "And he isn't lying."

Jegud looked his brother over before turning away as well. Neither of them admitted aloud what this meant. If Michael had pocketed Erika's children without telling his most loyal brother, then the children were never coming back.

Gabriel waited for Jeremiah. As the brothers rolled down the road to the king's sixth house, they could make out his profile through the window of his own carriage. His favorite hunter, a pearl gray dog with salt-and-pepper ruff, lay at his feet. They rose, dog and master both, at the advance of Jegud's coach.

"Where have you two been?"

"Visiting Uriel," Jeremiah said, as Gabriel ducked through the door of his carriage. Jeremiah stepped out to join him. Jegud nodded at Gabriel and then signaled his own driver to move on.

Gabriel and Jeremiah watched Jegud's carriage disappear into the city before turning back to each other.

"Were you apologizing?" Gabriel asked.

"Hardly."

The crown prince looked his little brother up and down. "Are you afraid that you'll hurt me, Jeremiah?"

"Is that relevant?"

"What is it that you know?"

"No more than you. But I happen to think that it matters."

Gabriel shook his head. "I wanted to give you this in person." He took out a sealed envelope.

"What?"

"A permit to stay in the Kingdom. I wrote it myself, after I saw your letter. No brother of mine, recognized or not, should have to go below for compassion. I'm so sorry about this."

Jeremiah was still confused over the news from this morning — that Michael's girl had gotten the Sickle as well. He knew that Gabriel would understand better than any of them.

"Hadn't you heard?" he ventured, clinging to his last threads of hope. "Erika won the Sickle."

"Everyone won the Sickle," Gabriel said, shrugging. "It's just a consolation. Father said that he would be happier to go a widower."

"But your coronation —"

"He plans to go to services."

Jeremiah felt as if the breath had been knocked out of him. "No."

"I tried to talk to him," Gabriel said, his voice thick. "He told me that he's been overlucky. He would rather go now than have that luck run dry. He wanted me to let you know that he was sorry. For everything."

"I've never blamed him."

"Yes, you have, Jeremiah. You've always blamed him." Gabriel pressed the envelope into his brother's hands. "I'd like for you to be there when he passes. It's tonight at sundown."

"So soon . . ."

"It isn't our choice to make."

"Can't the laws be changed?"

"He doesn't want them to be. He's always been a purist, you know that. He's always said that rules shouldn't be distorted once they've been written. What kind of a hypocrite would he be if he changed that now?"

Gabriel climbed back into his carriage. "We'll see you?"

"I'll think about it."

"You're always welcome, Jeremiah."

"I don't think that everyone feels that way."

"Why shouldn't you be there on the day your father frees himself?"

Jeremiah locked eyes with his brother. "Because," he said, "I'm not so sure that I want to join him just yet."

Gabriel nodded. "That was politics," he said. "Politics are always cutthroat."

He dropped the curtain to cover his window and called to the driver. With the crack of a whip, the pair of horses picked up their feet and carried away the crown prince's private box.

Jeremiah went around to the back gardens, trying to avoid Erika for a few minutes more. He was afraid to face her, now that he knew the worst, especially when his thoughts were filled up by his father. He'd lost her, he knew. She could never forgive him for what he'd done to her, and even if she could, he could never forgive himself. He was descended from a long line of men infamous for tearing apart the women who loved them best, and he now realized that he wasn't any different.

Jeremiah wandered down a dirt path, thinking about death. A nip of frost, lingering from morning, hung sharp throughout the air. It had been a long time since anyone except for Simon had come back here. Fishponds and flower beds were scattered over the sweep of hand-clipped grass. The year was too far gone for flowers; their leaves had stiffened up, as if arthritic, and were beginning to lose their color. Winter was a sad season in the Middle Kingdom. Snow never came, just a frost that spiderwebbed the whole city each night and a cold sun that glowed, weak as a fever patient, behind a sheet of white cloud.

The first time Jeremiah had left the Kingdom in order to collect a human soul, it had been early December in Edo, long since renamed Tokyo. Snow fell thick, coating roads and houses, working its way into shoes and clinging to hair as if afraid of letting go. He'd been so preoccupied, he'd almost forgotten his charge. *So this is it*, he'd thought. *Even their air is alive.*

Jeremiah stood over one of the fishponds, hands deep in the pockets of his trousers. A family of koi floated near the surface: pretty, flecked calicos with black and white, red and gold, each one costing a fortune because life was so precious in the Kingdom. Wealthy families paid in solid silver for birds, rabbits, baby mice, just to feel them breathing. These fish would go to the bottoms of their pools in a few days, trying to survive beneath a sheath of ice. Simon came out each morning and chipped a hole to bring them air, but sometimes it didn't matter. Jeremiah could remember one season when every fish had died before spring. It was the same year that they had taken his mother's coffin from the family crypt and moved it to the Colonies. The stone they gave her was inscribed with her name and nothing else. Jeremiah had visited a few times after the interment, and, once, he'd used his knife on the soft sandstone to carve a picture of the emblem that his stepmother had always worn, and that Martha had fished from his birth mother's sheets, and had kept for him until he was old enough to understand. A thin ring crossed by a pair of sickles.

Now it was only a picture, less than symbolic, because his

father had taken the meaning from it that morning when he'd sent away those charms as if they were immaterial. As if they had always been immaterial.

"You're going to the service tonight."

Jeremiah turned. Selaph stood behind him, as still as one of the bronze garden statues.

"I haven't decided," Jeremiah said.

"You're going, Brother."

For the first time, Jeremiah realized that Selaph had always been sidelined by his own silence. The brothers hardly ever considered him, because he had given them no reason to. He was soft-spoken, and what he did say was always noncommittal. He treated all of his brothers as if they were older than himself, letting them find their own way and, more often than not, letting them make his choices for him. It was because he never gave absolutes that they had gotten used to walking all over him, and because he never seemed to mind that they had never even noticed.

"Why should I go?" Jeremiah asked.

"Because Michael will be there," Selaph replied. He made it sound so simple. Predetermined.

"And when have I ever wanted to see Michael?"

"You used to," Selaph said. "When we were younger. Remember how we thought he was a king? More of a king than our own father?"

"I do."

"Gabriel was the crown. He always shut himself up with his books and his lessons. Michael was . . ."

"The second?"

"Except to us."

"Except to us," Jeremiah mused. "It's funny how the tables turn, isn't it?"

"He has Erika's children."

Jeremiah blinked. His mind felt numb — as if every rational thought had slipped away.

"How do you . . . How do you know about them?"

"Word travels fast here, as you should know by now. I've been keeping an eye on them, to make sure no one abused them too much. They're only children. It's not their fault."

"And you know where they are now?"

"Didn't you notice that I was gone from the ball last night?"

Jeremiah flushed, because he hadn't.

"Of course, Brother," he said. "Of course I did."

"He had me take them last night. He didn't think that it should be someone they already knew. I listened because I thought that it might keep the family together." He paused. "Both theirs and ours, Jeremiah. They came willingly."

"But why would Michael want them in the first place?"

"He's baiting you," Selaph said. "He's after your soul."

Jeremiah felt suddenly cold. He considered the statement for a moment, afraid to speak. "Hasn't he got his own?" He'd meant for the question to be light, to ease the sting of such a hard situation. Selaph didn't seem to take it that way.

"I'm not always sure," he said. The look he gave Jeremiah was filled with so much sincerity, so much sadness that it forced his little half brother to turn away. "He's the one who moved the council against you."

"I know," Jeremiah said, surprised with the thickness of his own voice.

"You never meant for this to happen, did you?"

"Of course not."

"You still love him."

"How can I? After what he's done. After everything that he still means to do."

"He's your brother."

"Not by much," Jeremiah said. "Besides, I doubt he feels the same way."

"Are you taking your lessons from him now, Jeremiah? You used to call him a god."

"He used to be one, for me."

"What happened?"

Jeremiah looked back at Selaph, unsure as to whether or not he expected an answer. Anticipation filled his eyes, as if he honestly didn't know. All that Jeremiah could see, apart from Selaph's expectant face, was an old memory from his childhood. The edges were faded, the sounds were muted, but Michael's face came through clear. He was young and petulant and jeering as Jeremiah backed himself into an alley. Gabriel had come to save him just in time. If he hadn't heard the shouting, perhaps it would've all ended there.

"My mother, I guess," Jeremiah said.

"That didn't change who you were."

"It did for him."

Selaph turned to leave. "You didn't fall out of favor," he said. "Michael did."

"Father hasn't ever seemed to think so."

"Father's isn't the only voice that matters," Selaph told him, and then he walked away.

Erika opened the front door before Jeremiah even put his key to the lock.

"Where are they?"

"I don't know how to tell you this, Erika —"

"Don't play with me, for God's sake. You owe me more than that."

Jeremiah held back a rush of self-hate. Of course he owed Erika more than this. She deserved more than any of this. He found his voice. "Michael's holding them," he said, "to get to me."

Erika pressed her fingers against her forehead. "Oh, thank God."

When Jeremiah stayed quiet, she dropped her hand. A challenge flashed through her eyes.

"You *are* going, aren't you? I mean you're not . . . you're not just going to leave them?"

He waved his hands in front of his face, palms out. "No, Erika. Of course I'm not going to leave them. Listen, my father is . . ." He took a shaky breath. "Is going to free himself tonight."

"What?"

"It's a service. It's . . . complicated."

"But I thought —"

"So did I. I was wrong. I'm going. Michael will be there. Gabriel will be there. I need him to see what Michael's done. I need him to know. After our father goes . . . well, then Gabriel will be the one with the power to stop Michael. Gabriel will be the one with the power to send your kids home."

"I'm going with you."

"No, you're not."

Erika grabbed his hand.

"This isn't about me. This is about my *children*. So yes," she said, "I'm going."

Jeremiah ran a finger over the spines of a row of books, deliberating. He took one down and set it in the wooden crate at his feet. An identical box, already full, waited by the door of his study. Close to that sat a locked pine-and-iron traveling chest with his mother's portrait perched on top.

Gabriel's proclamation lay unopened on the desk, and beside it, a note sealed with a splatter of blue wax.

Gabriel —

I'm sorry to write that your first wish as king will never be bidden; I have given up living on anyone's charity.

Take Kala, who has lived too long below her place, and let her remind you ever of the boys we used to be.

Erika I leave also in your care, for I would be a poor host to bring her where I plan to go. I realize that she will not understand. Tell her that I'm sorry for all the pain I fed her. Tell her that I am afraid of being too much my mother's son.

I wish for peace, Gabriel, and a long reign to the new Throne.

Do not look for me.

Yours, humbly,

Jeremy

Jeremiah drummed his fingers on the glass front of the next shelf. At last, he sighed and pulled down a five-volume series. He frowned, thumbing through the pages, and tossed aside three of the books, each making a loud *crack* as it hit the tile. The last two he dropped into the crate.

"Are you happy, Mother?" he muttered. He felt the Sickle's weight in his left pocket, and reached in to feel the cool metal. "Would you be happy if I wanted you to be?"

He took down another armload of books. As he stared at them, a breath of air, half-laugh, half-sigh, passed over his lips.

"For my eleventh birthday," he said to the first cover, "from Armen Firman." He flung it against the wall. *SLAM.* The next book was embossed with red velvet and gold thread. "For my thirteenth, from the dear lady Hildegard von Bingen." *SLAM.* "From Gottfried Leibniz — a parting gift." *SLAM.* "For top scores in mathematics, from Shen Kuo." *SLAM.* "Here, from the queen herself, a very patient woman. She even signed it." *SLAM.* "And this." Jeremiah waved a slim leather-bound book over his head. "This was the first book I ever stole, after Father turned me out." *SLAM.* He turned to his mother's portrait, which smiled softly at him. "I hate you, Mother. I *hate* you." He grabbed another book and threw it at the portrait. "*I HATE YOU.*" Another. The corner broke the canvas, ripping through the side of her face. "You *LEFT me.*" Another. It sank into the cinched waist of her gown.

"YOU."

Another.

"LEFT."

Another.

"*ME.*"

Another. Gone were her pale fingers, where the Sickle had hung before someone filched it away.

Chest heaving, Jeremiah brushed his wrist across his eyes. He dropped the books that still dangled from his other hand.

"Why couldn't I have been more like you?" he moaned. "You, who couldn't love your own son?"

He looked one last time at the clean, empty green of his mother's eyes and then walked away, the study door thudding shut behind him.

Chapter Thirteen

Jeremiah and Erika arrived at the common just as the sky began to bruise. A halo of crimson hung over the building, a flush cast by the dying sun. A line of empty carriages waited along the sidewalk. Erika recognized Jegud's black coach and Gabriel's white one. A pair of trotters drew it today, instead of his hounds.

After stepping down, Jeremiah peered back into his own unlit carriage.

"Are you sure about this?" he asked.

Erika gave him a hard, cold look.

"Fine," he said, and shoved his hands into his pockets. "Wait here." He went down the sidewalk alone, horses whinnying and tossing their manes as he passed.

The archway that surrounded the common was lit by lines of gas lamps, and the smooth cut of the stonework became a mirror under their flickering glow. Jeremiah followed the hallway into the main room, where the altar stood ready for services. The king waited behind the podium, in the same place he'd stood to conduct services every morning for millennia. He ran his fingers back and forth over the silver edges of the ceremonial dagger. It had gained new meaning for him, since the handle now had his own death note carved into the bone. It was fitting, maybe, to be set free by the same knife that he had used so many times before. He looked up when the door opened and saw Jeremiah walking toward him. The king smiled, or tried to, and set the knife back on the podium.

The princes were the only ones in attendance.

Jegud walked over and clasped Jeremiah's hand, leaning in close to his ear. "What the hell are you doing?"

"Michael has the kids," Jeremiah said.

There was a pause.

"Don't ruin this for Father." Jeremiah pulled back a little in surprise, but Jegud kept hold of his arm. "Did you hear me?"

"Yes," Jeremiah said. "I'm going to wait until after the service."

Jegud nodded and stepped away.

Jeremiah took the hands of his other brothers, wondering if this wouldn't be the last time he was ever allowed to do so.

At the end, he came to his father, who stayed an arm's length away from his youngest son.

"You came," the king said.

"I did."

The moment stretched awkwardly.

Then the king reached for Jeremiah and pulled him to his chest, hugging him as he'd never done before.

"I loved your mother," he whispered. "I would have done anything to save her. I would have done anything."

"You exiled her."

"I know. There are things you do as a leader that you would never dream of doing as a man. I had to."

"You didn't do it as a leader," Jeremiah said. "You did it as a coward."

The king drew back. His mouth was open, his eyes half closed as he stared at the ground between them.

"If your stepmother had stayed, then it would be different now, Jeremiah," he said. "Do you see how history can be twisted? How intentions can be perverted by time? You *are* right to call me a coward, but only because my wife ran away."

"Put my mother back in the crypt."

"Oh, Jeremiah." The king shook his head. "We all have to fall into our places as they come. That is no longer mine."

"Would you, if it still was?"

"I'm not a man for hypotheticals," he said. "But yes. That was my one great mistake in life. Can you understand that?" He looked his son in the eye. "I made her into a whore instead of a queen. For that, you can blame no one but me."

Jeremiah reached for his father's arm, but it was too late. The king had already turned away. That was one thing that, Jeremiah could see, would never change.

The king picked up the dagger. His old fingers traced the bone handle, thanking it. The carvings felt alive in his hands, electric and comfortable. He brought it to his eldest son.

"Please," he said. "I'm ready, Gabriel."

The eldest prince took the knife from his father and weighed it in his hands. He had seen these services every morning of his life, but this was different. Everything that he had ever heard about being freed no longer applied. No longer mattered.

The king lay down on the altar, resting his neck against the raised cradle. He smiled.

"Do you know," he said, "I've probably been in the common a million times. But I've never really seen the sky from here."

All six sons turned their eyes to the open ceiling, where a blanket of stars winked down at them like a silver city. When they looked back at the altar, their father had faded into a blur of white mist.

Gabriel crossed the room, his brothers close behind, and leaned over the king.

"Go to peace," he murmured, lifting the knife above his head.

He brought it down with all his strength. The blade slowed when it sank into his father's soul, but, with a quiet grunt of effort, Gabriel forced it toward the stone beneath. There was a *click*, as the tip of the dagger touched the bed of rock, and then Gabriel sprang backward and the king's soul rushed up through the creamy handle of the knife and swirled skyward, churning like the slender tail of a cyclone. When the last of it was in the air, the knife clattered against the altar and a rush of wind spat the funnel out through the open roof. The soul split overhead with a crack like dry thunder, and the pieces drifted, as fine as gold dust, back into the soil of the Middle Kingdom.

Gabriel carried the knife back to the podium and laid it down with gentle respect. The altar had collected a thin layer of powder-fine dust, which he would gather and send to the crypt for interment.

He could hear his brothers behind him, coming out of their own separate thoughts, but he didn't feel up to facing them just yet. Instead he stared at the cold blade of the dagger and at his hands, thin and pale in the lamplight. He tried to remind himself that this was what his father wanted. That he had only ever done what his father wanted.

Michael and Jeremiah were bickering in low voices as they passed by behind him, but still, Gabriel held himself from turning. Perhaps it was for the best that they were being split by law. He knew that it had never been Jeremiah's fault, but it remained that the simple fact of his existence had always been a strain on the family. His father had tried to ignore it, but the weight settled on his own shoulders now.

He felt that he had to do what was best for the Kingdom as a whole.

Michael and Jeremiah stepped out of the common, still bickering.

"Why would you even bring them into this?"

"Why not?" Michael asked. "*You* did." He shook his head, laughing softly to himself. "When you tried to marry off their dead mother, you made the entire court concern itself with the well-being of the children. How would it look if we let them starve alone in the Passing Woods?"

"You're crazy, Michael," Jeremiah whispered.

"I'm the mad one now? And who brought a human soul into the picture? It wasn't me, certainly."

"Erika has nothing to do with it."

"Erika has everything to do with it. A human in the palace. You've been trying to corrupt my family all your life, Jeremiah, ever since you wormed your way into the cradle. But then, I guess that it comes from your mother. You inherited something other than guile from her after all. It's a pity that it was still something filthy." A footman leaped down to open the carriage door, but Michael waved him away. Instead, he took the brass handle in his own hand and gave Jeremiah a long stare.

"What do you want me to do?"

Michael laughed again. "Nothing, Jeremiah," he said. "I want you to do nothing but leave us alone. Have a nice life in the Colonies. I hope that there's nothing catching."

"I'm sure that you won't leave me long enough to find out."

The second prince grinned. "You're probably right. But only time can tell."

"And what are you planning for the children?" Jeremiah asked.

"That's no longer of your concern."

"Do I need to remind you that your duty is first to the people?"

"You need not remind me of anything, Jeremiah, because you are wrong. My duty is first to my family. Besides, the children of that woman are not my people." He smirked. "Well, other than the little one, I guess."

He ducked into his carriage, but the lamps near the opposite door cast a flickering glow into the box, and Jeremiah could see the face of Rebecca Stripling, bent forward in sleep.

"You bastard." He grabbed Michael by the back of his coat and pulled him out of the carriage and onto the walk. Michael slammed against the cobbled ground. He lay there for a moment, motionless, and then let out a low, rolling laugh as he ran a hand through his hair, where his head had hit the stones.

"Oh, Jeremiah," he said, propping himself up. "You're going to regret that." He transformed into a cloud of twisting vapor and sped away.

Jeremiah didn't pause to check the children. He sprinted back to the entrance of the common, almost toppling Uriel, Selaph, and Jegud in his break for the door.

It didn't take much for them to make up their minds, and the three of them turned en route and dashed after their half brother, none of them really knowing what he was after.

Erika had been waiting just outside of Jeremiah's small carriage when she saw the scene, and she pulled her coat tighter around her waist and ran over to the open door of Michael's coach to see what the matter was. As she drew closer, the footman turned and looked down his nose at her. She ignored him and stuck her head into the carriage.

She clapped her hands to her mouth at the sight of her children.

"Megan?" she gasped. Relief swept over her, making her heart pound hard. Suddenly everything made sense, everything was right.

Rebecca and Shawn were sitting at the front end, side by side, eyes closed and shoulders moving in slow, sleepy breaths. Megan, on the other hand, lay curled on the floor, with her knees under her chin, wearing a high-collared dress a size too small for her and looking very pale.

Erika reached in and ran the tips of her fingers down her son's cheek. His eyes fluttered open as sleep slipped away, and he took a moment to adjust to the dim light.

"Mom?"

"Shawn." She pulled him out of the carriage and wrapped her arms around him, rocking him like a crying child against her chest. She almost laughed with the release, she felt so free. Shawn melted against her.

"What happened?" she asked him, allowing herself a smile. "How did you get through?"

"There was an angel," Shawn said. "Mom, we —"

But Erika's eyes flew open and she jumped away from her son.

"You!" she called to the footman. "Your master — what was he thinking before he left?"

"He was thinking about a knife, madam."

Erika gasped and felt Shawn push her toward the common.

"Go, Mom," he said. "Hurry."

He didn't wait to watch her leave. Instead, he turned back to the carriage and shook Rebecca awake. Megan he was more careful with. He had seen her breathing a few hours ago, before they had been put to sleep, but he had also seen her die. He did not know which would be the more permanent.

Jeremiah came back into the hall with pounding footsteps. He saw Gabriel first, standing behind the podium with a hand over the blade of the knife. Then he saw Michael, who waited, arms folded, a few feet away.

"You don't know what you're saying, Michael," Gabriel warned. A tinge in his voice suggested that, in reality, they both knew what Michael argued, but that the ground was too dangerous for Gabriel to even consider it. "You're tired," he said instead. "We're all tired. Go home. Rest yourself. He'll be gone by week's end and you won't have to think about it any longer."

He looked over when Jeremiah walked into the room.

"This is a bad time, Brother," Gabriel said. "What is it?"

"Listen to you," Michael spat. "Calling him brother as if you claim him. You're just as bad, Gabriel. You're the crown prince and you're just as bad."

The doors thumped shut again, and Uriel, Selaph, and Jegud came running down the hall. They froze at the threshold of the room.

"My God," Gabriel snapped, the first touch of anger that any of them had heard from him in a long time. "Why are all of you so determined to make this as difficult as possible?"

"What are you doing, Michael?" The outburst came from Uriel, and all eyes turned to him.

"I'm *fixing things*," Michael barked. "I'm doing what everyone else is too weak to do."

"You didn't tell me anything about this."

"It was unplanned."

"You can't do this," Uriel hissed through his teeth, gaze flicking to Gabriel. "Not here."

"It's not about what you think."

"Excuse me?"

"It's never been about what you think." Michael turned away from his baffled little brother and began an advance at Gabriel. "Give me the knife, Brother."

"No."

"Give me *the knife*."

Gabriel picked it up from the podium and pointed it at Michael.

"Go *home*, Michael."

"Are you threatening me?"

"As the Kingdom's heir, I order you to forget about this and go home."

"Kingdom's heir?" Michael quipped, chuckling. "Take it back please, Gabriel. You don't deserve to call yourself that."

"And *you* do, I suppose?" Jeremiah asked.

"I suppose so, yes," Michael replied, without taking his eyes away from the dagger.

"Stay out of this, Jeremiah," Gabriel said.

"Yes," Michael said. "Stay out." He took a step forward, and Gabriel took a step back.

The other brothers began to fall away themselves, trying to stay out of range of the impending scuffle.

Michael took a few more strides toward his older brother, and Gabriel answered them by retreating even farther. Michael laughed.

And then, without warning, Michael ran.

He tackled Gabriel and pinned his arms against the cold marble.

"You wouldn't kill me, would you, Gabriel?" he whispered.

Gabriel forced himself back up, but in doing so, he lost his grip on the knife, and it skidded out of his hands. Michael scooped it up and leaped back to his feet. He cradled the blade between his hands. Carefully. Lovingly. He held it up.

"The one mirror in our family's entire Kingdom," he said. "Remember the legend? That the dead always see their reflections in it before they give up their souls?"

Erika burst through the doors at the end of the hall.

When she saw Michael with the knife, she froze.

"The muddy little whore is here," Michael announced. "Tell me, Jeremiah, what did you *do* to make her seem so like your own mother? Or do all sluts just look the same?"

"Leave, Erika," Jeremiah ordered.

"No," said Michael. "Stay, Erika. Since this is all about you and your battered soul."

Erika took a cautious step forward.

"Don't," Jeremiah said, desperate.

"Ignore the rogue, dear," Michael said. He retreated a few paces, giving Erika a wide berth for moving into the room.

She darted forward.

Jeremiah groaned.

"Don't be so distraught, Jeremiah. It's only because she loves you." Michael chuckled. "But that's right, isn't it? You can't love. How ironic that your own mother's curse would come back to you. But with a bit of a downgrade, if I might say so."

"I can love," Jeremiah said. "I loved you, Michael. Or have you forgotten that we used to be brothers?"

"Brothers," Michael spat. "Wipe your mouth, Jeremiah. It's bad to lie on judgment day."

"Michael," Gabriel said. "Put down the knife. Please."

"Oh, shut *up*, Gabriel. You've ordered me around plenty enough. You were lucky to be the firstborn. Your soul's too haughty for anything but."

The doors opened again, and the Stripling children came in, looking wary.

"What a pretty little party," Michael said. "Come on, then. Join the grown-ups."

The children started forward, more because they saw their mother than because they were listening to Michael. Shawn set Megan on her feet next to him. His first mistake. He let her run along ahead, arms open to their mother. His second.

Michael scooped her into his free arm and knelt down beside her.

Rebecca screamed.

Shawn saw the glint of the knife and knew better than to try anything. He grabbed Rebecca by the arm and dragged her on to the cluster of princes. Erika took Rebecca into her arms and pressed her, shaking, to her chest.

"What do we have here?" Michael breathed, his cheek close to Megan's. "A little dead girl."

He spun her around and ripped open the top buttons of her dress, showing them the clean cut through Megan's back. Off to the side, Selaph flinched and looked away, as if wounded himself. Erika tightened her grip on Rebecca. The world disappeared around her and she felt herself going limp, her knees beginning to buckle. "No," she moaned. "God, no. Oh God, *no.*"

Rebecca gripped the front of her mother's blouse and sobbed into the black silk. "I'm so sorry, Mom," she said. "We didn't know. We came so far, but we didn't know."

Erika heard the voice of her eldest daughter, but couldn't process the words. She was focused on Megan's pale skin and the thin line that went down into muscle. Down into her spine. The room was spinning.

Michael twirled Megan back to face their audience.

"You see," he said to Jeremiah. "I needed to get to you, and so I had to get to her." He pointed the tip of the knife over Megan's shoulder at Erika. "Has it worked, Erika?" he said, with a smile. "Do I have your attention now?"

Erika buried her face in Rebecca's hair.

"And you, Jeremiah," Michael went on. "Do I have yours?" He twisted his free hand through Megan's hair and jerked her head toward him. Skin stretched white across her throat and eyes forced to look at the city of stars, Megan began to cry.

Selaph and Jeremiah stepped forward in the same instant.

“Please, Michael,” Selaph begged. “Some time to think. There is no turning back from where you are going.”

The second prince looked at his little brother as if charmed by his innocence. “There has never been any turning back,” he said. “That’s the best part; I can’t lose ground.”

“Stop speaking to me like that.” Selaph’s voice had grown bitter. “Don’t send me off to kill a child and then act like I’m still one myself.”

Jeremiah stepped ahead again and Selaph turned away, knowing his moment was lost.

“Trade places with her, Jeremiah,” said Michael.

“What?”

“It’s you I want, not the little brat.” He put the edge of the knife to Megan’s throat. “She’s gone if I press at all. I’ll drink her up like breakfast. But I’m not even hungry. Give yourself over, Jeremiah. You saw Father go. It isn’t hard.”

“Don’t,” Jeremiah said.

“Don’t *what*?”

“Don’t be stupid.”

“I don’t think that label applies to me of all people, Jeremiah,” he said. “After all, it’s you who just keeps trying and trying and trying and falling on your face every time. Aren’t you damaged enough by now?”

Jeremiah jerked forward. “Michael —”

“Ah, tsk, tsk, tsk.” Michael clicked his tongue against the roof of his mouth. “Let’s not be rash anymore. Go slow.”

Megan’s face was damp and flushed, but the skin of her bare neck was stretched pale. A bubble of spit formed on her lips. “*Please*,” she whispered. “I’m *sorry*.”

“Oh, darling,” Michael crooned. “It isn’t your fault. It’s *his*.”

Jeremiah asked the question that had haunted him since the first day Michael had turned on him: "Brother. Why do you hate me?"

"I don't hate *you*, Jeremiah. I hate your worthless mother. And, unfortunately, I could never live happy with you alive. With you keeping *her* alive. So don't blame me for this. Blame her."

He brought the blade down, with all his strength, and dropped Megan's body on the floor.

"Michael, no!" screamed Uriel. "What have you done?"

Erika was too devastated to make a sound. She collapsed to the ground, choking on her own breath. Rebecca went down with her, hitting the marble hard with her knees.

"Mom, what's going on?" The panic was thick over Rebecca's voice, but Erika couldn't bring herself to answer. Clean as morning mist, Megan's soul rose from her slashed throat. Erika watched, helpless, as Michael opened his mouth.

Jeremiah dove. Michael fell backward as his brother tumbled over him. The knife clattered from his grip and skidded across the polished floor.

Michael struggled to his feet, dragging Jeremiah up by the shoulders, and slammed his brother against the wall. "But now," he said, "all the Striplings have come through the gate. And all it took was one little cut. Why didn't you think of *that*, Jeremiah? They always said that you were the clever one."

The room fell silent. All eyes were on the two brothers, and on Uriel, who drew up behind them. His footsteps came soft on the marble, so quiet that Michael was surprised to feel his little brother's breath against his ear.

"You said that it was just politics," Uriel said. His voice trembled on his tongue, teeth, lips. "A game."

Michael felt the prick of the ritual knife through his jacket, against his spine. He tried to slow his breathing. "Kingdoms don't always have to battle for power, Uriel," he said. "We can fight for family too."

"No one should die over it. No one should die for blood ties."

"And they should over a chair?" Michael laughed. "A chair and a title. Don't be so superficial, Brother."

Uriel punched forward with the dagger, but Michael had already twisted away.

Jeremiah's eyes widened as the blade sank into his own stomach, pinning him against the wall.

Uriel's mouth fell open and he stumbled back, frightened.

"Uri —" Jeremiah gasped. Shock gleamed in his green eyes — his mother's eyes — and, worse, his mouth twisted with panic. "Uri . . ."

Uriel trembled. "Jeremiah," he said. "Jeremiah, I'm sorry. Jeremy. Jeremy, forgive me."

Jeremiah's hands went to the hilt of the knife, but he didn't try to pull it out. He looked frightened, like a wounded animal, but he could tell that the terror of the moment would be nothing next to the pain of his end. He'd been running for so long. Running and running and running. He didn't know what to do when cornered.

Uriel dropped to his knees in front of his youngest brother and bowed his head, shaking hands shielding his face. He couldn't look at what he'd done. At the mistake he'd made. He was breaking down. "Jeremy." Each word tumbled out with a sharp gasp. "I'm . . . so . . . sorry."

"Uri," Jeremiah whispered, forcing out the last breath his spirit could manage. "It's —" He shivered, his body spasming.

"It's — okay." Jeremiah's head tipped forward, a line of spittle creeping toward his chin. His soul seeped out through the handle of the knife, pulling his body with it. He seemed to peel away from the wall, sucked forward into the fountain of pale smoke that rushed out in a column.

It hovered above the crowd, as if unsure, and then shot toward Erika and streamed a clean spiral around her curled and devastated body before erupting through the open ceiling and exploding, like a single blue-white firework, with a blast that knocked everyone off balance.

The knife clattered against the floor.

Michael was the first to pull himself back onto his feet. He was laughing. He staggered to the podium and settled his weight against it, looking down at Gabriel, who was just sitting up.

"I give you the keys to the Kingdom, Brother," he said. "Bless you."

"You killed him," Gabriel said. "He was your brother and you killed him."

"That bastard was no brother of mine," Michael said. "He was an accident. A slip. I only cleaned up Father's mess, since he could never be bothered to do it for himself."

"The Furies will come for you," Gabriel said. "Tisiphone will come."

"Tisiphone is myth."

"What else is myth, Brother?" They all turned to look at Jegud as he spoke. "Furies are legend. That does not make them lies."

Michael laughed. "I'm not so superstitious as you."

They watched, puzzled, as Selaph stepped up behind Michael and leaned in close to his ear.

"Take my hand, Brother," he said. "I think you may be dying."

Once more, Michael could feel the knifepoint through his clothes. "I always loved you best, Selaph," he whispered. "Is this your idea of loyalty?"

When Selaph pressed forward, Michael didn't fight.

It no longer mattered.

In the years since my car wreck, I've learned more about living, and more about love, than I ever knew existed. I can tell you now, without flinching, that I *am* dead. That my children buried my body with flowers and cherrywood and that a desperate prince pulled me from the wreckage he'd created. He did it for his own neck, I know now, but I've seen enough to move past that. We all have to fight for the things we love most, and, in the end, Jeremiah wasn't fighting for himself any longer.

I saw his face when they pinned him to that wall, and I've never felt so lost. He was terrified and trapped, and I felt that knife in my own stomach, taking away all the things I'd ever learned to love. But there was no regret in his eyes when he looked at me. He was born into war, after all, and not from it. He'd always been a lover.

He saved my little Meg.

Gabriel did also, to give credit where it's due. He pushed her soul back into that delicate, broken body and carried her to me. He said that she was mine now. I cried because I didn't want her.

I didn't want her like this.

She was supposed to go home, with Shawn and Rebecca, supposed to grow up.

She was supposed to live again.

Shawn told me that when he first woke in the hospital, he thought that he was dead. The doctors were thrilled that he'd come out of the coma. Smoke inhalation, they said. He hates how Judy-Garland-in-Kansas it was.

When they thought that he was well enough, they told him: His sister Rebecca had just opened her eyes in the next room. His sister Megan hadn't made it.

Matt was there, God love him.

John stayed away from Meg's funeral. In the weeks he left the kids to grieve, Shawn had his eighteenth birthday. He and Rebecca found an envelope on the porch, propped up against the storm door. Inside were the house title, signed over and witnessed, and a card with a watercolor rowboat. Rebecca went off to college and Shawn kept the house until he did too. Now it's gone to some family with a baby and a dog that barks too much. Or this is what Shawn tells me, when I see him. I slip in, sometimes, when he's sleeping, and so far he accepts it. Though I think the dreams of dying have begun to get a little old.

He's grown now. He's beautiful. He used to tell Rebecca how I was, but she's too afraid to hear it. She says that she's trying to forget, and I can't blame her. I only hope that she thinks of me sometimes, and smiles.

Megan doesn't talk to either of them, though she asks me how they are. I know that she remembers what those dreams are like. I see her through her open bedroom door, sometimes, staring out the window as Simon clips the hedges. Rakes the leaves. Trims away the dead. I wonder what she's thinking.

When she comes to me at midnight, slinking under the covers that, by now, I'm used to sleeping in alone, I know that I should teach her to let go, even if I can't, and wash away her body and the face that she's too old for. No one should be trapped at the age of eight for so many years.

But I also know that I'm greedy, and that she's smarter than her round cheeks and big eyes can tell you. These days, she creeps into my bedroom not because she's frightened, but because I need her. She's turning into a little rogue herself.

Sometimes I think that I should just let go and leave my crooked mother love behind, but, honestly, I'm afraid to. "Better the devil you know" and all that.

At least I've seen what death means.